A MEI ODYSSEY

Adam Carter

A Mermaid's Odyssey

Copyright 2019, © Adam Carter. All rights reserved. No content may be reproduced without permission of the author.

Cover by Covermint Design.
www.covermint.design

Visit: https://www.facebook.com/OperationWetFish for news, illustrations, previews and short stories.

For Paul

A Mermaid's Odyssey

Also available by the same author:

Dinosaur World books:
- Excavating a Dinosaur World
- Dinosaur Fall-Girl
- Dinosaur Plague Doctor
- Ike Scarman & the Dinosaur Slavers of Ceres
- Dinosaur Prison World
- The Dinosaur That Wasn't
- Awfully Wedded Strife
- Tales of a Dinosaur Prison World
- Deities of a Dinosaur World
- Return to the Dinosaur Prison World
- Nikolina Finch & the Dinosaur Utopia
- Of Stags, Hens & Dinosaurs
- Dinosaur World Gladiator
- The Wounding Tooth
- Dinosaur World Massacre
- Dino-Racers
- Dinosaur World Unscripted
- Christmas on a Dinosaur World
- Utara the Savage

Sheriff Grizzly:
- Book 1: Sheriff Grizzly
- Book 2: The Horse Thief Honey
- Book 3: The Coyote Colt Kid
- Book 4: Joins the Circus
- Book 5: The Haunting of Athelstan Swift
- Book 6: The Santa Claws Showdown
- Book 7: The Kangaroo Claim Jumpers of Crumbling Gulch
- Book 8: Gets a Reality Check
- Book 9: Bets Against the Card Shark
- Book 10: The Hairy Walrus of Truespire Peak
- Book 11: The End
- Book 12: In the Afterlife

Knights of Torbalia gamebooks:
- The Return of the Stolen Jewel
- Into the Massacre
- March of the Demon Trees
- The Thief of Tarley Manor
- The Class War
- The Haunting of Past Wraiths
- The Hunt for the Adulterous Bard
- A Peacock in the Den of Foxes
- Attack of the Demon Trees
- The Slave Scandal of Torbalia

Miscellaneous gamebooks:
- Lost Treasures of a Dinosaur World (300 paragraphs)
- The Underworld Horror (300 paragraphs)
- Sheriff Grizzly: The Good, the Bad & the Grizzly
- Sheriff Grizzly: The Wild West Dungeon Adventure
- The Christmas Adventure of Sam and Klutz
- Operation WetFish: Vengeful Justice
- Operation WetFish: A Wealth of Sin
- Jupiter's Glory: Oppression of the Press
- Dinosaur World: The Forest of Fiends
- The Temple of Death: The Villain's Gamebook

Adam Carter

Hero Cast trilogy:
- Book 1: The Villainous Heroes
- Book 2: The Heroic Villains
- Book 3: The Forge of Heroes

Jupiter's Glory:
- Book 1: The Dinosaur World
- Book 2: The Pirates and the Priests
- Book 3: The Obsidian Slavers
- Book 4: Just Passing Through

Detective books:
- Detective's Ex
- One-Way Ticket to Murder
- Who Slew Santa?
- The Curse of the Genie's Detective
- The Woman Who Cried Diamonds
- The Murder of Snowman Joe
- The Murder of Loyalty
- The Prostitute Butcher
- The Santa Worshippers

Dinosaur Frontier:
- Book 1: The Lightning Angel
- Book 2: Lightning Strikes Twice
- Book 3: The Law of Ceres
- Book 4: The Silk Caves of Ceres

Operation WetFish, Vampire Detective:
- Book 1: The Power of Life and Death
- Book 2: Chasing Innocence
- Book 3: The Hunt for Charles Baronaire
- Book 4: Christmas on the Kerb
- Book 5: A Necessary Evil
- Book 6: No Comment
- Book 7: Fear and Ecstasy
- Book 8: Call of the Siren
- Book 9: Happy Families
- Book 10: A Step in the Right Direction
- Book 11: What Money Can't Buy
- Book 12: 'Tis the Season
- Book 13: The Power Trip
- Book 14: Trust and Betrayal
- Book 15: A Gathering of Minds
- Book 16: The Pain of Life
- Book 17: The Happy Place
- Book 18: The Terrible Truth of Barry Stockwell
- Book 19: The Apex Predator
- Book 20: End of an Era
- Book 21: He Who Kills the Killers' Killers
- Book 22: Bad Day at the Office

Miscellaneous:
- Holding the Nuts
- One Week to Love: Speed Dating of the Gods
- The Trojan Ant
- Gauntlet of Daedalus
- The Faerie Contract
- Token Love
- Sleigh Ride Slaughter to Saturn
- Have Imagination, Will Travel

A Mermaid's Odyssey

Adam Carter

A MERMAID'S ODYSSEY

CHAPTER ONE

There was light above me. In my emotional, near-delirious state, I had little conception of anything else, yet I instinctively headed towards that light. It was too bright to be starlight, for I knew starlight. I had many happy memories of basking on a rock whilst gazing into the night sky, my mother beside me telling her little girl all sorts of amazing stories about knights and princesses and brave dragons. Even with the storm raging in the sea around me, I should have known the lights were manmade and that by being manmade they were to be avoided.

As I broke the surface, I screamed, my tears streaming from eyes so used to immersion, my voice rumbling thunder across the black sky, my heart cracking angry lightning. I had never known such anger, such sorrow, such fear, and with my head above water at last, I released my emotions upon the world which had never been my own.

Then a dark shape came at me with the tumultuous rise and fall of the monstrous waves and a boat hit me in the face.

I went under, stunned but not dead. Had I been human, no doubt I would have had my skull smashed into splinters, turning my brains into pulp; but my kind were made of sterner stuff. Instead, I turned over and over beneath the water, buffeted by the waves even as the dark shape of the boat blocked out the light which had enticed me to the surface. My head swam with pain just as my heart swam with my mother. I would have to put both behind me if I intended to survive the next few hours.

The return of the light signalled the passing of the boat and, having regained my senses, I placed my arms to my sides and shot upwards. The evil of men knew no bounds, yet if I could keep close enough to the boat, I would deter my pursuers long enough for me to compose a plan to save my life.

Breaking the surface, I obtained my first proper look at the boat. It was fairly large and would have been crewed by around half a dozen people. Beyond this, I knew little about boats, for I had only ever seen them from a distance. Human beings (colloquially called men, despite half of the species being female) used such boats to harvest fish from the ocean; I had watched them do this many times in the past. They used a variety of means, although their main method was to hurl a great net into the water and trawl for fish, bringing them still wriggling with life onto the deck of their boat. No nets were being thrust out that night, for with thunder in the air and the storm tossing frothing madness all around, not even human beings would be foolish enough to steal from the larder of the gods.

Rain battered my face, although seeing through water had never been a problem for me, and I set off quickly for the monstrosity. Swimming swiftly to the side of the boat, I knew I would have to get much closer than I had ever dared before. There were dangers beneath me and I did not feel safe in the open. Even as my hand touched the wet wood of the boat, however, I knew the threat would not long be put off by the nearness of men.

My fears were focused too much on what was below, however, for I failed to notice the actions of the fishermen above. Something struck me and I panicked; and the more I panicked, the more my arms became entangled in the thick rope. It took me a few moments to realise the humans had dropped a net upon me and that my struggles were only entrapping me further. I looked up to a face at the side of the boat. Strong arms were hauling upon the net and as my panic turned to terror, I glanced down to see the dark form of my pursuers making a final effort to reach me.

Abandoning my struggles, I clung to the rope net and hoped the sailors above would not be half as monstrous as I knew those beneath me to be.

It seemed to take an eternity to draw me up, perhaps because the storm was working against the efforts of the fishermen, and several times I slammed into the side of the boat or else scraped cruelly across the wood. Free of the water, the rain set upon me in force, and I felt more self-conscious than ever before, for, while I had been out of the water in the past, always had I done so through my own choice and never at the behest of another. I worried I had made the wrong decision, yet it had been a decision I had been forced to make quickly and there was no backing away from it.

At last, I felt coarse hands grab me. The slickness of the rain caused them to slip away, but those same hands found purchase on the equally coarse rope and with an almighty heave I was dragged over the side and dumped ungraciously onto the decking. All about me, people were shouting, attempting to keep the boat upright, and now that I was lying on the deck, I could feel the intense motion of the vessel and wondered how anyone ever kept their footing.

While the majority of the sailors concentrated on keeping everyone alive, one man had knelt beside me and was busy cutting through the net with a knife. As with the others, he wore waterproof attire which likely provided some protection against the storm, yet did not to my mind bring him any degree of comfort from the cold. He worked furiously to get me freed of that rope net, his eyes never once falling upon me. I watched him work and wondered how soon it would be before he despised me for what I was.

The man was a sturdy fellow, large of frame and full of beard, although his head was entirely bald. I almost spoke to him, yet there was nothing I could have said which would have made him trust me, so I maintained my silence in the hope he would turn out to be blind.

He sliced through the final section of rope and I saw him freeze. His eyes widened, a prayer was visible upon his lips, and his eyes focused upon the lower section of my body.

Someone's shouts snapped him out of his trance and he wasted no time in removing his waterproof coat, even through the freezing hammer of the driving rain. As he reached for me with the coat, my heart stopped, but after a moment I realised he was not attempting to smother me with it, but that his intention was to hide everything below my waist.

"Mallok," a woman shouted above the storm as she skidded towards us across the deck. "What are you doing? Get her into the cabin and get a hand on the sail."

The big man, Mallok, hefted me in powerful arms as though I was a babe. He replied to the woman and with a fast pace which denoted him as being used to such rough weather, took me to the cabin. Shouldering the door, he took me into a small room with a few bunks and a table fixed to the decking. A lantern was nailed to the table and covered with waterproof materials. He set me gently upon one of the lower bunks, taking care not to allow his coat to slip; then hurried back outside.

I could not believe what had happened. Always I had seen human beings as cruel beasts, yet here was one who had not only drawn me from the dangers of the ocean, but had concealed me from his mates, even at the expense of his own comfort. The storm would be harsh upon this man and my emotions churned for him, which only made the storm rage harder.

Remembering there was a reason for the storm, I lay there on that hard bunk and attempted to control my emotions. I practised breathing techniques my mother had taught me and forced my fears to the back of my mind. I pictured the boat and imagined the quieting of the thunder, the lessening of the rains. Then I pictured a large full-cheeked being to the west of the boat, billowing great gusts of wind eastward, and was rewarded with feeling the rise and fall of the boat grow steady, heading in the direction I had chosen.

Exhausted, I kept my eyes closed and must have fallen into a much-needed sleep, for after this I knew no more. I could not say whether I was safe, only that the greatest danger I had ever known had passed.

I awoke to the gentle rocking of the boat upon calm waters. I had slept well, which was the reason for the passing of the storm. Affecting the weather is not something I have ever intentionally done, yet I've never had much control over my emotions.

The room was as I remembered it. The table and lantern were still bolted down, although some of the bedding had fallen off the bunks. There was water over the floor, sloshed in from the storm, although there had been some effort made to mop it up. I looked down and saw the cold, wet coat was still over my lower section and I slowly peeled it off to reveal two pale, naked legs. Tossing the coat away, I swung my legs over the side of the bed and placed my feet upon the floor. From there, I took a deep breath and rose to a standing position, using a conveniently placed bar for support.

My experience with legs was not extensive and I allowed myself a few minutes to gain confidence in standing. I was alone in the cabin, so felt I likely had the time to prepare myself.

When I was relatively steady, I moved across to the door and reached for the handle. I had it half-turned before I realised I was naked and that humans had a strange aversion to nudity. It was something my mother tried to explain to me one time, although I had never understood it.

Looking about the cabin for something to wear, I located a ghastly cloth formed into double tubes, and I struggled to fit my legs into them. Tumbling about the room, I almost crashed into the lamp and found it much easier to slip into the things whilst seated. After that, I looked about for a means to cover my chest and found something which I believed was called a shirt. It lacked arms, which made it easier to get on over my head, yet I worried my bare arms might not be proper in human society.

Finally, I donned a cap and moved back to the door. Here I stopped, for there was a mirror set into the wall. It was not large, but the glass was crooked so that it was possible to see a full miniature image of myself.

What I saw gazing back at me was not the young woman who had left home only a short while earlier. The trousers were tight, the shirt baggy, with fine golden hair spilling out from the hat. Beneath the rim of the cap I saw the remnants of the real me – the slightly chubby cheeks and piercing blue eyes. Even my usually wide smile had been replaced with a thin slit of sorrow.

Turning from the nightmare figure, I opened the door and walked out into the bright sunshine. There were people on deck and two more up the rigging. It was the first good look I had of the boat and I took it all in quickly. The boat was longer than it was wide, with the cabin situated close to the front, or the prow as I knew it to be called. There was a massive hatch in the centre of the vessel, stretching towards the back, although it was presently closed. I knew this was where the mariners would drop their fish, into the cargo hold within the belly of the beast. There was a main mast stretching high into the sky, with smaller ones offering support, and a great many ropes stretching out between them, holding the massive sheets of cloth in place. The cloth would catch the wind and the amount of sail shown would determine how fast the boat would travel, and whether it would tip over in a storm.

"You're awake," a young lad of around eleven or twelve said at my feet. For an instant I thought he was praising me, that this was some strange human custom; then I thought he was washing my feet, that this was an even stranger custom. My mind quickly made sense of him, however, for he had a bucket of water and a mop and was clearly washing down the decks. He was a scrawny lad with large eyes and gangly limbs, but he looked harmless enough.

"She's awake," he called across the boat. "Captain, she's awake."

I half expected everyone to come running towards me and was thankful they did not, for I would have found such overwhelming. Instead, most of the crew continued with their work, although I did notice a familiar large man approach with a smile to his eyes.

"You survived, lass," he said. "And I see you found your sea legs."

My lips parted, although I did not quite know what I was going to say. He had seen my true self, knew I was not of his own species, yet he was not immediately revealing my secret.

A moment later, a woman hopped down from the rigging and stepped around the large man. She was short but had the bearing of an octopus – a confident predator with so many limbs there was no sense of instability or uncertainty about her.

She looked me up and down in an instant and said, "You're wearing my cap."

"Sorry," I said automatically.

"And my trousers."

I removed the cap and was trying to struggle out of my trousers when the woman gave a cry of alarm.

"What are you doing, girl? I have fishermen on this trawler who haven't seen a woman in two months. Keep your clothes on."

I stopped, uncertain what to do right, since I had no idea what I had done wrong. The large bald man chuckled – I remembered his name was Mallok – which only infuriated the woman.

"Get back to work, Mallok," she said as she walked off. "And give our drifter something to do, if she wants to stay on my boat."

I parted my lips again to speak, but Mallok raised a finger to his own until the woman had departed. He placed a hand about my shoulders and steered me away from the cabin doorway. "Don't mind the captain," he said. "She's just worried about that storm last night. Thinks the gods are against us."

"What's a drifter?"

"Hmm? Oh, that's you. We plucked you from the ocean, like driftwood, so you're a drifter."

"Thank you. You saved my life."

"Couldn't well have let you drown out there."

"I wouldn't have drowned. I …" I shut my mouth.

"It's all right," he said. "I know you can breathe water. And I haven't told the captain, before you ask."

"Why?"

"That's a big question. Why what?"

"Why are you being nice to me?"

"Why wouldn't I be? I have a daughter around your age and I'd hate for someone to put her in danger. How old are you anyway?"

"Eighteen."

"In human years or faerie years?"

"Isn't a year the time it takes for the planet to go around the sun?"

He laughed. "That it is. Never understood myself why dog years were different, but there you go. What's your name?"

"Misako."

"That's a beautiful name. I'm Mallok."

"And the captain?"

"Tyburn."

"Your Captain Tyburn, he looks like a woman."

"Captain Tyburn *is* a woman."

I frowned. "But she said the fishermen on this boat hadn't seen a woman for two months."

"Her little joke. One of many none of us understand. But she's the captain, so she's allowed her little eccentricities."

"Oh. Are all captains like that?"

"Probably."

I nodded. "I'll remember that."

"Uh, are you taking everything we say literally?"

"Should I not do that? I'm confused."

"This is your first time talking with a human, isn't it?"

"No. Yes. Not exactly. I've spoken with humans before. Sort of. I've practised singing to them."

"You mean because mermaids entice men to watery deaths with their beauty?"

"Ah. Yes."

I did not know how he was going to react to that, and it seemed he did not know, either, for we did not speak for several moments. Once we reached an untidy pile of rope, he said, "Would you mind taking a seat and trying to sort all of this out? It got tangled in the storm last night."

I sat without a word, using a small box for a stool. There was a lot of rope and I could imagine the task was going to take me hours. I wanted to talk with Mallok, to tell him that not all faeries meant ill of humans, that many of us simply wanted to be left alone. But I knew about the war, had experienced the distrust from both sides, and there was nothing I could have said which would have meant much to him.

So I sat in silence and worked while Mallok went to tend to his own duties.

Two hours later, I had made a fair bit of progress. First, I sorted the rope into piles of what could be saved and what would have to be discarded; then I disentangled all the smaller lengths so they could be of use to the crew. I was just starting on one of the longer pieces of rope when I realised the lad with the bucket was sitting cross-legged opposite me. He was staring, more inquisitive than anything, and I continued working for some moments without either of us saying anything.

"You don't talk much," he said at last.

"I'm a little overwhelmed to do much talking. My name's Misako."

"Hallen."

"Pleased to meet you, Hallen."

He narrowed his eyes. "Why?"

"Why am I pleased to meet you?"

"Yeah. What are you after?"

"Nothing. I just … I was trying to be friendly."

"Uh huh. No one wants somethin' fer nothin' in this world, lady."

"That's a very pessimistic outlook for someone so young."

He still stared at me darkly, although it was more cautious than hateful. "Some of the other men have been looking at you funny."

"I haven't noticed."

"I think yer trouble."

"All I'm doing is mending rope."

"I still think yer trouble."

He yelped as the captain clouted him about the ear and he scampered off.

"Get back to work, ya lazy swab," she said.

"I didn't stop," I protested.

"Not you." She looked at me with venom in her eyes, although her expression softened after but a moment. Looking around, she pulled up another box and sat opposite me. Whether the boxes contained anything, I did not know. She regarded me for several moments and, feeling distinctly uncomfortable under her gaze, I focused exclusively on my work.

"Here," she said, tossing me something. I caught the pouch and opened it to examine its contents. Within were slivers of dried meat and some form of biscuit. "You're a good worker," she said. "You need something to eat." She held out a flask and I took that also, grateful to discover it contained water. I had not noticed until that moment, but in the afternoon sun I had become dehydrated. Chugging down the water, I would gladly have exchanged the food for another flask.

"I'm sorry you're cranky about the storm," I said as I handed back the empty flask.

"Why? It's not like you caused it."

"No," I said so quickly she looked at me oddly.

"What were you doing in the water?" she asked.

"Trying to stay alive. My mother ... my mother was killed and ..." I took a deep breath, trying to work out how much I could tell her while at the same time fighting to control my emotions. Thunder rumbled in the distance and I fought harder. "The people who killed my mother were after me," I said. "I swam as hard as I could, but they ..." I looked her straight in the eye, determined not to be a weakling my whole life. "You saved my life. Thank you."

The captain snorted. "That was Mallok. Me? I would've let you drown."

"No, you wouldn't."

"No? You know me so well after two minutes?"

"No. But Mallok respects you. I could hear that in his voice. And someone who risked his own life in a storm to rescue a stranger must have a decent captain."

"Maybe I've fooled him."

"Maybe pretending to be grouchy is just a captain's eccentricity."

She smiled. "This conversation isn't going quite the way I expected. Aside from Hallen and Mallok, I have four men on my boat, and I've been watching them. The boy's right: they've been taking an interest in you. That makes you trouble, even if it's not your fault. But you're a hard worker and I think you can look after yourself. If you continue to work, I'm willing to let you stay on board until we get back to port."

"Thank you. I'll work hard for you."

"Do that. And eat something before you get so skinny your trousers fall down. Like I said before," she said as she rose, "that's something I could really do without my sailors seeing."

CHAPTER TWO

The following month was blissful. I still worried about pursuit, still thought about my mother, but I kept myself too busy to dwell on anything. The mariners were a friendly sort and there was nothing menacing about them, despite what Captain Tyburn would have me believe. Mallok took me under his wing and taught me how to lay nets and trawl for fish, and how to properly bring them on board and dump them in the hold. One time I caught him drawing up a string of pots and kettles from the ocean floor and he explained this was the best way to catch crabs. He was providing the animals with somewhere dark to crawl into before drawing them all up together and seeing whether his strange traps had borne fruit. With a little squid in each trap for bait, Mallok's method was surprisingly effective.

My natural litheness and strength made me the perfect choice for climbing the rigging and dealing with problems with the sails, and on more than one occasion I noticed the captain watching me with approval.

We worked by day, and come the evening we would sit together on the deck and eat. We would share stories and jokes; it was not long before Mallok convinced me to sing, although I kept the tone light, for there is nothing more dangerous than a mermaid's song.

Then, on a day which began as any other, I was standing at the edge of the boat, leaning on the railing as I watched the distant horizon, when Mallok came to stand beside me. He rested against the railing so his back was to the sea, which was a sign that he wanted to be able to see the crew in case anyone should overhear us.

"You've fit in well with us, Misako," he said.

"I like it here. It feels like being in a family."

"If the captain knew what you were, she'd kill you."

The comment made my heart leap. "She wouldn't. She's kinder than you think."

"The problem with war, Misako, is that the people on both sides tend to think the worst of the enemy. Propaganda kills peace, and every time we hit a port, there are people who congratulate us on surviving. The ocean isn't our native element, it's yours. Fishing boats exist at your sufferance, Misako. If the captain knew there was a faerie on board, I think you'd find she's a different person than you hope."

"You haven't told anyone," I said, refusing to look at him. The seas were calm and so was I, for I trusted Mallok. "You clearly don't believe every faerie to be evil, Mallok."

"I heard one time that faeries don't have a concept of good and evil."

"Oh, we have a concept of it. I'm not sure we understand it, but we know it exists. There's a tale that goes back long before I was born, when the creatures of faerie ruled the land. The story says that the world was at peace. Then the humans came. A fast-lived race who spread so quickly that the faeries blinked and were suddenly overrun. From the humans, the faeries learned the word good and the word evil and they understood those terms through a simple means – they looked to how humans were and saw evil; and they looked to how humans wanted others to see them and saw good."

"You have a low opinion of us, Misako."

"It's just a story. I'm sure you have equally bad tales of my kind."

"Yes. We tell of how mermaids entice our menfolk to the depths and drown them."

I said nothing. The silence stretched for half a minute.

"Why do you do that?" he asked at last. "I'm genuinely curious."

"Why do we drown people? Maybe it's to save lives."

"Explain that."

"When you were a child, did you ever play by the stream?"

"No. My parents would tell me the stream was the home of Greenbeard the Gruesome. Every town, every society, has similar stories. It seems most bodies of water are named after water deities or spirits. There's even a long-held tradition of tossing in a coin before drinking, in payment to the water spirits that they might not drown us as we slake our thirst."

"There are parts of the world, Mallok, where people have forgotten mermaids even exist. They toss coins into fountains to make a wish, not remembering that the wish was always to stay alive, that in the old world all waterways were linked and that sea serpents could easily appear up a well. Yet, even though those people have forgotten, their rivers are still named after water deities."

"What's your point?"

"Fear of water, Mallok. Children don't play near rivers and streams for fear of being grabbed by demons. Whether those demons are real is irrelevant, for it keeps the children away."

"So you're saying you draw men in and murder them in order to keep the myth alive?"

"That's one theory."

"And the truth?"

"The truth is many mermaids are lustful, sinful creatures and some even devour human flesh."

I could tell by his shudder that it was not an answer he had much liked, but it was a truthful one. "How do you affect the weather?" he asked.

"I'm a teenager. I throw a strop and everyone suffers."

He smiled at that answer at least. "And your legs? When I pulled you out of the water, you had a glistening tail. It was beautiful."

"You think so?"

"How did you turn the tail into a pair of legs?"

"You really think my tail's beautiful?"

"You're not going to answer my question, are you?"

"I'm tired of questions, Mallok. I've spent a month with you and your crew. We've eaten the same food, toiled at the same work, avoided the same captain. I've enjoyed my time here, amongst all of you. Please don't treat me differently now."

"I'm sorry. You're right, it's none of my business. I'm just insanely curious about you."

I glanced to him. "Well, you'll just have to stay curious, because I …"

There was something strange on the horizon, something I had never seen before.

"Because you what?" Mallok asked.

"What's that?"

He looked out to sea and strained to make it out. "A ship. Bigger than ours. Probably nothing, but I'll go tell the captain."

I could tell he was nervous and as he moved off, I held onto his arm. "What is it?"

"Like I said, probably nothing."

"Mallok."

"All right. As we've already discussed, the ocean isn't our natural element. There are water spirits out here, so most people tend to avoid being on the sea at all. It's why being a fisherman is such a well-paid job. But there's more to fear out here than faeries."

"Believe me, I know all about what there is to fear out here. Are you saying that ship might attack us?"

"With people, sometimes it's best to assume the worst. Piracy is a crime seldom investigated. If a fishing trawler doesn't make it home, everyone assumes it was water demons anyway. Look, I have to tell the captain."

He hurried off and I was left looking at the distant ship. Mallok used a lot of words indiscriminately, but then I had been guilty of such as well. Faeries, demons, spirits and deities. They were each vastly different things, yet my kind was considered all of those. Mallok had said propaganda killed peace, yet I felt ignorance did a good enough job of that all by itself.

I watched as Mallok informed the captain as to the potential problem. She utilised a telescope to better see what we were facing, and as she lowered the tube she swore. That told me she had seen the flag the other ship was flying.

"Listen up," she called out to us all. "Gather round and listen. That ship means us ill, but we have a great deal of distance between us. They're bigger and faster, but beyond that I can't tell you anything about her. The clever dogs have painted patterns across their hull so I'm having a difficult time telling how heavy they are. I'm surprised Mallok was even able to notice the ship at this distance."

For the briefest of moments, I was annoyed that Mallok had taken the credit, but then I realised he was only doing it to protect me. Having spent my entire life underwater, my muscles were stronger and my senses more honed; he knew if the captain thought it was I who had spied the distant vessel, she would be suspicious.

"If we can keep our distance," the captain continued, "they'll lose interest in us. We only have fish, anyway, so once they see we're a trawler, they won't want to waste the effort in chasing us down. Now, get to work, people."

Everyone moved to whatever duty they were best at, which meant I was up the rigging. For the next six hours, we watched as the pirate ship came closer and closer. We tried every trick we knew to gain more distance, but the pirates were determined to see what was in our hold. Their ship was like a city to us, for while it was formed of the same basic shape as our own boat, it was a mass of sails both large and small and was formed of at least three levels of deck that I could see. There was the main deck, at either end of which there rose a staircase leading to another section. From the rear one, mariners controlled the rudders; from the fore one, they handled the wheel. There were also steps leading down from the main deck to a lower area, where fully a hundred people were rowing as hard as they could. Whether they were slaves or fellow pirates, I could not say, yet the effort they were putting into their work had me worried.

After a while, it became clear the pirate vessel would catch up to us, and I could see concern in the captain's face whenever I looked down to the deck. The pirate vessel was so large in our sights by this point that it was liable to catch us within the hour – I could even hear the cries of the overseer for the rowers to stroke, stroke, stroke.

Sliding down the rigging, I moved to the edge of the boat and gripped the railing with trembling fingers. I heard the wood crack and wished there was another way out for us.

"Misako?" the captain asked from behind. "What are you doing? Get back up the rigging."

"Captain," I said through gritted teeth, my eyes upon the pirate vessel bobbing up and down on the waves. "Captain, what if there was a way I could save this boat?"

"What do you mean if there was a way … Just get back to your post."

I turned to face her. My heart was hammering, for I really did not know how she was going to react. I watched Mallok hasten towards me, although Captain Tyburn stopped him with a raised arm.

"What is it with you people deserting your posts today?" she said.

"Captain," I said, loud enough to be heard over the roar of the waves, "I can save us. But you might hate me for it."

"Girl, if you can save my boat, I'll name my first-born after you. Now, what are you talking about?"

In answer, I closed my eyes and concentrated. At first, nothing happened, purely because I was far too nervous. My stomach was dancing and I was concerned too much with how the captain was going to react. Then I reminded myself it was my emotions, not my level of concentration, which caused the storm.

Raising my psychological dam, I allowed a torrent of fear and sorrow to wash through my mind and the first spots of rain fell even as the heavens rumbled in distress.

The rain intensified until it was pelting my skin, bouncing from the deck in frantic applause at being released. The winds howled about me, bright flashes of lightning illuminated my closed lids, and I felt the boat surge forward.

As I opened my eyes, it was to see the mariners scurrying about as they kept the boat focused in one direction, the wind of the storm filling our sails. Looking back out to sea, I watched the pirate ship struggle on the tossing waves, the stirrings of a maelstrom appearing in the water upon which it sailed. I could not create a massive whirlpool under them without also destroying our own boat, but what I had managed would suffice. Our boat moved with such speed that within half an hour the pirate ship had become a speck upon the distant black horizon.

Now that we were safe, I tried to still my hammering heart, for I needed to lessen the storm before stopping it completely. However, I had revealed myself to the crew and was terrified of how they would react, so controlling my emotions was far from easy.

"You did good," Mallok said, and with him by my side I gained strength enough to bring the storm to a close.

The crew avoided looking at me and kept themselves busy at their posts. I could not blame them, for they were likely as afraid as I. It was the captain I was concerned about, for if she took a dislike towards me now, not even Mallok would be able to save me.

She was standing several paces away, staring at me without emotion. I could see she was thinking, but that she had reached no decision. I took that as a good sign.

"Yeah," I said to break the ice, "I'm a mermaid."

She stared some more. "You don't have a tail."

"Not at the moment, no."

She continued to stare. It was becoming uncomfortable. Then she turned to walk away.

"Captain," I called out and she stopped but did not turn around. "Captain, are you going to throw me off your boat?"

She did not answer for several moments. "I don't know." Then she carried on walking.

The crew was arguing. It was as though they did not know I was there, curled up on the floor, my knees brought up to my chin, my arms wrapped about my legs as I tried not to make contact with anyone. Some of the fishermen wanted to toss me into the sea, one wanted to cut open my chest and sacrifice my heart to the gods. Hallen kept trying to venture an opinion, but no one paid the boy any mind. Mallok was silent, offering me no defence at all. He had not turned against me, for he had positioned himself by my side that he might react should someone attack me. He knew nothing he could say would make a difference and that the captain would have to make her own decision.

As for the captain, she was quietly listening to all the arguments. We had found some rocks in which to hide and had moored the boat, although the pirate ship was far behind us. Therefore, her full concentration was upon our situation. I only hoped I could control my emotions long enough not to brew another storm.

"She's a faerie," one of the fishermen was saying. "We're at war with her kind."

"I'm not at war with anyone," Captain Tyburn said. "I'm a sailor, not a soldier."

"We have to kill her," another said. "They're unnatural."

Shouts and grunts of agreement accompanied this opinion.

The captain waited for quiet before saying, "Misako has been with us for a month. She's worked with us, bled with us, laughed and cried with us. Does it matter that she's a mermaid?"

"You're defending her?"

"I'm asking a question," she replied. "Human beings tried to murder us today and a mermaid saved us. Yes, she's been lying to us all this time, but we'd all be dead if not for her actions. It would have been easier for her to have leapt into the water and abandoned us, but she didn't. Instead, she revealed herself to us, knowing we would hate her for it."

"Sure sounds like you're defending her."

Tyburn looked at me directly and I raised my teary eyes to meet hers. "Misako, you're running away from something. Whatever's after you, is it worse than anything pirates could do to you?"

"I don't know, ma'am. I don't know what pirates could do to me."

She considered my answer. "What are your plans?"

"My plans?"

"Once we return to shore, what do you intend to do with your life?"

"I'm searching for my father. He's a human, a soldier. My mother's gone, he's all I have left."

"So you're half human."

"It's why I'm being hunted. I was protected up until I turned eighteen."

"A spell?"

"Yes. A spell which bred superstition. On my eighteenth birthday, the other mermen and mermaids descended upon us. My mother fought them and told me to swim. I ..." Thunder rumbled in the distance and I closed my eyes until I could force it away. "She's gone, Captain. I don't have anything now."

Tyburn thought long and hard about everything I had said. "I won't harm you," she said at last. "But I don't want you on my trawler. We'll return to port, we should be home within a couple of weeks. After that, you leave and never come back."

Unable to speak, I merely nodded.

The captain ordered everyone back to work and Mallok moved over to lay a reassuring hand upon my shoulder. "It'll be OK," he said. "It's a better deal than you could have got."

"They still hate me," I said, seeing the derision in the eyes of some of the fishermen.

"They'll always hate you. It's just the way things are. Now, go get some sleep and we'll put all this behind us."

As ever, I did as Mallok told me, for he was, it seemed, my only friend.

The following week was difficult. No one would eat with me in case I infected their food, no one would talk with me in case I bewitched them, no one would look at me for more than a moment in case I cursed them. I went about my duties, staying in the rigging as much as I could, all the while counting down the days in which I would have to leave my family. During this week, we caught sight of the pirate vessel again, although it was some way off and the captain ordered me not to cause a storm to help us outrun it. The fishermen worked twice as hard to evade the pirates under their own labours, so they would not have to resort to trusting an unnatural hybrid beast for their survival.

One night, I descended the rigging and returned to the pile of rope which had become my bed, for I was no longer allowed to sleep in the same cabin as the rest of the crew. I lay on my back, staring at the sky and wishing the world would not hate me, all the while holding back my tears. I thought about what I would do once I reached the shore, but had no conception of what land-based human society could be like. I had heard there were many hundreds of thousands of human beings and hoped I would be able to lose myself in one of their great cities.

A movement to the side caught my attention and I saw Hallen approaching in a crouch. The boy was one of the only ones who still spoke to me, although he had become guarded over the last week, and I knew the other fishermen had been telling him foul stories of me.

"Hey, Hallen," I said.

"Hey, Misako."

"It's all right, you don't have to skulk."

He came close to me and sat just outside of my rope bed. There was concern to his face, fear as well, and I could see he had not simply dropped by for a chat.

"What's up?" I asked.

"Miss Misako, are you evil?"

"Do you think I'm evil?"

"Some of the others, they … they say you steal young men and … and do horrible things to them before you kill them."

I wondered precisely what the sailors had told the lad. At eleven or twelve, he might not have reached puberty, so if they were feeding him horror stories there was a chance he might not even have understood. Still, I was not going to lie to him.

"Some of my kind are cruel," I said. "Just as some humans can be cruel. We can't all be alike. Look at Tyburn and Mallok. They're different, aren't they?"

He nodded.

"It's the same with all the races. I'm not a monster, Hallen."

"They say the gods will be angry."

"The gods are always angry. It's what makes them gods."

"They say bringing a mermaid back to port will make them angrier."

"I wish there was something I could say to change your mind, Hallen, but you're just going to have to accept there are people on this boat who really need to mind their own business." I lay back and closed my eyes, hoping he would get the message, although I could sense he was still there. Then I heard the scrape of metal on wood and opened my eyes to see Hallen lunging for me with a knife.

Gasping in shock, I caught his wrists but could not prevent the knife from slicing down my arm. Pain and terror shot through me so suddenly that rain battered the deck as though it had been the sky which had been torn an injury. Hallen was screaming something, there were tears in his eyes, and I knew he was afraid. The men of the trawler had fed him lies and half-truths, maybe even some truth, and they had sent him to do their dirty work. We struggled for but a moment before I was able to throw him off me; yet in my panic and through the rush of adrenalin I had failed to take into account my greater muscular strength. Hallen struck the side of the boat with a sickening crunch and collapsed.

Booted feet were racing across the deck. One mate went to the boy, two more hauled me to my feet.

"He's dead," the mate with Hallen said. "The witch killed him."

"Hang her!"

"Burn her!"

"Hang and burn her!"

"What's going on?" the captain said, pushing past the mob and shielding her eyes from the storm. "Misako, cut the rain out."

But my eyes were fixed upon the broken form of young Hallen, dead because of my unnatural state.

The captain saw him also and was stunned, but even as the shouts for my execution resumed, she cut them off. "What happened?" she asked; and, when further voices were raised, she said, "I was asking Misako."

"He ... I ... I killed him."

The knife was long gone but I could see in the captain's eyes that she did not believe I would have murdered the boy. Yet she was the captain of her vessel and there was a dead body on deck. It was something she had to deal with.

Mallok stepped between us and this time came not only to my rescue by to Tyburn's as well.

"Misako," he said, "dive."

"Dive?"

"Get in the water, go!"

The captain stood emotionless, not wanting to order an attack upon me yet unable not to. The crew ran for me, but Mallok stood resolute, preventing them from reaching me. I watched as he bodily picked up one man and hurled him into another, but the crew were relentless and as they swarmed over my friend, I knew it would only be a matter of time before they overpowered him.

Mallok's only chance for survival was if I did precisely what he was telling me.

Wiping the tears from my eyes, I turned and vaulted over the side of the boat. I struck the water like an anchor, plummeting deep into the brine. I broke the surface a fair distance from the trawler and could see the fighting had stopped. Of Mallok I could see no sign and only hoped he had survived. The only face I could recognise from that distance was that of the captain, leaning against the railing and watching me, making sure I was not coming back.

Mallok had told me to swim for it, just as my mother had before him, and I had lost them both because I had obeyed. Turning away from them, I swam farther out to sea. Within a month of turning eighteen, I had lost two families.

CHAPTER THREE

I spent the next few days underwater. With the lower half of my body back to being the glistening sleek tail of a fish, I moved with streamlined grace, although found nothing poetic about being a hybrid freak. I spent much of my time in tears and wallowed in enough self-pity to drown my heart, if a mermaid could ever be drowned. It was during one of my tearful, wailing episodes that I fell foul of trouble. Floating on my back and staring at the unforgiving sun, I had not noticed the approach of the rowing-boat and as the net fell upon me, I struggled in panic.

This was not the life-saving net of Mallok. As I thrashed madly to escape, a body collided with mine and strong arms encircled me. Fighting back, I cracked my elbow into the man's face, bloodying his nose and sending him reeling. But there was another man, and another, and then someone was punching me in the face and my senses reeled in pain.

My attackers bundled me into the rowing-boat, clambering in after me. Those already within the boat hammered at me with their oars and I curled up in the bottom of the boat, holding my arms above me that I might protect myself. Searing pain shot through me at the landing of every blow, although I received no satisfaction from hearing one of the oars break against my arm, for all it meant was that one of the men began to stamp on my face with his boot.

I must have drifted in and out of consciousness, because everything after that was a blur. My first cognisant moment after this was of being thrust to the decking of a larger ship and of a booted foot slamming into the back of my head to press my face to the sodden wood.

"So, this is the mermaid what conjured up a storm."

I craned my neck to take in my surroundings. The ship was larger than the trawler I had departed and there was something familiar about the loose garb of the sailors. It was as my eyes found the slaves that I realised I was on board the pirate vessel.

"Get her up, let's take a look at 'er."

Hands grabbed me by my armpits and hauled me to my knees, or what would have been my knees if I had taken the form of human legs. A large crowd of unsavoury characters had gathered before me – there must have been upwards of fifty of them. Some were missing ears, others eyes, and there was a foul stench on board coming not only from the pirates but also the slaves. At their head was an old man, possibly into his ninetieth year. He was short, with wispy white hair and only a single tooth. At either side of him were two women: brutish thugs who were likely twins. I surmised the man to be the captain and the women to be his bodyguards.

"Unnatural filth," the captain said, leaning forward to spit in my face. I closed my eyes as the foul glob struck me and dripped down my chin. For some reason, the gathered pirates found this hilarious.

I was no longer as I had been on board the trawler. Having departed Mallok's company, I had shed my clothes and regained my fish tail. As such, I was entirely naked before the pirates and could see excitement in the eyes of many of the men and heard a great deal of coarse muttering.

"Quiet," the captain barked. "I know what yer thinkin', but no one touches this thing. It's an unclean horror a nature an' you'll get more than the pox if ya surrender ta yer base natures. It may look like a woman, but it's one a them. A faerie. We may be thievin' murderers, but at least we're human."

"What do you want?" I asked. My body was sore from the beating I had taken and my pride was bruised, but I was wound tight enough to snap.

"Yer a cursed, foul thing, mermaid. I don' want nothin' from ya. Durin' that storm ya created, ya caused us ta lose our figurehead, an' that's goin' ta cost ya. Figureheads are an important part of a ship, mermaid. Do you know why?"

"I don't care."

"You should – yer kind is the reason we have 'em. Throughout the years, women have been offered ta the sea gods for appeasement, an' figureheads figure inta that tradition. Stick an image of a naked woman onta the prow of yer ship an' the water deities take it as an offerin'. Imagine how much favour we'll be in when we give them an offerin' of a different sort."

He nodded to the two men holding me and they dragged me upwards, perhaps thinking my legs would magically appear. However, the pirates had not reckoned on my strength and I yanked downwards, dragging the two men over my shoulders to strike the deck hard. Sliding for the edge of the ship, I almost made it overboard when rough hands grabbed me and yanked me back. The pirate captain's bodyguards threw me to the deck and lay into me with fists and feet. The force of their attack was so hard, so painful, that I could do nothing against them and after the first few blows, I lacked even the ability to scream. Within minutes, the pain had numbed my senses and while I could see the women landing blow after blow upon me, I could neither feel nor hear anything.

My eyes found the row of slaves just beneath me. For a moment, I hoped they might help, but I could see their derision matched that of the pirates. Slaves they may have been, but they felt safer with their murderous masters than with me.

Succumbing at last to the pain, I blacked out, feeling only resentment for this strange, disgusting species.

I awoke to a pain so intense I wondered that I was not dead. My head pounded, my belly and torso were sore, while my muscles screamed in agony. I realised my hands were bound behind me and as my senses began to clear I realised with horror what the pirate captain had ordered.

I was tied to the prow of the ship, bound with thick rope even I could not break. My tail was still that of a fish, of which I was grateful, for it was bad enough being naked from the waist up around the pirates – there was no way I was going to drop my fish tail and reveal the remainder of my womanhood.

Testing my bonds only renewed my pain, so I hung there for a long time, trying to regain my strength even as the unforgiving sun dried out my skin and baked my mind. Over the next few hours, I deeply contemplated everything I had gone through since my eighteenth birthday. My mother had always warned me against the evils of humankind, and it was only then, as I hung near-delirious and dehydrated, that I realised she had known all along that the other mercreatures would come for us. She knew my eighteenth birthday would mark the end of her life and she had been preparing me for this, my epic journey into the world of the humans.

I thought about Mallok, of how he had protected me even from the moment he had brought me onto his trawler. I thought about how I had failed him, how I had likely ruined his life. The faeries hated me for being half human and the humans hated me for being half faerie. I had no home, no people, nothing to call my own.

Which led me to thoughts about the pirates. As despicable and foul as they were, they were also right. I was a monster, a cursed hybrid, a being of two worlds yet belonging to neither. The captain had said I might look like a woman but that I was nothing short of a monster, and that was precisely what I was.

In my life, I had known love and fear and loneliness and despair; I had known happiness and sorrow and jealousy and desire; I had known friendship and loyalty and betrayal and remorse. But I had never before wished it would all end, that I could be baked to death by the sun and cease to be anything at all.

Something struck me across the face, tearing me away from my destructive thoughts, and I looked around. My face was dripping and it occurred to me that someone had hurled a bucket of water over my head. There was a young woman nearby, sitting on a plank of wood and gently swinging close to me. Two lengths of rope rose vertically from the plank and I assumed this was a means the pirates used to clean their vessel or to fix the figurehead. Or, in this case, to torment me. Beside her, an empty bucket was held up by a third rope, which she would likely move around with her as she pleased.

"What?" I asked, for the woman was staring. She was not much older than me and was wearing a loose shirt and trousers. Her dark hair was cut short and her eyes were intense. She was not afraid of me, yet nor was she especially curious. It was as though she simply had nothing better to do with her time.

"Why are you naked?" she asked.

"I'm a mermaid, what do you expect?"

"I thought mermaids wore shells."

"Wore shells? What does that mean?"

"You know, over your breasts."

"And how would I possibly fix shells over my breasts?"

"Or necklaces of stones."

"What are you talking about?"

She swung absently. I came to understand she was doing this on purpose and that her movement was not simply through the motion of the ship. "What's your name?"

"Misako. You?"

"Kuara. I've never seen a mermaid before."

"I've never seen a pirate before, so we're even. Why did you throw a bucket of water over my face?"

"The first mate told me to water you, like you're a pansy or something. None of us have ever seen a mermaid so we don't really know how to treat you."

"Throwing water in my face isn't going to keep me alive."

"You drink water?"

"Everyone drinks water."

"Everyone human, yes. But you're not human."

"I'm half human."

"You're half slut, is what you are. Seriously, get some shells."

"If you've just come to mock me, clear off."

"Maybe I've come to set you free."

"Have you?"

She laughed. "No, of course not."

I wanted her to leave. My body ached and I was in a bad mood, but she was the only one who was talking to me and I had to try to use her to my advantage. "Kuara, why are you a pirate?"

"Because of my parents, I guess."

"They were pirates?"

"No, but they were killed by pirates. I was taken alive, you can probably guess why, and now I have a job cleaning and repairing this ship. Which is fine by me, since it keeps me away from the other pirates most of the time."

"Why don't you leave?"

"And go where?"

"Anywhere. Dive into the ocean, if that's your only option."

"Kill myself? As bad as life is, suicide's hardly the answer."

I was about to tell her it was a pretty good answer, but stopped myself. If Kuara was telling the truth, she had known a hard life. If she was willing to carry on living, I should have felt ashamed. In truth, I did not feel much of anything.

"Still," she said, "however bad I've got it, at least I'm not a mutant freak like you." She said this so conversationally that she probably did not even realise she was being insulting.

"Why don't you just go?" I said. "Leave me to my own thoughts. They're much better than having to think about you."

"Hey, at least I'm not spitting on you."

"How about I put it this way: clear off or I'll curse you."

"Mermaid magic only works on men."

"Not the curses. Spend too long with a mermaid and we have the ability to swap your soul with a seagull's. One moment you're painting the ship, the next you're soaring overhead, panicking about having wings while all the pirates think you've gone mad because the gull in your body will be flapping her arms around."

"You're so weird," Kuara said, swinging herself away to get on with her work.

I blamed the sun for my delirium and the pain for my crankiness, but I achieved my goal, for the young woman had gone. Taking deep breaths, I found I was in a different mind to how I had been before Kuara had come along. My despondency had gone, to be replaced with a bitter anger over my situation. A part of me had come to accept I deserved to be tied naked to the prow of a ship, but speaking with Kuara had changed my mind. The pirates were the worst of humanity and I deserved nothing they had elected to heap upon me. In that moment, I was resolved to escape, if not to gain vengeance upon them, but bound and bruised as I was, I was powerless.

Yet my words to Kuara returned to badger me. I may have been joking about the curse, but as I had already proved, my emotions could become a powerful tool.

Closing my eyes, I allowed my memories to flow, to wash over the sand of my emotions. I was angry over the injustice, sorrowful for my loss and concerned for Mallok. Yet I knew I could not do this in halves and forced myself to relive every blow I had taken, every fist and boot which had landed upon me. I recalled the oar shattering against my elbow, of being assaulted in the water, of being strung up like some meaningless sacrifice. My rage burst through my mind, mingled with fury and exploded outward.

There came no distant thunder to herald the coming storm; the storm simply opened all about the pirate ship. Rain battered the decking, winds tore down the masts and a churning maelstrom opened a great maw beneath the vessel.

I heard pirates yelling, saw bodies tumble from the ship into the Stygian depths, but I did not care. I would have killed them all if I was able and been glad for the opportunity. Someone was shouting, someone had realised I was to blame for what was happening and was ordering me shot or hacked to pieces or something. I dug deeper for more fuel for my rage and with an almighty lurch the pirate ship turned over. Men and women screamed, chains rattled as the slaves wailed without any means to free themselves. I smiled a mirthless smile as the prow of the ship slammed into the water, the sheer force of the plunge strong enough to loosen my bonds.

I was away, bulleting through the water, heedless of the mighty whirlpool I had created, uncaring of the carnage I was leaving behind. I did not stop, did not look back, did not care. I had suffered the worst humanity had to offer and I was scarred for it.

I did not stop swimming until land came into sight and at last I allowed my weary body to shut down as once again blissful unconsciousness seized me.

CHAPTER FOUR

I awoke to the gentle lash of the waves upon my naked body and never a more blissful feeling had I known. The aches and pains from my encounter with the pirates remained, although I had no broken bones and I was confident all the physical scars would heal. Had I been human, no doubt I would have been writhing in agony, I would probably even have died, yet those of the faerie races are stronger and far more resilient. Perhaps that was one of the reasons humans had always hated us, perhaps they were not only fearful of us but also jealous.

I lay for some time in a state of half-wakefulness, basking in the sun and stretching my limbs as I turned over. I could hear the distinct cawing of gulls and the gentle thrum of the waves. Behind all of that were whispers, which was odd, and, lying on my belly with my chin resting upon my hands, my elbows bent to the side, I opened a lazy eye to find myself upon the shale of a beach. There was a wall not far ahead of me, upon which wooden beams and buildings had been constructed, with walkways and piers encrusted with barnacles and hanging seaweed. I saw a few people standing on one of those piers, while a few more faces looked down at me from the buildings.

I had come, then, to a wharf, and judging by the discarded and broken detritus of rowing-boats and other rotten wood scattered across the shale, it was not a well-used one.

Rising, I finished my stretching and checked to make sure I had human legs, for the sight of a mermaid on the beach would have brought the humans running with their knives and staves. Giving a hearty wave to the people on the pier, I was a little offended as one woman covered her son's eyes and hastened him away. At least one young man had the decency to wave back, while motioning to his friends to come look at me.

It was at that point I remembered the whole obsession human beings had with clothes and that a woman walking naked from the sea was likely just as bad as a mermaid having washed up.

Hurrying to get beneath the pier, I was cut off from the warm sunshine, but at least I was out of sight of the gawkers. Looking around, I contemplated garbing myself in seaweed, but doubted that would give off an image of an ordinary young woman. My toes brushed against a large shell and memories of the pirate ship returned, of Kuara asking me why I wasn't wearing seashells over my breasts, and I kicked the thing in anger.

Thunder rumbled in the distance.

An idea formed in my mind and I returned my thoughts to the pirates, to how they had treated me, to how they had made me feel worthless. I felt tears well in my eyes and a lump form in my throat, and I opened my eyes to find the clouds had opened. Above me, I could hear people running for cover, for on such a bright sunny day no one had expected a swift onset of rain.

A Mermaid's Odyssey

Poking my head out from beneath the pier, I could see no one around aside from a couple of hardy fishermen up on the wharf. Taking my chances, I grabbed the supports of the pier, used the seaweed to steady myself as though it was a rope, and scuttled to the top. I could see people rushing to get out of the rain and thankfully no one was close enough to pay me any attention. Running down the pier, I cut down the first alleyway I found and disappeared between two large wooden buildings.

Behind me, the rain ceased, the clouds parted and the sun shone down once more.

Shaking the water from my long blonde hair, I slowed my pace and pricked up my ears. There did not appear to be anyone around, but I could have done without bumping into people. The buildings either side of me did not have any doors, although there was a window up ahead, boarded over and useless since it faced the alleyway. Hearing footsteps coming from ahead, I ran for the window, leaped, used a handy box as a springboard and stretched with my hand. Catching hold of the window frame, I hauled myself up, rolled through the wooden barrier as easily as if it had been formed of sand, and tumbled into the building.

I fell farther than expected and ended in an untidy heap on the floor. My body ached anew, but it was not the shameful pain of being beaten half to death. Staggering back to my feet, I found I was in a dark place, with shafts of light striking through from whatever windows were around. It was large and mainly empty, although there were crates scattered around. Most were open, all were empty, and I wondered where I had found myself.

A faint scratching sounded to my right and I stared in that direction, allowing my eyes to become adjusted to the gloom. There was a rat clawing at some sand which had spilled from a box, searching for material with which to build its nest. I had seen rats before, although only seldom, and I slowly lowered myself until my knees were touching the ground. The rat was several paces away and ignored me entirely, so I was able to watch, fascinated. Its large, bulbous body was coated in a thick dark fur which appeared coarse and dull in the gloom, while its unblinking eyes and sharp teeth lent it a truly horrific appearance.

Placing my palms to the floor, I slowly made my way over to it. The rat continued to ignore me. Perhaps it did not recognise my scent, perhaps it just did not care. Either way, it could not have predicted my speed.

When I was but two paces away, I controlled my breathing, levelling out my inhalations and exhalations until my heart was beating normally. Then I snatched out with my right arm, caught the rat by the tail and swung it around, smashing its head upon a crate. It emitted a little shriek but was silenced the instant its brains splattered across the wooden floor.

Drawing up my legs, I crossed them beneath me and sat with my back half inside the crate of spilled sand. Taking the rat in both hands, I tore into its flesh with teeth which had become instantly sharp enough for the task. Warm blood splashed across my face, bathed my arms and dribbled down my chin to drip onto my naked breasts. If anyone could have seen me in that moment, they would have labelled me a monster and even Mallok would have had a hard time reconciling me with the young woman he had come to love. But the truth of faeries is that we are not human and cannot be judged by human standards. After my ordeal with the pirates, I was famished and exhausted, and the rat offered me sustenance of both meat and blood.

I sucked all the goodness I could from the bones, crunching them and removing what little marrow could be found in the skeleton of a rat. By the time I was done, all that remained was a collection of broken bones and tufts of black fur my teeth had shorn off to get to the yolk inside.

Satisfied, I leaned back against the sand and breathed deeply of the salty sea air. I had food in my belly and my head was beginning to clear. By this time, my teeth had returned to their human-like nature and I sat there for some time contemplating what I was.

The transformation from faerie to human was not something to which I had ever given much thought, yet now that I was in human territory, I would have to be careful. My tail would cause great trouble if I forgot about it, but there was far more fey about me than the tail. The teeth of a mermaid are necessarily sharp, in order to shear through our human prey if we choose, yet they cannot remain so, else we would never entice people into the water in the first place. As with all faeries, much of what made me a mermaid was my glamour. From changelings to vampires, from succubi to will-o'-the-wisps, it was the very nature of faeriefolk to deceive humankind.

After my rest, I decided I had best begin my search for some clothes. Moving about the building, I found a lot of the floorboards were rotten and some of the internal walls had collapsed entirely. The sea air had done a great deal of damage to the place and it was clear it had been abandoned.

As I searched, I became aware of a presence and tried to work out where it was. There was something else alive in the building and I was reasonably certain it was a person. It took a great deal of time, but I eventually managed to locate the correct part of the building. It was no different in appearance to the rest of the place, save that I could sense the steady breathing of someone within. Casting my eyes about the floor, it was not long before I found him.

He was a man of wiry, unkempt appearance. He was not old, although the harshness of his life had aged him prematurely. He lay on a crude bed of straw and had a small metal case sitting beside him. It was old and battered but seemed to be all the man possessed.

As for the man himself, he was snoring gently and I could not understand why he was sleeping in an abandoned building. From what I knew of them, humans slept in beds which were found in houses. Also, he stank terribly and clearly had never been down to the beach to wash himself. On the trawler, and especially on the pirate vessel, the unwashed bodies were curiosities to me, but those were people who spent a long time at sea and could not simply bathe whenever they wished.

I could not understand the man. He did, however, possess clothes, and I wondered whether he would be willing to trade something for them. That I had nothing to trade made my situation somewhat precarious, but I had little to lose so decided to give it a go.

"Excuse me," I said, prodding him. "Sir?"

He stirred but all I achieved was that he turned over in his sleep.

"Sir?" I shook him by the shoulder and must have exerted more pressure than I had intended, for his eyes snapped open. He stared at me, leaning over him, and opened his mouth to scream. Perhaps his tongue had caught in the back of his throat, for no words came out. Scrabbling backwards, he struck against the wall and could move no farther.

"I'm not going to hurt you," I said. "I just … well, I'd like your coat, if it's all the same to you. I'll return it, I promise."

He tried to say something, pointed at me with a shaking finger, and I unconsciously looked down at myself, wondering what his problem was. Then I realised. It was not just that I was naked, but that I was covered in rat's blood. I could only imagine how red my lips were and how much dried blood must have been smudged across my face.

I tried to think of something to say which might reassure him, but honestly my mind was blank.

The man tore off his jacket and hurled it at me, which was precisely what I wanted. I thought about asking him for his trousers and shirt as well, but did not want to upset him more than I already had. Thanking him, I moved off, shrugging on the jacket as I went. The material was coarse and felt heavy upon my shoulders. It also itched and I did not doubt there were lice nesting in the thing. The smell was worse than the man himself, for it was probable the jacket had been washed less frequently than its owner. It would, however, protect me from most of the stares.

Locating a door, I re-entered the outside world and clutched the jacket about me. I was conscious of my bare legs and feet, but was hoping this would not appear so odd. As I moved away from the building, I approached some dock workers tying off rope or carrying heavy equipment, and none of them paid me any attention at all. Keeping my head down and wishing I had a cap, I moved at a pace neither too quick nor too slow. I had no destination in mind, for I knew nothing of human society, and as I rounded the next corner I stopped and stared in disbelief at the veritable world laid out before me.

I stood upon slightly raised ground and stared in awe. The city stretched east and west as far as the eye could see, while in the distance, to the south, it was as though the entire world promised to be this one sprawling network of human beings. The buildings were amazing. Some were small, others huge, while rows of houses snaked their way through everything, with shops scattered around and merchants plying their wares from carts. A few of the buildings rose to two, possibly even three storeys, while thin towers stretched even further to the heavens.

Then there were the people. My wide, awestruck eyes must have picked out thousands in my first sweep alone. Some worked shirtless on the docks, others ran between alleys, while men and women of all ages and sizes mingled on the streets, moving about their daily business. There were strange animals, too – large four-legged beasts with long faces which pulled carts – and I wondered what other marvels the city held.

Someone moved past me and I broke from my reverie. If I wanted to fit in with the human society, I could not stand there staring all day. Keeping my head bowed again, I made my way slowly down to the street level, where my excited heart beat fiercely at the thought of becoming one with the crowd.

At first, I kept to the shadows. The noise was deafening, for the sea was essentially a quiet place and I was unused to the clamour of human voices and actions. Peering from the shadows, I watched as two small boys danced between the legs of some passing women, evading a man chasing them and crying out that they were thieves. I saw a young man hopelessly trying to talk to a woman who held her chin so imperiously high that she could have done with a good slap, while two more women gossiped and giggled as they watched a shirtless man heave timber.

I could not step out into them, for my stomach was filled with butterflies and I was suddenly well aware that I was garbed in a filthy, lice-ridden jacket.

"Hey," someone called. There was a woman storming over to me. She was dressed in tight trousers and a loose blouse which revealed bare shoulders and an ample amount of cleavage, even though she didn't have much to speak of. Her face was painted with some form of oil in order to mask her true looks and her lips were blazing red. As with the man in the building, she looked older than she was, and I wondered whether human society aged everyone before their time.

"Misako," I said, extending my hand as the woman reached me. "Pleased to meet you." I decided I might as well be polite.

The woman stopped, stunned, and accepted my hand without meaning to. Then she drew her hand away and said, "This is my patch."

"Patch?" I asked, looking to her eyes. "Your eyes are your prettiest feature, ma'am, you don't need a patch."

"I ... huh?"

"Sorry. I'm new here, I probably spoke out of turn."

The woman's venom was dissipating, turning to confusion. "New? Are you trying to muscle in on my territory or not?"

"I don't think so. I just arrived and I'm a bit overwhelmed."

"Arrived from where?"

"The sea. I ..." I stopped myself. I may have been in shock over my first experience in a human city, but I could not blurt out to everyone that I was a mermaid. "I was captured by pirates. I escaped."

"Pirates?"

I shrugged.

The woman narrowed one eye and rubbed at her chin. "That's not lipstick, is it? That's blood."

I wiped at my mouth, having forgotten about the rat's blood. I could not imagine much of it came off.

The woman raised my jacket experimentally with one finger and wrinkled her nose. "You really don't want to be wearing that."

"No, but it's all I have."

Her ire had vanished entirely by this point. "All right, kid, it looks like I've adopted you for the moment. Come with me."

"Where?"

"Somewhere you won't get arrested for walking around naked."

"I'm not naked. I have a jacket."

"Just come with me, all right?"

"What's your name?"

"Salla."

I contemplated saying no, but my options were limited. It seemed I was making no choices for myself, but so far I had survived. "All right. I'm sorry if I infect you with lice."

She laughed at this and took me on a journey through the backstreets of the port. While we travelled, she revealed this was not a city, just a port, or a town, and that the cities were much bigger. The town was called Mrinth and its primary trade was the fishing industry. I asked Salla whether she fished and she laughed but did not give me much of an answer.

We came to a building with a blue door and Salla passed through, leading me into a long corridor with a great many doors. At the end was a staircase and it was up this that she led me. There was a lot of noise in the place, and I could sense a range of emotions from those who lived there. At the top of the stairs, we came upon another row of doors and Salla took me to a specific one. Inserting her key, she turned it before pushing the door open.

"Jacket," she said from the doorway.

"Hmm?"

Shaking her head, she slipped the jacket off my shoulders and, holding it between thumb and forefinger, took it to the end of the stairs, where she tossed it out the window.

"I'm supposed to return that," I said.

"Well, get used to breaking promises, kid." She looked me over briefly and I found it odd she was appraising me. I did not feel uncomfortable, for there was nothing lascivious or damning in her look, but I did wonder what she was doing. Then she motioned me into the doorway and I entered Salla's home.

It was small, formed of a single room with a bed and a few scattered possessions. There was a bowl of water sitting on a table and Salla told me to use it to clean myself up. She explained there was a communal bathroom at the end of the hall but that the girls who lived in the building generally kept a bowl in their room so they could freshen up in private. While I cleaned the blood from my face and chest, Salla moved across to one wall and opened a wardrobe, from which she removed some clothes and tossed them at me.

"They should fit," she said.

"I can't take your clothes."

"You took that jacket."

Holding the clothes in my hand, I composed myself, for everything was moving too quickly for me. "I don't have anything to give you in return."

"Just stay off the streets, that'll help me loads."

"How?"

"Pretty thing like you wandering through my patch? I'm never getting any work again."

I did not know what she meant, but she clearly did, so I slipped myself into the trousers and top. I had little trouble with the trousers, for I had experience with the things back on board the trawler, but the top had arms and that was something I was not used to. After getting stuck, unable to see and wandering about for a few minutes trying to get my arms through the sleeves, Salla stopped laughing long enough to give me a hand.

"There," she said as she smoothed down my attire and stepped back to admire me. "Perfect."

"Salla," a woman said, leaning against her open door. She was slightly shorter than Salla, with blonde hair like mine, although hers was dirty and stragglier. She was also unhealthily thin and I worried she was ill.

"Mirna," Salla said. "Misako, this is Mirna. Mirna, my cousin."

"Mirna's your cousin?" I asked.

"No, I was telling Mirna *you're* my cousin."

"Oh. Sorry. Pleased to meet you."

Mirna glanced at the hand I was holding out, but her eyes were filled with disdain. "You never mentioned you had a cousin, Salla."

"Why would I recite my family tree to you, Mirna?"

"Is Misako going to be working with us?"

"Gods no. She's just staying with me a while. Until she gets on her feet. She's new to Mrinth and doesn't know anyone."

"Why's she wearing your clothes?"

"Because hers wore out on her way here. Why are you asking so many questions?"

"No reason." Mirna cast me one final look of hatred before walking away.

"Wow," I said. "She's a mean one."

"Mirna's fine, once you get to know her. She distrusts people, that's all. The world let her down and she hates everyone for it."

"She said you work together? I could help. I like to work for my keep."

Salla's smile reached her eyes and I could see she found something extremely funny. "You're a swell kid, Misako, but I don't think you'd much like the work we do here."

"Here? You mean in this building?"

"No. The rule is never to bring our work home. This is just where we live. We all live together so we can keep an eye out for one another. That way if a girl goes missing, we can know about it right away."

"Is your work dangerous?"

"Yes. There are some sick people out there."

"You're doctors?"

"Are you joking with me?"

"A little." I must admit, I did not at the time fully understand what Salla did for a living, but then I had lived something of a sheltered life. Her profession did not exist within the realms of faerie, not as far as I understood, and with it being my first visit to a human settlement, my thoughts were not exactly intent on solving puzzles. That was not to say I was stupid, just naïve and with my mind elsewhere.

"I don't have to go to work until tonight," Salla said. "What say I show you around town?"

"Would you? That would be amazing."

"Sure." She ruffled my hair and I was glad she was happy. I had a saddening suspicion she did not get to be happy all too often.

CHAPTER FIVE

Mrinth was like nothing I had ever experienced before. Salla asked me what I wanted to see and I replied everything. We visited the marketplace and she bought me something to eat off a stall. It was cooked over a sizzling griddle and set upon a skewer, although I could not tell what the food was. Salla said it was a collection of meat and vegetables, but the smell alone was so divine I instantly forgot anything she was telling me. She introduced me to a horse, since I revealed I had never before seen one, and she laughed at my attempts at communication. She taught me to whistle at young men and how to add a swing to my walk which apparently accentuated my bum. We watched street performers re-enacting the fall of some pantomime villain named Clothos and sat through a puppet show about two women fighting for the affections of the same man; before the man got himself eaten by a crocodile. Children found that part funny and I laughed along with them, even though I thought it an odd and upsetting thing to be showing them.

We passed two uniformed soldiers who were sauntering through the streets and Salla bumped one with her hip. He chased her away with a grin and a half-hearted slap with the back of his hand aimed toward her general vicinity.

"Wasn't that dangerous?" I asked once we were away from them.

"Flirting with the town militia? They pay most of my wages, I flirt with them every opportunity I get."

"Then you're in the military?"

She laughed aloud at this but said no more. We came to another marketplace and Salla stopped to feel the material of some hanging garments, although did not appear to have any intention of buying anything. I copied her and found the material to be rather ordinary but did not wish to be rude and say so.

Then something did catch my eye and I found myself standing before another stall. Upon it were scattered a hundred sparkling gems set into earrings, brooches, bracelets and all manner of other pretty things. A suave, thin man stood behind the stall, talking about the rarity of his jewels and somehow managing to talk over the woman selling half-price strawberries down the other end of the market.

"I have my eye on this stall sometimes," Salla said, joining me. Now that he had two potential customers, the thin man redoubled his efforts and Salla smiled kindly, although she had no intention of buying anything.

"I've never seen anything like it," I said.

"Baubles are lovely," Salla said, "but they don't pay the bills."

I picked up a pearl and found it was attached to a necklace. There were many others strung to the same necklace and I played with it slowly, raising each hand so the beads would spill from one to the other.

"That's a bargain, that one, miss," the man said. "Only a hundred fetrekons."

"What's a fetrekon?"

He laughed, although stopped when he saw the confusion in my eyes. "Fetrekons," he repeated as though I was supposed to understand it the second time around. "Money? Little pieces of beaten metal imprinted with the seal of the kingdom?" He glanced to Salla for help.

"My cousin's not from around here," Salla said as she gently lifted the beautiful pearl necklace from my fingers and placed it back onto the table. "They have a different currency where she's from."

"A different currency? But fetrekons are universal. The only difference is the stamp on them depending on the kingdom it's from. Whatever kingdom you call home, miss, I'll gladly accept the fetrekons they mint."

"Maybe another time, thanks," Salla said, steering me away. I did not speak while she did so, for I feared I had made a grave error. It seemed humans exchanged pieces of metal for things they wanted. I had noticed Salla do this already, when we had got something to eat, yet had not paid much attention to it.

She released my arm once we had gained a little distance from the stall. "Sorry," I said. "We don't have money where I come from."

"You don't say."

She was amused by something; if there was one thing I was growing to like about Salla, it was that she was always amused. I knew it was my influence that had her in such high spirits and was glad I could bring some joy to her life.

She grabbed us some more food and made a point of showing me how she was paying for it. We took a big bowl of strawberries and sat on a wooden barrier overlooking the docks. There were a lot of people working down there, with boats coming in and out all the time. There were ships sailing on the distant ocean and I longed to be back out in the vast waters.

Salla bit into a strawberry and tossed away the green stalk before offering me the bowl. I took one tentatively and nibbled its end. It was sweeter than I expected and as I felt its juices dribble down my chin, I was reminded of the rat I had devoured earlier.

"So," Salla said, removing her shoes so she could gaily swing her bare legs, "you're a mermaid, then."

I choked on my second strawberry.

"Oh, don't worry about me," she said. "I'm not going to tell anyone. Nice legs for a mermaid."

"So I've been told."

A light flickered across her eyes. "Then it's true?"

I knew I should not reveal the truth, had been warned by my mother to hide my true nature from humans if ever I found myself among them, but I trusted Salla. She was a good woman and, more than that, she was my friend. "Yeah," I said. "How could you tell?"

"A lot of things. You don't know what money is, which is downright weird. Your face when you ate your first ever strawberry, the fact you can't even put on your top without getting lost and needing my help. Then there's the walking-around-naked thing. You were dressed in a homeless person's jacket when I met you, which means you came to Mrinth naked.

Sure, you had the pirate story, but everything about you screamed mermaid."

"The pirate thing wasn't a story."

"I'm sorry. Did they hurt you?"

"Yes."

"Then I'm sorry about that, too."

"Salla, just because I was walking around naked, the natural conclusion isn't that I'm a mermaid."

"No. But it's not such a stretch when you consider the talk."

"Talk?"

"There was a big commotion at the docks earlier. Apparently, a beautiful nude woman emerged from the water, basked herself on the beach for a while and then blasted everyone with a storm and vanished. From what I know of faeries, the only two types of people who can do that sort of thing are mermaids and vampires; and, last I checked, vampires don't like to cross water."

"There's not much difference between vampires and mermaids, to be fair," I said. "We're both elemental species who can control the weather, we can both change our forms at will, we're both far stronger than the average human being."

"And you both lure people of the opposite sex to their orgasmic doom."

I shuddered at the crudity of her words, but did not refute them.

"What?" she asked.

"Nothing. You're just very uncouth."

"You're saying you don't wrap yourself around the minds of young men and draw them into the water so you can have your wicked way with them?" She was teasing, but we both knew she was also being truthful.

"I've never had my wicked way with anyone," I said, feeling the blood rush to my face. "We're not all monsters."

"You being a monster never crossed my mind." She stared out across the water for a moment. "Gods, never?"

"Never what?"

She held up a strawberry she had bit vertically in half. "You know."

I blushed deeper and pointedly ignored her.

She laughed loudly and rolled onto one elbow, where she could more comfortably eat her strawberries. "Seriously, though, I respect that," she said. "My first time wasn't exactly memorable. My dad liked to keep it in the family, and we had a huge family."

"Salla, that's terrible."

"Mmm. I'm over it. What are you doing on land? And, I've been desperately trying not to ask, but where's your fish tail? I heard stories that you take it off and hide it and that if a man finds it, you have to marry him until you can find it again."

"That's mainly selkies."

"What's a selkie?"

"Like a mermaid, but more seal-like. Then again, there are tribes of mermaids who do that, so I hear."

"Mermaids live in tribes?"

"Not really. We usually live alone, or in small families. But we get together if there are more of us than there are streams. I've heard of a dozen mermaids working one stream, but then that's because they're the ones who eat human flesh."

"You haven't told me about your tail."

"It's ... complicated. I can change my form, like I said. There are lot of faeries who can do that. The more demonic ones pretend to be human, changelings resemble human children, vampires become wolves or bats or rats. Mermaids, we don't change our entire bodies, just the lower half. It's not something I can really explain to you; no offence, but you wouldn't understand it. It's just something we do."

"Uh huh."

I felt freer than I had in a long time. Talking with Salla was an amazing experience and sitting in the cool dockside air, it was as though I had shrugged off all the troubles life had heaped upon me. She was interested in me and she was not afraid at all. Even Mallok had been cautious of me, but Salla found me fascinating, which was something I had not expected from a human being.

"Are you really as beautiful as you look?" she asked.

"How do you mean?"

"Well, if you can change your appearance, surely you'd make yourself as beautiful as you could. Beauty can move mountains, Misako. With your face, you could be a queen."

"I'm not beautiful."

"Yeah, and I love my job."

"You do?"

"No, that was sarcasm."

"Oh. We don't have sarcasm in the undersea kingdoms."

Her eyes widened. "You have undersea kingdoms?"

"No, that was sarcasm."

She tossed a stalk at me.

I inhaled deeply of the warm air and lay down beside where Salla was still perched upon her elbow. I had never expected to feel so comfortable and a part of me would have loved to have stayed with Salla in the port of Mrinth for the rest of my life.

She fed me a strawberry while I lay there and I chewed it slowly.

"You didn't answer my first question," she said. "What are you doing on land?"

"I'm searching for my father. He's a knight, a powerful and important man. A long time ago, he was taking a drink from a stream, when he saw a beautiful face peering out at him through the water. He fell instantly in love and asked her to come onto land. The mermaid refused, for she knew the tricks of men, even though she yearned for him with as much passion as he did her. But the knight was no fool and knew not to enter the realm of a mermaid unless he wanted to die.

"So they hit on a compromise. The knight was also a powerful sorcerer and they agreed that he would place a spell upon the mermaid, one of decay. Over the course of the following year, the mermaid would age rapidly until she wasted away. The knight would lift the curse once he was back on dry land. It was his way of making sure the mermaid would not kill him and would allow him to return to shore.

"The curse in place, the knight felt safe enough to enter the water. They remained together for several days, although my mother never went into precisely what happened during that time and I never pressed. Eventually, though, the knight had to return home and it was with a heavy heart that he left the water. The mermaid leaned in for a final kiss and in that kiss the knight not only lifted the curse but also bestowed what he termed the 'child's blessing'. If the mermaid conceived because of their union, their child would be protected from harm for eighteen years, until she reached womanhood.

"It turned out the mermaid had indeed conceived, and when I was born, the other merfolk would not harm me for fear of exacting my father's curse. On the day of my eighteenth birthday, then fell upon my mother and murdered her. I escaped. Now, without my mother, without a home, all I have left is the image of my father and the amazing man he is."

There were tears to Salla's eyes when I finished my tale, although she wiped them away and pretended they had not existed. "The most amazing thing about that is that you mermaids consider eighteen the end of your childhood."

"It's not that way with humans?"

"It differs from place to place. You're lucky with your dad: mine thought my childhood ended when I was twelve. What's his name?"

"I don't know."

"You don't know?"

"He never told my mother. I don't think she asked."

"Oh."

"I have a description of him," I said. "He's a soldier with different-coloured eyes. One brown, the other green. And he has a scar over his right eye."

"That probably explains why his eye changed colour. Is that it? Don't you have anything else to go on?"

"No."

"Do you even know which kingdom he was fighting for?"

"No."

"And you say he's a knight? Are you sure he's not just a soldier? A mercenary?"

"My mother filled my childhood with so many wondrous tales of fabled kings and heroic beasts that he just has to be a knight."

"Uh huh."

"You don't believe he is?"

"I … I don't know. Sorry, I'm not going to lie to you, honey." She played another strawberry across her lips while she thought. "Misako, I want to ask you something and I want you to seriously consider it."

"What?"

"Stay here in Mrinth. Give up this quest of yours and stay. You could be happy here, Misako. It's not a bad place to live. You could get a job in the bakery or something."

"Why don't *you* get a job in the bakery?"

"Because I'm too used to popping down the clinic to get the buns *out* of my oven."

I shook my head. "Sometimes, I honestly have no idea what you're talking about."

"And that's what makes you sweet, Misako. Just promise me you'll think about it. We could come here every afternoon, we can bring something different from the market to try every time. And we could talk. It's nice to look into the eyes of someone who's not judging me, Misako."

"Salla, don't take this the wrong way, but I think you're a very lonely woman."

"I don't have to be. Stay here. With me."

I looked back out to the sea. It was tempting to discard my heart and agree to what she was offering, but my father was out there somewhere and I was determined to find him. "Sorry, Salla," I said. "But, once I find my father, I promise to bring him to see you."

Her face fell, although she masked it well. Her smile did not disappear, for she had spent her entire adult life pretending to be happy about something which made her miserable. It was more the slump of her body and the general energy falling away from her soul that gave it away. I felt terrible for having hurt her and wished I could make it better.

"We can still be friends," I said hopefully.

"Yeah," she said, trying to believe it. "I'd like that."

We did not speak much after that. We simply lay there together, yet apart, watching the boats and listening to the roar of the ocean. We had both lost interest in finishing off the strawberries.

CHAPTER SIX

Salla had said she needed to go to work in the evening, so as darkness fell I knew I was about to lose her for a while. It had been strange to spend the day with another woman, to chat and laugh and talk about inconsequential things for so many hours. Salla said she would drop me off at her home before she went out to work for the night and that I would have to keep myself amused. I said I was thinking of taking a look around the town at night, but Salla advised against it.

"It's not that the streets are rife with crime," she said while we walked back through the marketplace, "but I don't think you're city-savvy enough to be alone at night."

"I'm tougher than I look."

"That I don't doubt, but you're also not used to people. Here," she handed me some money. "Go buy us a few oranges. I'll be along in a minute."

I held the coins tightly in my hand and moved over to a fruit stall. Life under the water had not prepared me for all the human food and I found myself at a loss as to which fruit might have been an orange. There was a tray of orange fruits and I assumed these had to be the ones I was after, so I asked the stall owner for a bag of them. Handing over my money, I waited a few moments for Salla to catch up so I could show her my stash.

"At least they're orange," she said, taking one out of the bag and biting into it.

"I take it I bought the wrong thing."

"They're apricots, but who doesn't love apricots?"

We walked back to where Salla lived, eating the flesh of the juicy fruits and tossing away the stones. Our talk was light but I could tell Salla was sad that I had decided not to stay with her. In truth, I was debating whether to change my mind, for life with Salla would not have been bad at all and perhaps she was right. Perhaps I would never find my father. After eighteen years, there was no guarantee he was even still alive, although I firmly believed I would have felt it in my heart if he had passed away.

There were a few women on the street when we reached Salla's building. They all lived inside and were getting ready for work. They gossiped behind concealing hands as we approached and it seemed my arrival was causing a stir.

"Mirna's been brewing trouble," Salla said icily.

"She doesn't like you?"

"Mirna's an odd one. She keeps to herself mainly. There's clearly something wrong with her, but then that's to be expected. Her main problem is she sees threats everywhere, she never got the hang of trusting anyone. One time, I offered to do her laundry, just to be neighbourly. She didn't talk to me for a week, but I saw her staring daggers plenty of times. Like I was going to steal her dirty underwear or something."

"Maybe I should have a word."

"That wouldn't be a good idea. Like I said, she sees threats everywhere and pretty girls are a threat to her livelihood."

"You mean she might act more aggressively to me than *you* did when we first met?"

"All right, I deserved that. And you deserve this."

She held something out and I accepted it quizzically. It was a thin chain, upon which was strung a single pearl.

"I couldn't afford the whole necklace," Salla said, "but I scraped enough together for the one pearl. I figured it was better than nothing."

"But, Salla, even one pearl must have been expensive."

She nervously rubbed the back of her neck. "Yeah, well, you're worth it."

"It's beautiful."

"It's a pretty little thing cut off from the rest of her people, all alone and being strung along through life."

I hugged Salla. It must have come as a surprise because she stiffened and did not know where to put her hands. Then she hugged me back and I could feel her trembling.

"No one's ever bought me anything before," I said, pulling away and looking into her kind eyes. "I should get you something."

"You don't have any money."

"Then I should make you something, or do something for you. What don't you like doing? I'll do it for you for a month."

"You intend to stay with me for a month?"

I had not known I was going to say that, but did not regret the words now that I had said them. I had remained on board the trawler for a month and much preferred the company of Salla, so there was no reason not to spend an equal amount of time with her.

I had waited eighteen years to find my father, I could wait a little longer.

"I intend to stay long enough," I said, "to make you the happiest woman in the world."

She embraced me again, so hard I yelped, for I still had yet to recover from my mistreatment by the pirates. "Oh, Misako," she said, and I could hear the tears in her eyes, "you already have."

"Well, isn't this sweet," Mirna said, approaching with a small crowd of women. "Salla the social worker and her pet project."

"Leave us alone, Mirna," Salla said irritably.

"Sorry, have I ruined the moment?"

"What do you want?"

"Security, money, a life where decent people can walk the streets."

Salla's laugh was short and without mirth.

"I'm serious," Mirna said. "Society looks down on us, sure, but only when they're not paying us. Creatures like your Misako there, they're ten times the filth we are."

"I'm not filth," Salla said, looking at each of the women in turn. "None of us are. Misako hasn't done any of you any harm, why don't you just leave her alone?"

"She's a faerie," Mirna said, to several nods from the crowd. I had seen before where this mob mentality had gone and it had not ended well the last time. I had fled Mallok to hold off the other mariners and could not bear to think of abandoning Salla in the same way. Mallok had been a mountain of a man and could handle himself, but Salla would be swamped by these people if they attacked her.

"She's a person," Salla said through gritted teeth.

"No, she's a thing. And dressing the thing in your clothes and buying her trinkets isn't going to change that. We're at war with the faeries and here you are having an affair with one."

Salla took a swing at her. It shocked all of us, most of all Mirna, who dropped like the bag of apricots I was carrying. The other woman backed off, muttering, aghast by what had happened. Mirna groaned where she lay, rubbing her aching jaw and fighting through her surprise.

"She's not a thing," Salla spat. Her body was tense with anger, her finger was stabbing out at the women and I could feel the rage waft from her in waves. "She's a young woman who needs guidance, she's a lost soul who needs to be shown the way. It doesn't matter what you think of her, she's better than any of us."

"She's bewitched," someone said. "The mermaid's cast a spell on her."

"I don't cast spells," I said, stepping forward. "I'm not even sure I can. Look, I don't mean anyone any harm and I'm not here to interfere with your work. What's your problem?"

"Our problem," Mirna said, rising, "is that you're inhuman filth and if you're sleeping with the enemy, Salla, it makes you even worse."

"We can talk about this," I said. "I can prove myself to …"

"So you can bring us all under your spell?"

"I don't cast spells."

"It doesn't matter, anyway. It's too late."

"Mirna," Salla cautioned. "What have you done?"

"My duty as a human being."

Salla looked around and her eyes widened. Grabbing me by the arm, she turned me around to see a dozen uniformed soldiers appearing. At their head was a woman in armour and upon seeing us she gave an order to her soldiers.

"Run," Salla said.

"No," I said, shaking my arm free. "I ran before, I'm not doing it again."

"Run, Misako. Don't be a fool."

"I'm not a fool." I stood facing Salla, pushing down my fear as best as I was able even though Salla's own terror was not helping me any. "I may be young, I may be naïve and I may not understand much of human society, but you're my friend, Salla, and if I run, bad things are going to happen to you."

"Please, Misako. They're going to kill you."

"They can try."

Salla's hand caught me across the face so hard I staggered. My cheek stung with pain, but it was the emotional pain of betrayal more than physical hurt. Her lower lip was bleeding from where she had bitten through to steady her teeth and her eyes trembled with terrified tears.

"I know what you're doing," I said. "You're ..."

"You don't know anything about me, Misako. I'm a screwed-up mess and always have been. You think I liked you? I liked the idea of you; the innocent, naïve beautiful girl I was before my father started handing me around to my relatives like some pass-the-parcel where everyone gets a feel of the prize. You're a comfort blanket, Misako, a doll I was clinging to because it prettied up my own dirty, despicable life."

"You don't mean that," I cried.

"Get out of my life," she said, shoving me with both hands. Tears filled her eyes but her attack was forceful. "I don't want you, I don't love you, I can't even stand you. You're not human, Misako, you're a thing, a monster. A half-breed freak I spent the day with because I had nothing better to do."

"Salla, please."

"Just go, Misako. Please, just go."

I looked over my shoulder to see the soldiers had started running towards us now. They were still half a minute or so away and were having trouble getting through the crowds which had gathered to wonder what the soldiers were doing there.

"Salla, I ..."

She hit me with her fist, catching me on the side of the head and sending me crashing to the ground. There, she kicked me and I was suddenly back on board the pirate vessel, being kicked and beaten and spat upon by the foul, uncouth monsters of the sea.

Rising slowly, I tried to say something else, but no words came. Salla shook her head, unable to speak either, for she had become a destroyed mess. Mirna was too astonished to do much of anything and the other women chattered all over again.

I sent one final pleading look into Salla's eyes, searching for the love she had since denied, but all that stared back at me was disgust.

Turning, I fled down the street. Behind me, I heard the soldiers' captain give a shout and her troops gave chase. I did not stop, did not have any need to. There was nothing for me in Mrinth, no one to care about, and as I fled through the streets, I paid no heed to anyone or anything about me. I shot through the marketplace, overturning stalls, barging through people of all sizes and status. I saw oranges spill across the ground from where I had accidentally destroyed a stall, and heard the angry cries of the owner in my wake.

I ran for over two hours, heedless of the direction I was taking, oblivious to my surroundings. The soldiers had long since been lost behind me, although there would be others. I had the impression there would always be soldiers.

Finally, I stopped, exhausted, and collapsed against a small vertical stone standing half my bodyheight from the ground. Leaning against this, I wept bitter tears for the unfairness of life. I must have remained there for a long time, I don't know how long, and when I had no more tears to shed, I realised I was still clutching the pearl necklace Salla had given me. Angrily drawing back my arm, I made to hurl it away; and stopped.

Salla had spent her hard-earned money on that pearl, money she had gained from the job she hated. I thought back to the time we had spent together, however brief it had been. Buying me dinner, the mix-up with the oranges and the apricots, lying on the docks while Salla fed me strawberries and spoke of my innocence. Those were not the actions of someone who was mocking me, just as the pearl was not a gift to dress up a favourite doll. I realised in that moment how naïve I was, how blinded I had been by the strangeness of human society. I knew precisely why Salla had been kind to me, and why she had ultimately pretended to hate me.

I felt heartless for having doubted her and I hated myself because she believed she had fooled me – because she believed I now must hate her, too. But there was no returning to Salla. I could probably have found my way back to her, but she had made her decision and if I turned up in her life again it would ruin her. As things stood, she could mend things with Mirna, she could explain herself away to the town militia, claiming to have been under my spell, and she could get her life back in order. If I returned, I would not only ruin all of that, I would likely get her severely punished, perhaps even executed.

I had known there was a war on between humans and faeries, that it had been raging for generations, but its depth and complexity had never occurred to me. Humans would hate me simply for being me, as my mother had always said.

Slipping the pearl necklace over my head and fluffing out my hair, I set it against my breast and gazed upon it in sorrow, for it was all I had left of my friend.

"Are you all right, miss?" someone asked. I looked up to find a kindly old gentleman reaching down a helping hand. Refusing his aid, I used the vertical stone to get back to my feet.

"I'm fine," I said. "Leave me alone."

"Are you hurt?"

"I said I'm fine."

"I know you did, but you're crying and girls who cry aren't fine."

I wanted to snap at him again. He was, after all, a human and therefore an enemy who wanted nothing more than to destroy me. But he did not know my origins, nor my nature, and as such he was being kind. I did not want his help, but my mother had taught me better than to be rude to people.

I noticed there was writing on the stone and asked, "What does this say?"

"That's a touchstone, miss. It marks the edge of the town."

"A touchstone?"

"If you touch the stone on your way in, all your sins and troubles are drawn from you and into the stone. If you touch it on your way out, you absorb all the sins folk have put in there." He paused. "Or, it might be the other way around. I'm not sure."

I had already pulled myself up by it and decided I had already touched it. One way or another, I was likely cursed, so I placed my palm against it and closed my eyes. I felt nothing, which probably meant it was just a stupid human superstition. Strangely, most human superstitions grew from faeries, and this one probably had some root in my kind. I could almost hear the faeries laughing at me for my idiocy.

"Anything?" he asked.

"No." I took a deep breath. "Thank you."

"For what?"

"For giving me some measure of hope for your species." Looking to the south, I saw that indeed the town did end, for there was a well-travelled road heading away, with the settlements and roads becoming smaller and of fewer quantity as the way wore on. Placing one foot before the other, I began to walk. To where, I could not say. I could only be certain I was leaving Mrinth forever.

CHAPTER SEVEN

To the south of Mrinth, the land became more rugged. It was the first time I had been unable to see the ocean in any direction and I felt as though I was lost in a desert. My mother had told me stories about deserts, but I did not know precisely what they were. All I knew was that they were areas devoid of water and that my kind would surely die if trapped there for any great period of time.

Sleeping on the side of the road, I regained my strength before attempting to cross such a vast tract of nothingness. I had nothing to eat and nothing to drink, but knew I did not deserve anything. Salla would be miserable and I had no right to be happy.

After a couple of hours, the road ended completely and I saw no one and no sign of anyone for some time. As unsteady as I had been when first using my legs, I felt like a child all over again as I attempted to navigate the jagged rocks underfoot. Ahead, I could see giant rising mountains and it was to these that I veered purely because I was using them as a navigation tool. When in the ocean, I could travel in a straight line by keeping my eye fixed upon one single star, and this was no different. It was as I reached those mountains that I reasoned I had a puzzle to solve, for there was no easy route around them.

There were many of the things and it seemed they were connected somewhat at their bases. Steep valleys wound their way through the mountains, in some instances creating vast tracts of land, filled with sand and dust. I wandered around for several hours, until the sun dipped low, blocked by the mountains and creating a swift evening. I was still no closer to finding my way through than I had been when I started.

The growing darkness did not overly bother me, for my eyesight was exceptional, and I was able to explore a while longer. Eventually, I decided I would simply have to work my way through the valleys and hope for the best. The sand was trickier to walk on than I had expected and the rising mountains blocked most of the heat, allowing the cool wind to rush through. Living in the depths of the ocean, I knew all about extreme cold, yet could see how such a landscape would be considered inhospitable to humans.

Thirst was my main concern. My stomach rumbled in hunger, but my throat was dry and I was feeling light-headed from so much walking without being able to slake my thirst. After a while, I began to recognise landmarks in the valleys and knew I had been walking around in circles, for there was little chance of guiding myself by the stars when all the mountains blocked them from sight.

Feeling defeated and dejected, I collapsed against a rock and rethought my strategy. Thus far, I had been attempting to get around the mountains, and then to go through them. All I had left to try was to go over them. Looking up, I reasoned that to be a difficult proposition, yet with my heightened strength I felt reasonably sure I would be able to make a good go of it.

Steeling my nerves, I began to climb.

It was the first time I had ever attempted such a thing, for while we had mountains in the ocean, they were all underwater and I had been able to swim around them. We even had volcanoes at the bottom of the ocean, which may be dangerous things but they're also quite beautiful. There was nothing beautiful about the mountains I was climbing, however, for they were ugly grey eyesores which stood between me and my father.

By the time I reached a ledge large enough for me to stop for a rest, I was feeling the effects of my climb. Sweat poured off me in sticky, salty waves and I lay there for some moments catching my breath.

While I did so, I stared into the night sky, for as high as I had reached, I could at last see the stars again. Lying in the cool night air, it was comforting to see familiar sights, for the stars above the land were the same as those above the ocean. It made me homesick, but I refused to dwell upon them, for I was looking forward in life and leaving the past behind.

A strange scent was brought to me upon the wind. Something was burning. I remembered one time watching a ship which had caught fire. There had been oil spilled on the decking and the mast had caught alight, the sails going up in instant flames. The screams had been terrible and the sickly smell of burning flesh had reached me across the waves as I watched dying sailors tumble into the ocean.

This was different, for the scent was fainter and the smell of cooking meat was somewhat less sickening.

Moving across the ledge, I worked my way around the rocks, following the scent, and saw a crackling light some way ahead. Curious, I approached to find a small fire burning, trapped within a circle of stones. There were two pieces of wood standing vertically, either side of the fire, across which a horizontal beam had been set. There was something cooking on the spit – it looked like a rabbit – and my stomach gurgled at the thought of food.

There was a single man sitting beside the fire. He was old and gently stoked the fire without causing anyone any harm. I knew I could seize the rabbit without him being able to stop me, could even hurl him down the mountainside if I chose; but that was not the way my mother had raised me. I was wary about striking up a conversation with him, however, for my time with humans had taught me they could not be trusted.

"You don't have to stand there in the shadows, girl," he said in a low, scratchy voice. "Sit with me and make an old man smile."

Stepping into view, I moved to the fire and sat opposite him. Now that I could see his face, I noticed it was covered with a bushy, bristling beard. Upon his head was a cap to protect him from the winds, while his eyes were white and sightless. It explained how he had noticed me in the shadows.

"Do you have a name?" he asked.

"Yes."

He stoked the fire some more. "Would you like to share it?"

"Misako."

"A pretty name for a pretty girl."

"How do you know I'm pretty?"

"Your voice is young and confused, exhausted and afraid. But you didn't steal my food, so that makes you a good person. And good people are all pretty to a blind man."

"I've found humans determine beauty by what they see and what they are taught to believe."

"That's true. Fear and hatred are ingrained. Here." He handed across a flask and I took it quickly, eagerly raising it to my lips.

"Not too much," he warned. "If you haven't drunk for a while, it'll hit your stomach hard and cause cramps. We have all night."

I sipped and he was satisfied. My eyes were locked upon the rabbit.

"It's almost ready," he said. "Have patience."

"You're very perceptive."

"For a blind man?"

I blushed and wondered whether he could see that, too. "Sorry. Now it's me who's prejudging."

He shrugged and we did not speak for some moments.

"I haven't asked your name," I realised.

"No."

"Do you have one?"

"Troll."

"Your name is Troll?"

"It's how I'm known now. Apparently, there's a troll living in these mountains, although I've never found any trace of it. Therefore, the rumours must relate to me, so it's the name I've taken."

"What's your real name?"

"No one's left who needs to use my real name, so now my name is just Troll."

"That's so sad."

"Who is there to use your name, Misako?"

"No one. But it's my name and I'm not giving it up."

"Admirable. Naïve, but admirable none the less."

My stomach rumbled again. It must have been loud because Troll chortled.

"Is it funny that I'm hungry?" I asked.

"Everything's funny when you get to my age."

"You should stop being so mean to me. I'm not in the best of moods and I'm liable to snap."

"And you say that so politely."

"What if I was to tell you I'm not human? That I'm more troll than you'll ever be?"

"Then I'd say anything you do in these mountains will be attributed to me by the locals. Are you a succubus?"

"No."

"Shame."

I reached for the rabbit, deciding I had had enough of this man and his taunts. He whacked my hand with his poker and I drew back.

"It's ready when I say it's ready," he chastised.

"It's ready now, you old fool. You're burning it."

"Are you an expert in cooking hares?"

"No, I've never cooked anything."

"Then you'd make a lousy wife."

"I'd make a fine wife," I replied angrily. "What are you even talking about? If you think women are around solely to make your breakfast, no wonder you live alone in the mountains."

I reached out again and again he slapped at me with the poker. This time I caught it and yanked it from his hands. Tossing it to one side, I lifted the meat from the spit and settled back to eat it. Troll said nothing and I found I did not care. The meat was burned on the outside but the juices ran as I bit into it and the meat inside was tender. I was famished and did not share my meal. Crunching the bones, I tossed each one over the side of the mountain until I had consumed the whole animal.

"Was it good?" he asked once I was done. "Only, it was a little burned for my tastes. Besides which, I'd already eaten."

"You what?"

"That hare was for you. I heard you making a racket as you came up the cliff, figured you'd have worked up an appetite, so I put you on an extra hare."

"Then why did you keep hitting me with the poker every time I tried to take it?"

"Because I like hitting girls with pokers. It's one of the reasons I live alone in the mountains."

"You really are strange."

He leaned back against a rock and said, "Look at me, Misako. Tell me what you see."

"I see a blind, cantankerous old man filled with hatred for the world around him."

"Do you think it's a sham?"

"No, I think you really are a cantankerous, hate-filled old man."

"Maybe I'm a troll disguised as an old man. Maybe I'm cantankerous because I don't want you getting too comfortable around me in case you decide to go to sleep and I devour you."

As tired as I was, I suddenly had no intention of sleeping anywhere near him.

"Would you like for me to tell you what I see in you?" he offered.

"I don't care what you see in me."

"Nothing."

"Nothing?"

"I thought you didn't care what I thought about you?"

He was playing with my mind, which was infuriating. However, he did have me intrigued. "Go on. Why do you see nothing?"

"Because I'm blind, you daft mare." He chuckled at his hilarity. "In all seriousness, I don't see anything in anyone because I don't care to judge. Look at me, people think I'm a troll. They avoid these valleys because of the howls I make at night. They offer me sacrifices of goats because they think that's what trolls like to eat. One time, some zealots even climbed one of the mountains to chain a scantily clad girl to a rock. She stayed there for three nights before one of the sacrificial goats had wandered close enough to bite through her ropes. I have no idea how the girl convinced the goat to bite through her ropes, but I'm sure it made a fanciful tale once it reached the village. They probably thought the goat had been possessed by the spirit of the troll or something."

I reached the conclusion the man was insane, yet there was something about him which positively reeked of egotism.

"I think I'll go now," I said. "Thanks for dinner."

"Will you do something for me before you go?"

"That depends what it is."

"I want you to promise not to end up like me. I went through life taking things to heart, pushing people away who cared about me. Now I'm nobody, scaring folk because I'm bitter at the world. Don't become me. Make a friend."

"I had a friend."

"What happened to her?"

"She saved me. Both my friends saved me." I had not thought of that before. Salla, Mallok, even my mother … all had cast me away purely to save my life. It seemed I was destined to lose everyone I cared about purely because of what I was. The merfolk despised me for my human half and everyone else despised me for my faerie blood.

"Your silence is heavy like a raincloud," Troll said. "So long as you realise you mean something to people, you can survive."

"I should go."

"Then go."

And so I went. Troll had made me uncomfortable, but he had also given me a lot to think about. There was much wisdom in what he had said and he was right about one thing: I did not want to end up anything like him.

In the darkness, but with a full belly, I made my way back down the mountainside and wandered through the night before finally bedding down in a sandy hollow within some of the rocks. There I spent a restless sleep filled with nightmares of how my life had been and how much worse it could yet become.

CHAPTER EIGHT

The following day brought out the sun in earnest and as I finally made my way out of the mountain passes, it was to bathe in its glory. The mountains led directly into an area of land whose nature was vaguely familiar and I paused to examine my surroundings. Trees rose everywhere before me. To the right and left, as far as the eye could see, the trees spread out and I could not tell how far they continued ahead. I had known woodlands and forests in the past, for streams and rivers often cut through them and they offered a certain amount of protection if I ever wished to leave the water and sun myself on a rock somewhere. I did not recognise the trees before me and could not say whether there was any water running through them, but if I could find a stream or river, I would make swifter progress in the search for my father. That I had yet found no trace of him was worrying, although if Mrinth was anything to go by, the human world was far larger than I had ever imagined.

Deciding that the sooner I began, the sooner I would be done, I set off through the woods on foot. Having slept so fitfully, I had no hunger pains, yet knew I would operate much better with fuel so stopped to gather some berries. There would be animals in the woods as well, but I had eaten enough meat the previous night and sufficed with the fibre and vitamins of nuts and fruit.

I had been walking for perhaps half an hour when I heard a serene sound and strained to listen that I might place its origins. It was a soft and pleasing melody, falling from the lips of a truly beautiful being and at once I was reminded of home. That there could be a mermaid singing in the woodland might have boded me ill, but not every mermaid wanted me dead and most would not even know of my existence, so I followed the sound of singing until I scented the cool freshness of water on the air. Accompanying this was the low rumble of falling water and I became even more convinced that I had stumbled upon someone of my own kind.

Through the trees I spotted the stream and I followed it to a small semi-circular body of water, not quite a lake, into which tumbled a small waterfall. At the top of the waterfall, the stream disappeared into the woods, for this was just a small break in its passage and hardly the beginning. The waterfall rose less than a woman's height into the air, but it was precisely the correct height for someone to be standing underneath, the water rising to her chest while she washed her long red hair beneath its gentle motion. The rushing water frothed about the pool, concealing the girl's lower body from me, but I was certain she must have had a glistening tail.

The girl, or young woman I supposed, was about my own age of eighteen. Her auburn hair was silken and beautiful, while her face was soft and carefree. Her eyes were closed and from her throat there emitted that wonderful melodic sound which had drawn me in. Her skin shone with a natural radiance and what I could see of it was at the same time smooth and muscular without losing any of its femininity.

She stopped humming, opened her eyes and looked directly at me. I had not thought I had made much noise and over the roar of the falls about her, she must have had extremely acute hearing indeed. I noticed with a little trepidation that she had intense blue eyes, which, had she been human, would have made her a target for abuse since everyone knows humans with red hair and blue eyes generally return to life as vampires once they die.

"Morning," she said with a smile of greeting. "For a moment, I thought you were a soldier, looking for a bloody nose."

"There are soldiers around here?"

"There are soldiers everywhere." She continued to rub some kind of oil into her amazing red hair, frothing it up and washing it out with the fall of the water. As she turned to face me, she rose slightly from the pool and the water caressed her body in waves, but I was unable to see anywhere near her midsection to verify the existence of her tail.

"You can't believe how happy I am to see you," I said.

"Oh? Do we know each other? Uh, what are you doing?"

I was too excited to hear her, for I had already shrugged off my boots and was stripping off my trousers. The top came off a lot easier than it had gone on, although having been walking in it for days it had a ripe odour clinging to it. I had not until that moment even noticed the strange smell and I raised one arm to sniff at my armpit. It was not a bad smell, just an unusual one.

"Excuse me," the young redhead said, "but I don't generally have women strip off in front of me and then sniff their armpits."

"Do humans really perspire this much?" I asked as I smelt the other to check it was the same. My body was clammy with sweat and I could feel the dirt of the past few days clogging my pores. Spending most of my life underwater, I had never before had to worry about body odour, or really with keeping all that clean, and suddenly being human had more downsides than I had expected.

"Generally, yeah," the woman said.

"I wondered why Mrinth had that strange smell."

"You came from Mrinth?"

"Yes. Fabulous place." I dropped into the pool and found the water not as deep as I would have liked. When standing, the water rose to my chest, although once within the water I changed my lower regions to a tail, releasing the true me while I had the chance. Approaching the stranger, I noticed she had stopped scrubbing at her hair and was lathering oils down her arms. "You're very beautiful," I said without meaning to.

"And now you're coming onto me. Are you feeling all right?"

"I'm not coming onto you, it's a traditional greeting."

She raised her eyebrows. "Among?"

"Among our kind, silly. I reached out to grab her hips. She pulled back, her amusement vanishing in an instant, and I myself recoiled in horror, for my hands, however briefly they had touched her, had not come into contact with a fish tail. As I instinctively moved away, my own tail splashed upwards, breaking the surface.

"Oh," the young woman said, relaxing slightly. "You're a mermaid. I thought you were just being creepy." She went back to rubbing down her arms, moved to her chest and scrubbed at her armpits. "Would you mind doing my back for me?"

I stared in horror. My mind swam with panic, my every sense screamed at me to get out of the water, while a tiny violent part of my subconscious calmly told me the best thing to do in this situation was grab the girl's head and force it beneath the water. I was stronger than her and we were in my natural element. It would have been so easy to kill her.

"Are you going to float there all day gawping, or are you going to rub my back for me?"

Without a word, I moved forward and allowed her to squeeze some oil into the palm of my hand. She turned to face the other way and, using both hands, I rubbed the oil into her skin. Her back was not as smooth and supple as the rest of her body and my fingers found straight scars all over, as though she had been whipped. That she was a slave was my initial thought; perhaps she had served on board a pirate vessel.

"That's it," she said, relaxing as my hands rubbed the oil in. "You're good at this. Want me to do your back?"

I almost accepted, but reasoned this could have been a trick to get me to turn my back on her. Having realised she was out of her element, she could well have been attempting to lure me into a relaxed state so she could slit my throat.

"Suit yourself," she said, handing me the strange squeezy bottle. "Knock yourself out."

"Why would I want to do that?"

"Well, I could have said break a leg, but that would have been in bad taste."

"Why are all humans so strange?"

"Says the girl who introduces herself by sniffing her armpits?"

Self-conscious now, I squeezed out some oil and viciously rubbed under my arms.

"Better," she said. "Now, if you could just lose the attitude, we'd get along swimmingly. That was a pun, by the way."

"I'm not laughing."

"That's because you clearly don't have a sense of humour. My name's Braal."

"Misako."

"Is that Miss Ako or Misako?"

"What's the difference?"

"Nothing. I was just trying to make a joke."

"You did that once already. It wasn't funny so why try again?"

"Oh, I'm starting to like you."

I could not think why, since I was still debating on whether to drown this woman. "How can you sing like a mermaid?"

"I don't sing like a mermaid," she said. "Maybe mermaids sing like me."

"I'd say you have a beautiful voice," I said irritably, "but you don't appear to like compliments.

Why does everyone I meet have to turn out to be a jerk?"

"Ha! Yep, definitely beginning to like you. What are you doing wandering around the woods? I thought mermaids liked to keep to the water."

"I'm searching for my father."

"Oh. That's nice for you."

I did not feel like going into detail with this girl, since I was not going to be spending any great degree of time with her. I had pretty much decided not to drown her, but there was still a chance I could change my mind about that.

"What are *you* doing here?" I asked.

"Bathing."

"I meant what are you doing in the woods?"

"Bathing in private. Or at least I was."

"Oh, excuse me for breathing."

"You're a shirty thing, you know that?"

"And you're rude."

"Can I touch your tail?"

"You seriously just asked me that? And you said you thought I was creepy."

"Hey, you grabbed me by the hips, you owe me. I've never met a mermaid before. I touched a snake once and they're not slimy like everyone expects. You know what? I even …"

"Fine, you can touch my tail. Just shut up already."

"Nah, it's all right, I don't want to touch your tail. I just wanted to know whether you'd let me."

"I'm beginning to see why our people don't get on."

"It'd be nice if we did. I'm always saying that to people, that we should try to make peace with the faeries. But there's been too much blood spilled for that, apparently. On both sides."

"Your kind has hunted mine for generations."

"And your kind has preyed on mine for generations."

Neither of us was accusing anything, we were simply stating facts.

"As if you even know anything about the war," I said.

"Oh, I know plenty. I've seen the horrors of war when it only involves humans. Introducing faeries to the mix doesn't make it any more horrific, just more difficult."

"More difficult? Why?"

"Because this island we all live on, this one great land surrounded by the massive ocean, apparently contains all the humans the entire world over. I don't know how many of us there are, but there are seven kingdoms and at a rough guess I'd say there were a million or so in each kingdom. There could well be ten million people on this world, tops. But faeries? Scholars have estimated there are thirty trillion. Thirty trillion! I mean, that's a war we can't win. But we still fight it, because that's what human beings like to do."

"You sound like you don't have much faith in your own kind."

"I'm a realist. This isn't a war we can win so we need to find common ground. If we don't form a truce with the faeries, we'll be exterminated." She shrugged. "It's simple mathematics."

"Do you know why the war began?"

"I know what I'm told. That once upon a time there were no humans and the world belonged to the faerie races. Then, the faeries went away for a while and when they returned, they found the land infested with humans. Since faeries live a long time, what they considered a brief spell away was in human terms a few generations. By the time they realised we were a problem, we'd taken root. It's like if a family goes on holiday for a month and returns to find rats have nested in their basement. The obvious thing for that family to do is exterminate the rats."

"Then you consider your own species vermin?"

"I think that's the way the faeries see us. Sometimes I look at people and I can't say the faeries are wrong." She paused. "How about you? What do you know of the war?"

"Nothing. I've never really seen it. My mother always kept me shielded from the war, and all she ever told me about it were fanciful tales of derring-do and heroics."

Braal snorted. "There's nothing heroic about war and derring-do only gets fools killed. I'm eighteen. How old are you?"

"Eighteen."

"Do you think you're old?"

"No, I'm eighteen."

"I'm ancient. I never thought I'd reach eighteen. To be honest, I didn't expect to make sixteen, the rate I was going."

"What do you mean?"

She looked like she was about to answer in great detail, but said instead, "I've always been difficult. I had a view of life which wasn't the greatest and it turned out I was selling myself short in a number of ways. Luckily, I had someone good and decent step into my life who pretty much dragged me from the gutter."

"I have no idea what you're talking about."

"That's good. My point is, if you're eighteen and still innocent, good luck to you, girl. Have you ever killed anyone?"

I shuddered, thinking of the lad back upon the trawler. I had not meant to kill him, it had been an accident, yet he was dead because I had hurled him into the side of the boat. He had been trying to kill me and I had not taken into account my greater strength.

"Misako? Is that a yes?"

"No," I said defiantly. "No, I've never killed anyone."

"Not even in the height of passion?"

"Why does everyone I meet think I drag men to their deaths?"

"Because you're a mermaid and that's what mermaids do."

"If you think that, perhaps there's no chance for peace between our peoples after all."

"You're right." She sighed heavily. "I'm going to get dried."

I watched her wade out of the pool and hop nimbly onto the bank. Her entire body was lithe and well-toned and there was not an ounce of fat to her form. Her red hair spilled down her back, sticking to her in its sodden state, and I could almost have believed I was looking at some form of goddess.

Yet there were imperfections to her, scars. There were several scratches down one arm, a dirty bruise on one calf and a white slash to her elbow where the skin had not properly healed. While she dried and dressed, I stared hard at her back, which I had noticed earlier. It was covered with diagonal marks which looked both old and painful. She did not appear self-conscious about them, however, and soon covered them with her shirt as she dressed.

She wore thick and hardy boots and what appeared to be a blue uniform of quality material. She strapped on her belt, complete with sword and dagger, and tied a smaller band around her boot, in which she held a knife.

Sitting on the shore, she took a towel to her hair and fiercely scrubbed it dry.

"You want me to comb it for you?" I asked from the pool.

"I can comb my own hair, thanks." She ran her fingers through her hair and I imagined this was what she meant.

"You don't have a comb?" I asked.

"Why would I carry a comb?"

"Because you have such fine, silken hair."

"Aaand you're back to being creepy."

Placing my hands on the shore, I hoisted myself up, unconsciously changing my tail back to legs in the process. Braal tossed me her towel and I sat on the shore, drying myself. "How did you get the scars?" I asked.

"I was flogged."

"Pirates?"

"Pirates? That's a random thing to say."

"How, then?"

"I stood up for something I believed in. Some people didn't like that."

"What do you mean?"

She watched me curiously as she continued to brush her hair and I was surprised by how well her crude method was working. "It's not exactly a pretty story," she said.

"Please. I'm trying to learn about people."

"All right. I come from a small village called Varaton. We were stationed there at the time and I was given orders to do something I thought was wrong. I didn't do it. My superiors didn't like that I didn't do it, so they stripped me naked in front of the village – in front of my family – and flogged me."

"That sounds very cruel."

"That's because it was."

Something she had said clicked in my mind. "Hold on, your superiors? You're a soldier?"

"Knight Provisional Braal, Second Battalion of Royal Torbalia. Did I fail to mention that?"

I was on my feet in an instant, holding the towel before me as a weapon. Braal raised her eyebrows and did not stop brushing her hair.

Realising I must have looked a fool, I sank to my backside and put my trousers on. "You should have said," I grumbled.

"Why? So you could prejudge me just like you accused me of prejudging you?"

"You're a soldier. Your job is to kill my kind."

"No, my job is to keep the peace. Sometimes that means fighting, sometimes it means getting people not to fight. Yes, sometimes it means killing, but my boss doesn't take that route if he can help it."

"What's a knight provisional?" I asked as I finished dressing.

"A bone of contention. Basically, it means I'm not a knight, but that I'm supposed to go around showing people that they too can be a knight if they join the army. Which of course they can't, because that's a ludicrous idea. Knights own land, and I don't even own my horse."

"Where's your horse?"

"Back at the camp."

"There are other soldiers stationed nearby?" I asked cautiously.

"Sure. But far enough away for me to bathe in peace and sing to myself."

That made sense but did not make me feel much more relaxed. "Have you ever fought faeries?"

"Yep. Tenacious opponents, faeries. Big, small, bestial, meek. Some are invisible, others hypnotise you on the battlefield, some fly and some burrow. Fighting faeries is a blood bath, which is why we need to get a truce sorted."

She had mentioned the truce before and I at last began to believe her. I had been raised under the belief that humans were the enemy, that they were brutal and often mindless. They could not be trusted nor reasoned with, they could not be treated as equals and they certainly could never be called friends. Yet on my travels I had met humans whom I had indeed considered friends, and here was one who was a soldier – the worst of humankind – but one who did not want to kill us.

"Tell me about your father," she said.

"Why?"

"Because you were sad when you mentioned him."

I told her my story and she listened with non-judgemental interest. For the most part, her eyes were impassive, although they brightened when I spoke of the love between my father and mother and they saddened when I told her of their parting and of the eventual death of my mother.

"Then you're half human," she said when I was done.

"Not through choice."

"You hate us that much?"

"I don't hate anyone. I'm just leaning that way."

"Fair enough."

"Do you know my father?"

"Why would I know your father?"

"Like you said, there are so few humans on this land, and he's a knight and you're a ... not-quite-knight."

"Do you know which kingdom he served?"

"No."

"And you don't know his name?"

"No." I felt I had been through that conversation once already.

Braal considered the problem for a long while. Then she said, "I'll enquire."

I blinked, shocked. "You will?"

"Yep. I'll ask around, see whether anyone knows of a knight of that description. Or a soldier."

"My father is a knight," I said tersely.

"Doesn't hurt for me to ask. Besides, maybe someone saw him and thought he was only a soldier.

Maybe he's from a kingdom which has people like me: knights who aren't quite knights."

She was being kind, which I had not expected from her. Ever since I had learned she was a soldier, I had been extremely wary of Braal, yet she seemed to genuinely want to help. I did not know whether she was deceiving me, but there was something sincere about her.

"When do we set off?" I asked.

"Set off where?"

"To your camp."

"I don't think it'd be a good idea for you to come to my camp, Misako. If this was my regular battalion, maybe, but I'm on loan at the moment. Like I said, my battalion is something of a PR stunt – a recruitment drive. I'm working with some other soldiers at the moment so they can see how wonderful life in the battalions is." She smiled humourlessly to show what she thought of that idea. "Tell you what, I'll ask around and we'll meet up in a week. There's a stone lion downstream, that'd be a perfect place."

"Why would it be perfect?"

"Because it's distinctive."

"Do you think my father will be with you?"

She parted her lips to speak but no words came out. There was sympathy to her eyes which I tried not to dwell on. "No," she said at last. "But I may have an answer for you, who knows?"

"Thank you, Braal."

"You're welcome. Now, would you like me to comb your hair?"

I thought that the most ludicrous idea I had ever heard, but since I didn't have a brush or comb of my own, I decided to accept. Braal set herself down behind me and gently ran her fingers through my hair. She had a soft, feminine caress I would not have expected for a soldier, and I found Braal something of an enigma. On the one hand, she possessed so many kind and gentle qualities, yet her body was physical perfection for a soldier, which was not something she could have attained other than through hard training. I was well aware she had killed my people in the past – both faeries and humans – yet it did not bother me.

She began to hum and, without meaning to, I joined her. We stayed by the poolside for over an hour, singing and relaxing. When Braal had finished with my hair, we lay upon the grass completely in tune with our song. It was as though somehow our souls had become intertwined.

I thought back to Salla and her strawberries, but this was not the same. Braal did not want anything from me, did not see me as anything other than what I was. She was, like me, someone from two sides, someone who understood two aspects of the same whole. Where I was both faerie and human, Braal was both soldier and peacemaker.

If ever there could have been any hope for peaceful coexistence between faeries and humans, it would be at the hands of people like Braal.

I found myself not only content, but happier than I had been in a long, long time.

CHAPTER NINE

I had spent so little time with Braal, yet I found I trusted her. She had been different to all the other people I had thus far met and I knew she would try her best to find my father. I refused to face the possibility I would not find him, despite having seen in so many people's eyes that they believed my mission to be nothing more than a pipedream.

Before Braal had left me, she had told me to follow the stream, which I did for the first day. By this point, my curiosity had got the best of me and I longed to see Braal in her own natural setting. I felt if I could see her interacting with the other soldiers, I might get a better feel for who she was and why it was I trusted her so. To this end, I veered from the course the stream was taking and headed farther into the woods in search of Braal's soldiers.

I spent a day fruitlessly searching and by the time night fell I realised I had become lost. Bedding down for the night, I continued in the morning, yet after hours of further fruitless searching, I cursed myself for ever having strayed from the path. It was ironic that there were faerie legends about humans falling into trouble by straying from the set path, yet here I was in human territory doing precisely the same thing.

Towards the end of this day, I caught the hint of smoke ahead and followed this course. It was not long before I came to a small shack in the woods. It was a hovel formed of wood and mud, mainly twigs that had been stuck together like it was a house-shaped birds' nest. The door was comprised of a single slab of wood and the window was small, likely in order to deter predators. There was a plot of land directly outside the makeshift house, well-tended and weeded, surrounded by a tiny fence akin to those designed to keep the faerie races from entering a property. Within this patch poked the greenery of carrots and other vegetables, their white and purple heads peering out over the soil.

A small chimney chugged smoke from the house and I approached the door and called, "Hello. Is there anyone here?"

Receiving no answer, I drew the door aside, for it was not set upon hinges, and found a dark abode within. There was a pile of straw which served as the occupant's bed, a small table formed of a felled log, and a metal stove set into a stone hearth, up which ran the chimney. There was a fire burning within the hearth, but it was underfed and in fear of going out. Upon the log table was half a loaf of bread, some raw vegetables and a jug of water.

Sitting beside the warm stove, I ate and drank my fill. I knew I was stealing but did not much care. I had been walking for a long time and my legs were tired. As excuses for theft went, it was a poor one, but I had suffered enough by human hands so it was about time I took something back.

I stayed in the shack for some time, awaiting the return of its occupant. Since I was lost, I was hoping for directions back to the stream; perhaps the owner of the hovel had even seen the soldiers and would have been able to direct me towards them. During my time there, I kept the fire burning by gathering twigs from outside – I even did a little weeding of the carrot patch. After all this work, I finished off the bread and water and stretched out by the hearth for a rest.

After an eternity, I heard the approach of someone and bolted upright as a figure appeared in the doorway. He was thin, gaunt even, and incredibly tall. I would have placed his age to have been somewhere around twenty, although it was difficult to be certain since he was so strange-looking. His eyes were wide, his limbs long and gangly, his knuckles stretching so far beyond his knees they could likely drag upon the ground should he hunch. His ears were large, his head entirely bald and he was garbed in clean attire and clearly cared for his appearance.

"Sorry for invading your home and eating all your food," I said sheepishly. "Would you be able to show me where the stream is, please?"

His already wide eyes became veritable dinner plates and he backed away.

"Is that a no?" I asked.

Throwing his hands over his head, he wailed terribly and fell backwards out the doorway. I followed him but he back-pedalled furiously, ploughing through the fence to his carrot patch and destroying much of his hard work, and mine I might add. I could not understand what he was doing, but he was up and fleeing before I could say anything else and I was left standing there dumbfounded.

With nothing else to do, I left his shack and chose a direction entirely at random. Over the next few hours, I contemplated what had happened at the hovel and developed some disturbing theories.

He had been a young man who lived alone in the woods, which meant he was either a criminal or society had shunned him. That his appearance was so strange suggested the latter. He was no beast, nor was he mindless, for his clothes were clean, his vegetable patch well-tended and his house itself had been a construction of some intelligence. I deduced, therefore, that fearful humans had chased him away entirely due to his appearance. They likely thought him a faerie, a changeling child, and had persecuted him for it. That he was human was obvious to me, but it seemed it was yet another aspect of human cruelty that I had witnessed.

The thought that he would not return to his hovel upset me, for while I may have eaten his food, I felt terrible that I had also robbed him of his house. What he had thought of me, I could not say. Perhaps he had recognised me as a member of the faerie races, perhaps he had just seen me as a human and had feared me because of it. Perhaps he simply feared everything and everyone. I did not know and had no way to be sure of anything.

It was saddening to think humans could treat their own kind in such a manner, for the war had taken its toll on both sides and there was no reason at all to hate that poor man.

I heard a familiar sound ahead and knew I had found the stream again. Reaching it, I looked around but did not recognise the area. Knowing I would have to head downstream to the stone lion, I followed the path it had carved through the woodland, a little lighter in step now that I was back on track.

As I walked, I noticed indentations left within the muddy banks and paused to examine them. They were heavy prints left by boots and no doubt belonged to one of the soldiers Braal was with. I could identify several sets of prints, although as I continued downstream I noticed the majority headed back into the woods. I was not a good tracker and could not tell how old the tracks were, but I was hoping if I hurried I might run into some of Braal's unit.

Soon enough, I came upon signs that someone had recently been through the area. Bushes had been hacked away, grass was bent and there was the corpse of a rabbit which had been shot with an arrow. That the animal had not been taken as food was strange, and I assumed the soldiers ahead had been using it for target practice. It was an odd concept to me, that someone would kill an animal for such a reason, but I did not want to judge anyone too readily.

Ahead, I could hear someone whistling and a man soon came into sight. He was in his mid-twenties and wearing very mild and cheap armour over simple attire. His colours did not match Braal's, but then her uniform was probably of her own battalion and not this unit. He was a handsome man in a rugged sort of way and he was sitting by the stream, tossing in stones.

I watched him for some moments while I tried to think of what I should say, and I must have waited too long because he noticed me. He looked at me without fear or anger and did not stop whistling, so I walked over to join him.

"That's a pretty whistle," I said.

"Don't think I've ever been called pretty before. You all alone out here, miss?"

"That's an odd question to ask someone you've just met."

"I meant these woods are crawling with soldiers. I should know, I'm one of them. And soldiers have a bad reputation when it comes to girls they find wandering alone. I should know, I'm one of them."

He offered a lopsided grin as he said this and I knew a joke when I heard one. I sat beside him without being invited and took up a stone. "Is this a game?"

"I was trying to skim them but it's a bit difficult doing that sitting down."

"Then why not stand up and do it?"

"Because I stopped for a rest and if I'm going to rest I'd prefer to be sitting."

I drew back my arm, weighed the stone in my hand and swung my arm horizontally. The stone struck the surface of the stream, bounced twice and disappeared.

The soldier whistled again, this time in admiration. "Shoot, lady, you're something else. My name's Whistler."

"That's an army nickname because you like to whistle?"

"Looks like you're clever, too."

"Misako."

"Misako." He tried out the name. "Don't think I've ever heard of anyone called Misako before."

"Well, I've never heard of anyone called Whistler, so we're even."

"That sounds about right." He tossed another stone and entirely failed to make it do anything but plunge into the water. "Shoot."

"You want me to show you how it's done?"

"I reckon so."

Getting to my knees, I leaned in close to him and helped him draw back his arm. I showed him the angle he would need, explained the speed and level of force. The throw was about timing, finesse and balance, I told him, although I don't think he paid all that much attention because he kept looking at me instead of the water. Holding his arm for him in the right position, I brushed my cheek against his so our eyes were level and made him focus on the stream.

"Now, release," I said and let go of his arm so he could swing it himself. The stone he threw bounced once before going under, which was certainly a start.

"See," he said, "I was paying attention."

Sitting back beside him, I felt something strange happening within me. Whistler was funny, almost charming in his own way. My heart was catching in my chest and I felt far too pleased for him that he had managed to bounce his stone. I wondered why I was feeling so strange and put it down to the fact that I had met a human male I could sit and chat with. Ever since Mallok, all the men I had met had been the strangest people, most of them after whatever they could get from me or else they were trying to kill me. Aside from the old man who had helped me at the edge of Mrinth, but I had barely said two words to him.

"You're smiling," Whistler said.

"Must mean I'm happy."

"Every man should strive to make women happy."

"Women, plural?"

"Until he finds a special one."

I knew then what I was feeling and should have realised it sooner. Braal was right – we were both eighteen, but where she was a mature, experienced adult, I was more a fumbling innocent teenager. Whistler was fun to be around and if all soldiers were like him, I could not imagine why Braal had not wanted me to visit her troops; but I was not interested in pursuing that kind of thing. I was looking for my father and that took priority over everything.

Thinking of Braal raised an obvious question. "Are you in Braal's unit?" I asked.

"You know Braal?"

"We've met."

"Are you friends?"

"I think so."

"You think so?"

"We only met the once. What's she like?"

"Certain of herself. There are a lot of people in the army who'd like to take her down a peg or two. She comes across with all her battalion airs, like she's better than the rest of us. Believe me, there's serious talk of waiting 'til she's asleep and a dozen or so men going into her tent and ..." He stopped to compose himself, remembering I was sitting alongside him. "Sorry, she just gets on my nerves sometimes."

"Oh. She seemed really nice to me."

"I guess a lot of Torbalian soldiers resent taking orders from her."

"Because she's a girl?"

"What? No, what does that have to do with anything? I meant because she's practically a child and has a rank none of us will ever achieve."

"Ah, the whole knight provisional thing. Braal said it was a PR stunt."

"You can say that again."

"What's a PR stunt?"

"PR? Public relations. How can you not know that?"

"We don't have public relations where I come from, although now you've told me what it stands for, I get the idea."

"Where *do* you come from?"

"Mrinth."

"And your family's in Mrinth?"

"Yes."

"And all your friends?"

"Yes."

"Which means you really are travelling alone through the woods. I thought you were joking: no one travels alone through the woods."

"Why's that?"

"Because there are monsters out here."

"I don't believe in monsters."

"You want to see one?"

"You just happen to have one handy?"

"There's one real nearby."

I looked over my shoulder but all I could see were trees. "There are no monsters here."

"No? The scariest monsters are the ones hiding in plain sight."

I looked again. "There's no one here but me and you, Whistler."

He grinned and I did not like the face he was making. "That's so true."

Pouncing with the speed of a shark, he grabbed my arms with both hands and shoved against me with all his weight, forcing me onto my back. My head struck the mud and I heard it squelch even as I felt the mud seep through my hair, so neatly combed by Braal and ruined in an instant. Whistler was laughing as he forced my arms to my sides, holding me down as he placed his knees either side of my hips, holding me in place like a vice. I struggled, shocked by his sudden attack, and terror seized up my muscles, froze my heart and I found myself unable to move.

He slapped me across the face, hard enough to leave a coppery tang to my tongue, and laughed. "What's this stupid thing?" he asked, tearing away my pearl necklace. "What, some cheap boyfriend can't be bothered to buy you the whole chain?" He tossed it aside and punched me full in the face where I lay. Then he began to whistle.

For the next few moments I was powerless to do anything. Releasing my arms, he used his hands to work loose his belt, all the while whistling his merry tune. I stared into the stream, my body shaking, my mind hazing over. My mother had warned me about men and I had not listened; Braal had warned me about her soldiers and I had not listened; my own subconscious warned me about all humans and I had not listened.

Whistler grabbed me roughly by the chin and turned my eyes towards him. He had undone his belt and was in the process of bringing his trousers halfway down. There was anger to his eyes which I could not explain. "You could do me the decency to at least look at me," he complained.

That was when I snapped.

I do not recall what happened in the next few moments. I remember the rage seizing me, remember screaming something, vaguely even remember lunging at him with my hands. Beyond that, I have little recollection of how I got off the muddy ground. Yet I pounded him, that is a memory which will stay with me forever. I forced him to the ground just as he had forced me and I pounded his face with my superior fists, smashing again and again with knuckles as hard as steel until his face was a bloody pulp and bone and cartilage were embedded in my fists.

The rage passing, I drew back and Whistler scrabbled away. His face was a ruin, he was gasping for breath and he was trying to speak. And watching him, realising what he had tried to do to me, what he had threatened to do to Braal, what he had probably done to countless other girls in the past … it all settled in my soul and I felt hatred all over again for a human being.

"Braal wants peace between us," I said in a flat tone. "She wants peace and she thinks *I'm* the naïve one."

"Stay away from me," Whistler said, spitting a tooth and blinking away blood.

I grabbed him by the collar and hoisted him into the air. He shrieked and the sickening stench of urine soaked through his trousers. I was thankful he had not managed to lower them enough for him to have done me any damage with it.

"You said there was a monster in the woods," I told him. "You said there was a monster closer than I thought. You know what? You were right."

I hurled him forwards and he plunged into the stream, not bouncing even once. He floundered, tried to stand, but I had removed my trousers and was wading in after him. Seeing me, he fell back, tried to swim, but his legs were giving out beneath him. Then his eyes widened as he saw my legs change shape and I glided towards him, at home in my native element.

He screamed at me, flailed with his arms, but I seized his wrists and snapped them, the twin sounds like twigs cracking in the woodland. He pleaded with me, cried for mercy, and all I could do was snarl. My eye-teeth itched and I parted my lips to reveal to him the row of incisors which had formed within my mouth. He blubbered and wailed like so many of his victims must have, but I had no intention of biting him. I thought back to when I had devoured the rat. I had been famished then and the meal had satisfied me; but this soldier was beneath the rat. I could not digest something so vile, could not contemplate placing my lips anywhere near the thing I held.

Instead, I forced him down into the water. My tail wrapped about his body even as my arms held firm. He struggled madly, knowing he was fighting for his life, but I stared down through the churning froth of water, watching impassively as the precious bubbles of air escaped his lungs.

It was over within moments. Perhaps it was too short, perhaps I should have pulled him from the water and offered him the hope of life before plunging him down again, but I was not cruel. The man was a beast and did not deserve to live. It did not matter that I was in no legal position to judge him, for I was certainly in a moral one after what he had attempted to do to me.

As his body became still, I released him and he sank to the bed of the stream, for his belt contained weapons and they were heavy enough to keep him down there. Wading back to the shore, I paused only long enough to wash the mud from my hair. Once upon dry land, I reverted my tail back to legs and slipped into my trousers, uncomfortable in their wetness. I cast one final glance back to the stream and noted the surface had returned to being calm.

Turning from the sight, I continued to follow the stream, whistling dully as I walked.

It was many hours later that I realised I had not reclaimed the pearl Salla had given me and I wept true and bitter tears.

That night, I happened upon a slight waterfall and realised I had become far more lost in the woods than I had thought, for in following the stream where I ran, I had only just made it back to where I had first met Braal. It meant I was behind schedule, but at least I now knew where I was.

It was about a week later that I found the stone lion. Braal was right, it would have been difficult to miss. It was a cave through which the stream ran, to emerge upon the other side. A talented artisan had carved the image of a great cat into the rock so it appeared there was a petrified animal overlooking the stream as it entered the cave. Here, I settled down to wait for Braal, eager for any word she might bring of my father. There was a knapsack beside the cave entrance which a soldier must have dropped and I opened it to see whether there was anything interesting inside. There was a flask of water and a little food – some dried meat and nuts. I sat and ate while I rummaged through the rest of the pack, but there was only one other thing: some form of writing material upon which was scrawled some letters I could not decipher. Discarding the paper, I decided to keep the knapsack so, slinging it over my shoulder, I sat and awaited Braal while I ate and drank.

Four days later, I gave up. I had thought Braal different from the others, I had thought her special. I had thought her my friend. But she had lied to me, had let me down like everyone else. No doubt she was off somewhere, laughing with her soldiers over the stupid naïve mermaid she had met, whose hair she had brushed with her fingers, with whom she had sung by the shore. I could almost hear her laughter through the trees as she recounted how she had been confronted by a mermaid in the faerie's own element; of how Braal, naked and weaponless, had convinced the mermaid not to kill her, of how she had spoken of peace and love and how their two species could exist in harmony.

I hated her, or at least I tried to. I had thought she was genuine, but it seemed she was just like all the others. Eventually, after so long waiting for a friend who would not appear, I rose and set off alone through the woodland.

Alone, I knew then, I would always be.

CHAPTER TEN

The woodland came to an end and even before I reached the end of the treeline I could smell a strange odour on the wind. There was an intense heaviness to the air, as though the gods above were weeping without shedding the tears of rain, and there was an unnatural quiet settled upon the lands, split by the shriek of violent birds and the howl of dogs. I could not quite place the odour, but it was like warm copper and as I reached the end of the trees it became nauseating. I had one time come upon a fox which had been torn apart by a hunter's trap. It had been lying untouched for a week and there were flies buzzing about its injuries, settled in its flesh to lay their eggs. I had vomited at the sight and stench, and it was this very smell I could detect before me, although on a massive scale.

Ahead, the land stretched flatly. Upon the great field there rested the corpses of over a thousand fallen men and women. Most were armoured, some wore simple rags and may have been servants or slaves. A few of the bodies were small, and it seemed there had been children involved in the massacre. Weapons lay scattered, broken or discarded, while standards either lay upon the ground, soaked with blood, or else fluttered in the ghastly wind, flying from pikes which were stuck fast in the ground or within the corpses of the fallen.

I watched some wild dogs picking through the bodies, while vultures fought over scraps at the feast of death.

Holding my sleeve to my nose did not prevent the terrible stench from reaching me, but it saved me from vomiting as I made my way through the dead. I tried not to look at the faces of the corpses, but from their attire I surmised they were two human armies which had met in battle. There were no faeries that I could identify, which meant this was a purely human confrontation. The injuries were foul, many of them inflicted by untrained hands, and my heart cried out for a girl, no more than nine, who lay sprawled in a pool of blood, a knife still clutched in her hand, shattered armour about her chest. That at least one of the armies had recruited children made them either cruel or desperate, perhaps both, yet I was not familiar with the circumstances and wanted so desperately not to judge.

Not judging while standing amidst such mindless carnage was extremely difficult and I could not imagine two faerie armies ever going against one another like this. My mother had told me tales of some of the more extreme faeries, of how monstrous they could be, even to their own kind, yet nothing they could have done could surely have compared to what I was seeing that day.

I saw a child ahead of me, crouched over a body. I did not know what would happen to the orphans created through such violence, yet many would grow up with hatred in their souls. The child I could see would remain by the corpse of her father or mother for some hours, before finally moving on. As that child grew older, her fury would lead her to follow the path of her dead loved ones and ten, fifteen years from then it would be she who was lying dead on the field, with her own child bending over her.

Not quite knowing what I intended to do, I approached the child. I estimated her to have been around eight or nine years old. She looked up at me with a blank expression. Her clothes were ragged, her face dirty, her dark hair crinkled and thick like dried bracken. I struggled to find something to say; then noticed what she was doing. Bent over the corpse of the soldier, she was using the dead man's knife to slice through his finger so she could steal his ring.

Horrified, I simply stared, unable to say anything at all. Having paused in her work, the girl continued to look at me, her eyes unreadable. Looking around, I saw several other children picking over the corpses in a similar fashion. Two children were tearing a man's earrings from him even as the man writhed in the agony of a mortal wound.

This was not just a slaughter, it was not just a battle. This was war. It was something I had learned about as a child, but something I had reviled only in the knowledge that it was wrong. In my child's naivety, my daydreams had even sometimes glorified war. My fantasies of knights and dragons, of ogres and princesses; they were a young girl's whimsy compared with the brutal truth. Standing amidst the carnage, the reeking stench of death filling the air, the groans of the dying and the wailing of the injured … this was war as I had never known it before.

Tears came to my eyes and I savagely wiped them away. The girl seemed to determine that I was no threat and resumed her grisly work. Pocketing the ring, she rummaged through the pouches of the corpse and found a few coins, which she also took. Then, keeping in a crouch, she shuffled over to the next corpse and repeated the process. She worked quickly and efficiently, stripping the body of anything valuable, leaving anything useful but which could not be sold for much.

I followed her for several corpses, neither of us saying a word. Some of the other children noted me with interest, although it was not long before they too deemed me as no threat and continued with their work.

Licking dry lips and forcing words through the lump in my throat, I asked the girl, "Is this how you live?"

She ignored me.

"Can you talk?"

Again, she ignored me.

"What do you do with all the things you collect?"

This time she glanced up at me, but did not stop her work.

"Do you go to market and sell it?"

"No," she said, her voice rough and older than it should have been. "We give it to Switch."

"Who's Switch?"

"He sends us out to collect things. We collect them and give them to him."

She struggled with her words and it was clear she was not used to speaking. "Does this Switch look after you?" I asked.

"He gives us food, somewhere to sleep. I used to steal food." She shuddered at a memory. "I was caught sometimes. I used to sleep in alleys. I was caught sometimes."

"And Switch provides you with food and protection in exchange for you scavenging for him."

"The harvest."

By the girl's scrawny appearance, this Switch character did not give the children much to eat. Perhaps he gave them more depending on how much they collected, although it was more likely that he discarded the ones who did not collect enough. If he did not provide them with adequate food, I imagined the accommodation was not much better. A hundred children heaped in one pile, the ones at the bottom in danger of being crushed or asphyxiated, the ones at the top in danger of pneumonia or influenza.

It was no way to live, but it was the result of war. "Where are your parents?" I asked.

"Dead."

"I'm sorry you have to live like this."

She frowned. "Why?"

"Because you're a child and should be playing and dressing up and eating cakes."

Her frown deepened. She had no idea what any of those things meant.

"These armies," I said, "who were they?"

"Don't know."

"Were they Torbalians?"

She shrugged.

I looked around the bodies but could see no one wearing Braal's blue uniform. I was worried my father might have been among the corpses, but I was also concerned for Braal. Why I should even be thinking of her when she had abandoned me, I could not say, but her smile haunted my memories and I would have been distraught to find her dead.

"That standard," I said, indicating one of the flags still flying. "Whose is it?"

"Don't know."

Politics to any nine-year-old were an unknown concept; to someone like this urchin, they were even less. One day soon, she would be dead. Switch would find others to replace her, would probably not even notice she had not returned from the battlefield. If malnutrition and disease did not get her, other scavengers would, or roving soldiers like Whistler. I considered what Whistler would have done to this girl were he standing above her instead of me and I was glad I had killed him.

Then I remembered my knapsack and that I had been using it to gather food along my journey. "Here," I said, producing some nuts. "I don't have much, but ..."

The girl snatched the nuts from my hands and shoved them into her mouth so fast she choked. Other children looked up then and flooded me. I did not have much food in the knapsack but produced whatever there was. It was gone in an instant, seized by tiny, filthy hands and torn apart by the starving children.

Some dispersed, others looked at me with longing, expecting more, but I had no more to give. The girl I had been speaking with understood this, and in her I could see someone wise beyond her years. She may have only been eight or nine, but perhaps there was a chance she would survive after all.

"I'm looking for a knight," I said. "A man with different coloured eyes and a scar on his face."

"Don't know."

"A girl, then. My age, wearing a blue uniform. She may have been leading a charge of soldiers."

She thought about that one. "Don't know."

"Can you give me anything?"

She paused, then handed over a ring she had taken from the last corpse.

"That's not what I meant," I said, pushing the ring back. "You should keep it. Switch won't be happy if he finds out you're giving things away."

"Switch never happy."

"What happens when he's not happy?"

She rubbed unconsciously at her wrists and I could see the marks down her arms. No doubt those marks covered her entire body and I understood Switch was not a name but just something the children called him.

"You should come with me," I said. "I don't know anyone and I don't have anything, but it has to be a better life than this."

"We harvest or we're punished."

"You don't have to live this way."

She shook her head and went back to her work. I wanted to say something to convince her to join me, but there was no guarantee walking in my footsteps would grant her a better life than she was presently leading. At least with Switch she had something, even if it was abuse.

With a heavy heart and a hung head, I left the poor urchin to her work, to her life, and walked the rest of the way through the field of battle. It was a depressing walk, one which took a great deal of time.

By the end, there was a dull feeling in the pit of my stomach and all my fantasies had been dispelled. For this was war, human against human, and it did not matter that Braal had lied to and abandoned me, for she was right. This has to end, for if it continued, the only people left alive would already be half-dead.

CHAPTER ELEVEN

There was a town an hour's walk from the battlefield. It was not as large as Mrinth, yet it was even more populated. The houses were simple, mainly single-storey, and the roads were cruder. Bodies were propped against walls even at the outskirts of the settlement. They were living people, groaning near-silently as blood flowed down their bodies. The more aware were screaming, yet none of them were able to move. Their injuries were horrific. Some had lost hands, others entire arms. One had lost her leg past the knee, another was holding his head in place, his ear dribbling through his fingers. Some had been partially treated, with evidence of bandages and splints, but in the main they had been left to die.

Entering the town, I was greeted with the stench of death and bile rose in my throat. As bad as the battlefield had been, the town was worse, for here were not the dead of the battle, but the living of the aftermath. Out there, the corpses were beyond the pain and suffering of life, but within the town were those who had unfortunately survived.

As I moved through the streets, I noted the injuries of the corpses had been better treated and I surmised those outside were the soldiers who would not survive the night. The town would have only limited resources and someone was making conscious decisions as to which would be saved and which would be left for the vultures. I saw carts filled with bodies, with villagers trundling them off, presumably to burn or bury in a mass grave. Disease would be rife in the town and if the bodies were not quickly disposed of, everyone else's wounds would become infected; even the unwounded and any civilians not involved in the battle would be at risk.

It made me think about the townsfolk, for they could not have anticipated having to take on so many injured soldiers. There were no beds for them all, no resources to treat them, and many more would die. There would be some general out there somewhere, sitting in a cosy tent while drinking wine poured by a slave, totalling up how many soldiers had died in the battle, adding in how many would die afterwards from their injuries.

I wanted to help, but did not know what I could do. I knew nothing of medicines and little of human physiology. I crouched beside one man, he must have been a year or two younger than me, and readjusted his bandage. He licked cracked lips and rasped something. I realised he wanted water and produced my flask. The children had not taken the water and I offered it to him, but he was too weak to lift it. Raising it to his lips, I poured in a few drops and he closed his eyes, leaning back and sighing. I waited for his body to accept the water before giving him some more, for it would not do him any good to gulp it. I waited for several minutes before I realised he was not going to open his eyes again.

Rising, I felt my knees tremble and almost fell. I tried to take solace in the fact that in his final moments he had been shown kindness, but it did not make me feel any better.

Someone close by tried to speak and I noticed he was holding out his arm. I passed him the water flask without even noticing what I was doing and walked from the area. There was nothing for me there but pain and torment.

I wandered aimlessly through the town. No one paid me any attention. The wounded were in too much pain to notice anything and the civilians were busy either carting bodies or else distributing what aid they could. I came upon a man selling masks from a waggon, claiming they were the only thing to keep disease from your lungs. He was making a tidy profit, for he was putting the fear of the gods into his poor neighbours. Several streets down, there were some more urchins, although these were milling around in curiosity and were not robbing the dead and dying.

I came upon a large building with ornate and flowery designs carved into the brickwork. Stone creatures decorated the guttering, while large pillars led the way to the great front door. A steady flow of people moved to and from this building. Wounded were being taken in upon stretchers, the dead were being taken out on them, while townsfolk ran to and fro with buckets of water, towels and bandages. Even children were helping to carry things and my heart lifted somewhat at the sight. It seemed this was the centre of the efforts to save these soldiers and I assumed it to be a hospital or town hall.

Deciding this was where I could do the most good, I walked up the steps to the door and followed the townsfolk inside. Within, the building was formed mainly of a vast open space. Whatever furniture had existed within the great hall had been shoved to one side so beds and pews might be placed in even rows to maximise the space. The odour of fresh blood was in the air, just as it was upon the street, yet in the enclosed space the effect was stifling. There must have been upwards of two hundred wounded in that single hall, with dozens of townsfolk bustling about, doing whatever they could to help. I saw a young man tightly bandaging a soldier's arm, while in the next bed an old woman gently washed the blood from another soldier's head. There was a lot of talk in that hall, instructions were being barked out and obeyed, but there was no confusion. Everything was ordered, controlled, for otherwise all the soldiers would die.

Two men hastened past me, carrying a stretcher with a recent corpse, making room for another wounded soldier to lie in the same place as the one who had just died. I wanted to help, but as I stood there amidst the dying and the wounded, I had no idea what to do.

"You there," a woman said, "stop looking gormless and hold this."

She shoved some bandages into my hands and hurried off across the hall. Following, I was taken to a man of around fifty years. He had a bad cut to his forehead which was bleeding out, while a nasty gash to his thigh had sliced clean through to the bone. I saw the hard whiteness of the broken bone sticking out, although he did not utter a sound.

The woman went to work quickly, washing the man's forehead before stitching him up. She worked meticulously, with the speed of a striking cobra, and when she spoke to me, she did not even look my way. "Don't just stand there," she said, "tend to the leg."

I looked to the injury but did not know how to set a broken bone. Kneeling before him, I impotently held the bandage and wished I knew what to do. If I moved the leg, it would cause more harm than good, yet I could not see what bandaging the wound without first fixing it would do.

"Are you going to do anything?" the woman asked.

"I ... I ..."

"Give me that," she said, taking it from me without snatching it. "Don't go into shock, you'll be no good to anyone that way. Go boil water."

"Boil water," I said, nodding. "I can do that."

"Then go do it."

The woman wiped her sweating brow, leaving a trail of blood across her forehead she would not have cared about even had she noticed. She was working so hard she had switched off anything inside her which did not directly relate to her work. Once it was all over, she would not remember me, would not recall half the things she had done in that great hall. But she would have saved so many lives, and that was all that mattered.

I went over to where a stove was smouldering and blew upon the ashes until the flames grew bolder. People were coming to and fro, setting down kettles and bringing more. Nor were they limited to kettles, for they were using pans, pots and anything else which might convey water.

With the fire roaring again, I took up a bucket I found beside it and filled as many of the containers as

I could. Water splashed into the flames and sizzled, but my faerie strength enabled me to lift the bucket and not spill a great deal.

"Take some water over there," someone said, grabbing a kettle and rushing off with it. Picking up a pan from the stove, I followed his directions and wove my way through the moaning bodies on beds left untended. The injured outnumbered those working to heal them and many would die due to lack of attention. Ahead of me I could see a woman lying on a bed. She was screaming in pain as three people fought to hold her down while a fourth was doing something to the side with another stove. I took the water over and set it down.

The soldier on the bed screamed louder and struggled against those holding her. She tossed one away and struck out at another, wailing all the while as they tried to help her.

The woman at the stove noticed me and thanked me for the water. Her voice was cracked and husky, as though she had been inhaling too much smoke from the stove, but there was something familiar about it. Her attire was grubby and torn: her trousers were blue but she had removed her top and was working in a thick white undergarment, as dirty and bloodstained as her entire body. Her hair was thick with smoke, yet through its blackness I could see it was ordinarily red. The woman's face was slashed across the cheek and forehead, dirt mixing with the blood like tribal warpaint, while her eyes were dull and empty.

"Braal?" I asked tentatively. "Braal, is that you?"

She paused, equally surprised. "Misako."

The soldier on the bed gave another shriek and tossed her arms around.

"Quick," Braal said. "Misako, take over from them. You three, go tend to someone else."

"Are you sure?" one of the men holding the soldier asked.

"Just go."

The three released the soldier and I moved in to hold her down. Braal knew what I was and therefore understood I had a strength far greater than the three who had just departed. The screaming soldier almost made it off the bed before I pushed her back down. She flailed her limbs but I held her firm, refusing to allow her up. Her armour was cracked and pieces had torn away. Blood streamed down her side and her left leg was bent at an unnatural angle at the knee. Her eyes were feral, her mouth frothing with her own blood where she had bitten through her tongue, and even I had trouble keeping her down.

"Hold her steady," Braal said, removing something from the fire of the stove. It was a long piece of thin metal with serrations upon its underside, like shark teeth on a weapon.

"What are you doing?" I asked, my voice shaking.

"I got a few tools brought in from the wainwright. That leg has to come off and this saw's a much more precise way of doing that than using my sword."

"You have to save her leg, you can't just saw pieces off her."

"Misako," Braal said, her eyes boring into me, "just hold her down."

I did as I was told. Braal approached the task with grim determination and I could see then how she had risen to the rank of knight provisional at such a young age, and why Braal herself considered eighteen years to be a lifetime. The slick wet grinding of the saw was a sickening sound and the soldier screamed anew at the intense pain. The heated metal would hopefully help to ward off infection, or possibly it would aid in cauterising the wound. I tried to think of other things while Braal worked, but my eyes would not leave the saw.

Braal's rhythm was steady and within the span of half a minute she was entirely through. Nor was there as much blood as I had expected. The cut done, Braal set the saw back into the fire and moved the amputated leg aside, placing it upon the floor to spare the wounded soldier the sight of it. Pulling her sword from the stove, she told me to brace myself and pressed the metal to the raw flesh of the stump.

The soldier's screams filled the entire hall, yet there were so many others producing similar sounds that no one paid any attention.

Her work done, Braal replaced the sword in the stove and stepped away to breathe deeply. Her hands were covered in blood, her thick white undergarments were sodden with ichor, but she still had soothing words to speak to the wounded soldier.

An orderly took over to tend to the soldier and Braal and I moved to one side of the hall. There she dipped her bloody hands into a bucket of water and drank, heedless of what her hands were coated in.

My legs shaking, my head swimming, I fell against one of the chairs and vomited in the corner. Absently patting my back, Braal sank down beside me and closed her eyes. "Let it out, Misako," she said tiredly. "There's nothing to be ashamed of here."

We worked tirelessly for hours. I did not know how many hours, but candles were lit so we could better see and eventually they burned down and we no longer needed them because the sun was once again streaming through the windows. All too soon, more candles were brought in and still we worked. Eventually, though, all who had been brought in had been tended to, and any still outside had perished before they could have had their chance to be saved.

At last able to stop, Braal and I collapsed where we had worked. The hall was calm, there were few noises now, and there were people tending to those soldiers still with us.

"Get some rest, ma'am," someone said to Braal where she lay sprawled in the corner. "We'll find you a bed."

"If there's a spare bed anywhere in this town," Braal breathed more than said, "it should have a wounded soldier sleeping in it."

"At least use one of the prayer rooms."

She went to argue again, although nodded. I helped her to her feet. We were both exhausted but my faerie constitution made me stronger. That Braal was even still alive after all the work she had done was astounding, particularly since she had already been hard at work when I had first arrived. I led her through a door and into a small room. Within was an altar with some form of religious artefact sitting atop it. There were no chairs in the room but we sank to the floor wherever we could and closed our eyes while we recuperated.

My brain was a haze of nausea, conflicting emotions and weariness. It seemed an eternity ago that I had been anxiously waiting by the stone lion for Braal to arrive. Now we were reunited and I did not think I would ever be the same again.

"Glad to see you made it," Braal said after a while. Our bodies were still pretty much shut down, but our minds were far too active to sleep.

"No thanks to you."

She turned her head to me but lacked the strength to argue.

"I waited for you," I said. I would have been cross, but similarly lacked the energy. "You said you'd be there and I waited so long."

"I was there on time."

"I was a little late. Just a day or so."

"Oh. I was called away." She leaned her head against the wall behind her and closed her eyes. "Our scouts reported the army was trying to ambush a Torbalian unit. We snuck in with a pincer movement to cut them off."

In light of that, it was selfish to have expected her to stay behind and wait for me. "I thought you'd abandoned me," I said somewhat lamely.

"I left you a note."

"You did?"

"That's my knapsack, you must have found the note inside."

"I found some food. Oh, there was paper."

"That'd be the note, yeah."

"I can't read."

She laughed. It was a hollow sound, devoid of energy, but it was the first laughter either of us had heard in a long while. I would have laughed with her, but nothing that day made me want to.

"Who won?" I asked.

"Who won what?"

"The battle."

"Ask a general."

"I thought you were in command."

"I guess I was, after a fashion. But I'm also a soldier, a soldier who goes into battle and doesn't sit behind planning things. The only people who win battles, the only people who win wars, are politicians. I'm a soldier, so all I can do is lose."

"You were right."

"About what?"

"You really are an old woman."

She did not laugh at this, although I felt if we were still singing by the waterfall, she would have. "I enquired about your father," she said. "Nothing. Sorry."

"Thank you for trying."

"I'll keep asking around."

"What'll you do now?"

"I'm heading out in the morning."

"I think it might *be* the morning."

"Really?"

"Actually, I think it might be the morning after the morning. I lost track of days in there."

"Then I need to leave as soon as I can stand. I have to make my report."

"Right." I looked at Braal, lying there propped against the wall, eyes closed. She did not feel sorry for herself, did not dwell on how hard she had worked, did not voice a single word of complaint. She deserved to be whatever she wanted and if all humans were like her, the faerie armies would not stand a chance.

The thought of her leaving me again, just after I had found her, filled me with sadness, but if she had to make a report, then she had to make a report. I could not stand between Braal and her duty, no matter how I felt about her.

"What about you?" she asked without opening her eyes. Her voice was becoming distant.

"I don't know. I don't have anywhere to go."

"Want to come with me?"

"You mean that?"

"Sure. My unit's staying here, so it'll be just the two of us."

For the first time since leaving Braal at the stream, my heart was filled with warmth. "You won't regret this, Braal," I promised. "I'll follow your orders, do whatever you ask. I'll be the best travelling companion ever."

But Braal did not hear; she had already fallen fast asleep.

CHAPTER TWELVE

We were both glad to leave the charnel town behind us. Before we left, I was introduced to Braal's horse, which was a fine animal trapped in the blue uniform of her battalion and fitted with armour to protect him from enemy arrows and swords. Braal found it amusing that I was talking to the animal and asked me whether I could communicate with him.

"No," I said, "but animals can pick up on emotions and I want him to know I'm a friend."

Without a horse of my own, I sat on the saddle behind Braal and held on without quite knowing how to do so. At first, I held the saddle, but then I fell off the back of the horse so I didn't do that again. Then I encircled Braal's waist with my arms and almost crushed her to death, so compromised by holding her hips in order to steady myself. While we rode, we chatted about various things and I was amazed at how the rest had lifted Braal's mood. I asked her about it.

"If I let the war get me down," she said, "I'd end up drowning myself."

"If you tried that, I'd save you. I'm a mermaid; I can breathe underwater."

"Looks like I've got myself a bodyguard."

I did not know what to say to that, so instead looked out across the land. We were riding through beautiful countryside untouched by the war. The wind was light and warm, the birds twittered in the trees and wild flowers grew in abundance all around us. Some of the upper world was lovely and it was a shame the war was despoiling everything.

"Do you honestly think the war can be stopped?" I asked while we rode.

"I have to. Otherwise I'm fighting just so my children and my children's children will die in the war as well."

"You have children?"

"Not yet, but someday I hope to."

"How many?"

"Ooh, a dozen, at least."

"A dozen? Mermaids spawn by the thousands."

She cast me a strange look and I offered her a lopsided smile.

"Faerie humour," she said with a shake of her head. "I'm only gullible because I'm tired."

"Do you know any stories about mermaids?"

"You don't want to hear the stories I know about mermaids."

"Do you know any nice ones?"

She thought a moment. "Not really. There's one about a mermaid who thinks she's a princess, but it doesn't have a happy ending."

"Life doesn't have a happy ending. Tell me."

"It sort of ends with the mermaid realising she's worth less than swine and feeds herself to the pigs so at least she'll make a contribution as dung."

"That sounds like a lovely story."

"Well, it was made up by humans, what do you expect? I suppose you have a lot of bad stories about us."

I thought about that. "Not really. Faeries aren't an especially imaginative people. We don't make up stories."

"What about your mother and all that talk of dragons and knights?"

"They're not stories. Knights really did fight dragons."

"I don't think dragons exist."

"Only because the knights killed them all."

"I get the impression our parents may have been telling us the same stories, just with a different slant on the heroes and the villains."

"Tell me about your battalion."

"Tell a faerie military secrets? Do you want me to be executed for high treason?"

"Ah, I didn't think of it that way."

"It's funny, in a way. Right now, you're my best chance of survival because of your faerie blood. You're strong, you have sharpened senses and I like to think we're friends, which means we'd fight for each other."

"I'd like to think that, too."

"But when we get to Torbalia, you're going to have to hide who you are, pretend you're not a mermaid. No one will know, unless you tell them."

"What will they do if they find out?"

"Interrogate you, torture you, ultimately execute you." She paused. "Actually, it's probably not a good idea for you to come all the way with me."

"You just try getting rid of me now, Braal. I won't tell anyone what I am and I trust you not to, either."

"Once I've made my report, I'll go see my battalion. We travel a lot, it's part of our job description. Someone in the battalion must have heard something about your father."

"I appreciate everything you're doing for me, Braal. I wish I could put into words how much it means to me."

"You don't have to. What, have you never had a friend before?"

"Mermaids don't really have friends."

"Faerie humour again, ha!"

I did not like to tell her I had not been joking in the slightest.

We stopped when we reached a brook and filled our canteens. Braal had insisted on not taking any food or water from the town, saying the wounded had greater need for it, but we had had little to eat or drink for days. Upon leaving the town (neither of us ever knew its name), we had gathered some edible berries and those had sufficed. While Braal drew water from the stream, I stripped off and waded into the brook.

"Uh, Misako?" she asked. "If you're going to take a bath, could you do it after I've filled our canteens?"

"Shh."

"Excuse me for trying to be hygienic."

I noted she did not stop filling them, but in truth my concentration was elsewhere. Reverting to my mermaid tail, I lay in the water to face the oncoming tide. The brook was not deep – when standing, it would not have risen much past my knees. The water was clear and cool and I breathed it as easily as I would have the air above the surface. I was not there, however, to immerse myself in memory, but to make myself useful.

The flow of the brook brought me something almost immediately and I grabbed it, plucking the fish from its path before the surprised animal could understand what was happening. An instant later, I had one in my other hand, and I rose, breaking the surface as I laughed. Rolling on my tail towards Braal, I slammed the heads of the two fish onto a rock at the shore and held the two corpses dangling by their tails.

"Dinner," I said.

Braal stared at me with an unreadable expression. As she stoppered her flask, she said, "You might not believe this, but I've seen stranger methods of fishing than that."

Taking the fish from me, she took them over to where she had tied down her horse. Sliding out of the brook, I picked up my clothes and accepted a towel Braal threw at me. It seemed her horse's saddle-bags held a lot of useful tools and equipment, and I was seriously considering getting myself such an animal.

"They don't all come with magic pouches," Braal said while she set up the fire. I noticed she was using a ring of stones, much as the man in the mountain had done, and surmised it was a standard camp-fire trick. Not having fire beneath the water, I had little experience with such things.

"Are they expensive?" I asked as I finished drying myself and got back into my clothes. I was better at it now, more used to being in my human guise. It was strange to think of how much time I was spending walking around on legs.

"Horses? I'll say. I didn't have to pay for this one, which means I don't own him. He's property of the army. I still have to pay for his upkeep, though, all his health check-ups, his feed, his insurance ..."

"What's insurance?"

"It's a sum you have to regularly pay in case something bad happens. So long as I pay the insurance, if my horse dies I don't get billed for him."

"They'd bill you for a horse you don't own?"

"Everything's about money, Misako. The human world revolves around it."

"Do you get paid much?"

"No. And even then it's sometimes late. That's a trick of the people at the top, although my high commander is good with us. He insists we get paid on time, so we're usually OK."

"I don't understand, why's it a trick to pay a soldier late?"

Braal had finished constructing her fire and was setting it ablaze. Within the stones, she had set several small logs, as well as twigs and some paper she was using as kindling. She then rubbed two sticks together and blew on them to produce a flame. "The army's full of tricks," she said while she worked. "Let me put it this way: if you're a knight, living in the lap of luxury, and you're sending two thousand soldiers into battle, would you pay them before or after?"

"Before. That way, they could spend their money before they die."

"That's a sweet notion. If a knight is sending two thousand soldiers into battle and only one and a half thousand survive, that means the knight doesn't have to pay five hundred soldiers. So, yes, the soldiers are paid late."

"That's obscene."

"But also clever. The fact soldiers are never paid on time means their superiors don't expect them to survive. It's the same with food. That same army of two thousand soldiers? When they're sent out to march, they don't take enough food and water for two thousand people. They take enough for one and a half thousand. It's less to carry, which takes the pressure off the waggons."

"How can a knight know how many soldiers are going to be killed?"

"It's something they factor in. You'll always find the monarchs, the generals, the knights, they have a lot of experience in how many bodies to throw against how many enemy soldiers and know roughly what's going to come out the other end."

"What if all two thousand survive?"

"Then some would starve. Having every soldier survive a battle isn't a situation a knight would be happy with, because soldiers are costly. Human life is cheap, Misako, but food and water cost money. Besides, those in charge assume soldiers are going to spend all their money on gambling, cheap alcohol and even cheaper whores, so why pay them anything at all?"

One of the words Braal had used made me shift uncomfortably, for it brought back memories of Salla back in Mrinth.

"Where we just came from," Braal said as she secured the two fish in metal griddles she had taken from her horse's saddle-bag, "we lost upwards of six hundred soldiers on the battlefield. A further two hundred probably died through their injuries afterwards, and another couple of dozen are going to be executed."

"Executed?"

"There are always soldiers who drop their weapons in battle. In wartime, that's punishable by execution."

"You mean your knights execute the survivors in their own army?"

"I think the reason behind it is something to do with desertion. If you've dropped your weapon it's likely because you were running away, and if you were running away it means you've put the lives of your comrades at risk. I don't agree with it any more than you do, but I've seen it happen. I hide it whenever I can, but I'm only a knight provisional and I don't take commands like that very often."

"Has the high commander of your battalion ever executed anyone for dropping their weapon?"

"Ha, no. He spends so much time fighting for the underdog, it's a wonder he hasn't learned to bark."

"He doesn't kill for stupid reasons and he pays you on time. I think I like this high commander of yours."

"He *is* something."

I detected a strangely whimsical note to Braal's voice and watched as she turned the fish in their griddles. "Braal, are you sweet on him?"

"Leave off."

"Why are you blushing?"

"I made the fire too big, that's all."

"Why are you making excuses?"

"Why am I about to brain you with your dinner?"

I smiled. "I think it's good. It's nice you can experience positive emotions with all the death going on around you."

"Seriously, stop it."

I stopped, but only because I was insanely hungry. Braal finished cooking the fishes and unlatched the metal straps keeping them attached to the griddles. I reached to take one off her and screamed, dropping the thing to the ground.

Braal reached for her sword, her hand stopping only when she realised there was no external threat. I had taken the griddle from Braal and it had burned my skin as surely as if I had stuck my hand into hot coals. Holding my injured hand steady with my other, I could see blisters opening clear across my fingers and palm.

"I'll get some ointment," Braal said and hurried to the saddle-bag to bring out a bottle. She applied a few drops to my blisters and I bit my lip as I winced at the pain. Steam rose from the wound and the pain did decrease a little.

"You should wash it in the brook," Braal said.

"I don't know what happened. I touched the cool part you handed me."

"I don't know. I … Ah, hell."

"What?"

"The griddle, it's made of iron."

Iron. Iron was poison to faeries. In large enough quantities, it could even be lethal.

"Misako, I'm sorry, I just didn't think."

"No, no, I should have thought. I've spent so long as a human, it just never occurred to me that I …" I cut myself off, for I was not human. I may have been halfway there, but I was not fully a woman of humankind. The iron test was one reminder of how I could never truly be one of them, no matter how much I played at it. "I should wash it," I said stonily as I returned to the brook.

Braal did not know what to say. I could tell she felt bad for what had happened, that she blamed herself, but the fault was not hers. I was the fool who thought I could be someone I was not. It made me wonder whether my father would ever accept me as his daughter, with such reminders that I was not human.

Even washing my injured hand caused me pain, yet it was pain I richly deserved for ever believing I could be something other than what I was.

When I returned to Braal, she had a rabbit over the fire, stuck through a wooden spit.

"What happened to the fish I caught?" I asked.

"They're here. I'm going to eat them, but I thought you'd prefer rabbit."

"I'd prefer fish. Why would I prefer rabbit?"

Braal did not look at me as she turned the spit and I could see she was still upset. "Because I cooked the fish in iron, which means there are going to be traces of iron in them. Other than the iron which you naturally find in blood, I mean. If I irradiated your dinner, it would slowly kill you from the inside. Which is something I would have done, without even knowing, if you hadn't have taken the griddle from me."

I sank to the ground beside her, the shock of the realisation sinking in. "I never even considered that before."

"I almost killed you. I can't even apologise for that."

"You saved me."

She looked at me. "I what?"

"Now I know not to eat food prepared in iron griddles. I never would have thought of that, even after I burned myself. But you did. It means when I don't drop down dead from a mysterious illness twenty years from now, I have you to thank."

"You're going over the top."

"I owe you my life and you feel bad about it." I offered her an exaggerated sigh. "But then, I guess you're only human."

The quirk of a smile touched her lips and she handed me the rabbit. "Stop gushing over me and eat your dinner. I only did it so I could get both fish, anyway."

Grinning like a schoolgirl who, on her third term, has finally found her soul-mate, I settled down to eat. No matter how many times life kicked me in the face, from that moment on I knew I would always have a friend.

CHAPTER THIRTEEN

Over the course of the next month, I discovered more about Braal than I had anyone else in my entire life. We spent our days travelling, our evenings confiding secrets and our nights sleeping beneath the stars. Occasionally, we would happen upon a town or village, at which point we would be able to catch up on news and gossip. Braal could get her horse tended to by a blacksmith and properly fed, while the two of us could spend the night at an inn. For the sake of saving money, we shared a room and neither of us questioned the practicality of also sharing a bed. There was nothing sexual between us, there had never been any indication of such from either of us. As a faerie, nudity held no taboo for me, and I preferred being in the same room as Braal in case, alone, I made a grave mistake in the human world.

I did not like our times spent in these towns, for I relished the nights we enjoyed alone under the stars. My faith in people was not strong and I knew that should any of the townsfolk discover my true nature, I would be murdered. With Braal, her horse and the open lands, I held no such worries.

I broached the nudity subject one time while we were strolling. We did not always ride, for Braal did not want to tire her horse, knowing we still had a long way to go before we reached Torbalia; often, therefore, we would walk by the side of the animal, with Braal holding his reins. Clippety, too, appreciated this – Clippety being the name of Braal's horse.

"How do you mean?" Braal asked, which meant I had clumsily phrased my question.

"Well, even all that time ago back at the waterfall, when we first met, you didn't bat an eyelid about my being naked."

"You want me to bat my eyelids at you?"

"Stop that. I'm saying you're not bothered about being naked around people. It's a faerie trait." I thought back to the reaction I had received that time I had been sunning myself on the rocks when I had first entered Mrinth. "It's certainly not a human trait."

"It's a soldier's trait," she replied. "There are a lot of places with communal bathing, entire cities where no one looks twice at someone else just because they're not wearing any clothes. But with me, it's more necessity."

"Necessity?"

"As soldiers, we never know where we'll be, what we're going to be doing. Soldiers, through necessity, do whatever's most expedient or efficient. Worrying about little things like who's seen your girlie bits is a good way to get yourself killed."

"You mean it distracts you during battle?"

"Not really. I mean, if you're camped in a clearing and you need to relieve yourself, you have two options. You can leave the carefully established perimeter you've set up and squat in a bush, where anyone could ambush you; or you could hang decency and sit on a bucket."

"I've decided soldiers are very crude."

"Then there's my drill sergeant. He loves the rain."

"What does that have to do with anything?"

"Whenever the storms get really bad, he takes us all out into the training fields to do press-ups in the nude."

"Why?"

"Because he's sadistic. Also, because he's building up our immunity to harsh elements and wants us all in the same mental state. If we're hating him and freezing to the bone, none of us are paying any attention to the fact the people beside us aren't wearing any clothes."

"It seems nudity is a much more complicated subject for humans than I ever considered."

"There's nothing complicated about humans," she replied. "We're all pretty boring, really."

"There's something I've been meaning to tell you. It's about soldiers."

"Hmm?"

I had battled with myself as to whether Braal should know about this. Every time I considered telling her, I had been too afraid to get my words out. Some days I did not think of it at all, yet there were others when it ate me up inside. When we had stopped at the last town, I had lain awake all night, watching Braal sleep while working through so many scenarios of what she might say, how she could react. I knew her, I told myself I knew her like a sister, yet human reactions were temperamental and I did not want to lose her.

"It's about what happened in the woods," I said, not knowing how long I had paused.

"The woods? You mean the whole nude-bathing thing at the waterfall? I thought we just covered that."

"After that."

"After that?" She frowned as she strained to remember. "I didn't think there was an after that. I went off to my unit and you followed the stream. Or, you detoured, got lost and eventually followed the stream."

"I met someone."

"Met someone in a good way or a bad way?"

"A bad way."

That got her attention. Gone was the jovial, genial Braal I had come to rely upon and in her place was a serious, blank-faced young woman who had already accepted she was going to hear something bad.

"He was a soldier," I said. "One of yours."

"One of mine?"

"Whistler."

Her expression darkened. "I know Whistler. Thinks himself a ladies' man, but I wouldn't trust a girl alone with him for a … Oh, Misako, I'm sorry." Her face paled and she reached out a comforting hand but retracted it when she became instantly unsure whether that was the right thing to do.

"You're sorry? About what?"

"I know what he's like. He … he attacked you, didn't he?"

"He tried to do more than that."

"Tried?" she asked with hope shining through her eyes. It was then I understood what she thought had happened, and how she was truly worried for me. I did not want to continue, for I did not want to disappoint her.

"He didn't realise how strong I am," I said, not meeting her eyes. "I fought back. I killed him."

"Oh thank the gods."

My eyes snapped up to meet hers. "What? I killed him, Braal. I murdered him."

"Surely you killed him in self-defence."

"No. I was angry, furious at what he was trying to do to me, at what he'd likely done to so many other women in the past. I pounded his face into pulp and then drowned him." I had not meant to say all of that, particularly not with such venom, but my anger was returning, accompanied by the fear that Braal would hate me, and if I did not get it all out in one breath, I knew it would never be said.

Braal did not say anything, but she did blink in momentary astonishment. "Well," she said at last, "we've all had days like that."

"Days where you murdered someone?" I all but wailed, tears to my eyes.

"No, I meant days where we wanted to kill Whistler."

I stopped walking and Braal continued alone with her horse. "Braal, I killed him. I … I took the life from him with my bare hands. I watched it drain from his face as he realised he was going to die. And still I didn't stop."

Braal ceased walking. She released the reins of her horse and the animal shook himself to make himself more comfortable. She took a few steps back to me and I could see conflicting emotions to her face. She was frightened, I could see that much plainly enough, and it was because she now knew my true nature.

"That's who I am, Braal," I said, breaking into tears. "I'm capable of murder. I'm a monster."

"Hey," she said, taking me by the shoulders and squeezing until I met her gaze. "You think I'm not capable of murder? I've killed people, Misako. A soldier's job is to keep the peace and sometimes that means killing people. But I've never killed anyone unlawfully. That makes me a killer but not a murderer. Yet what exactly is the law? A load of rules made up by people above us in rank? Those same people who want half the army to die so they don't have to bother feeding them? Those same people who don't pay them so they can't enjoy their final night in life before they go out and die just so those superiors can sit back in comfort and safety? I obey the law because I'm a soldier, but that doesn't mean the deaths I've caused have been justified. In the eyes of the enemy, I'm a murderer, so many times over. You've killed someone, Misako, someone who was trying to rape you. I've killed men for exactly the same reason. Well, not exactly the same. I've killed them because we've been defending a town and there are enemy soldiers raping and murdering the people we're protecting."

"I'm a killer."

"You've killed one," she said seriously. "I've killed hundreds."

We stood staring at one another for several moments as the impact of that statement sank in.

"And," Braal said when she noticed I was about to say something, "never call yourself a monster. You are not a monster, Misako. In the time I've known you, I've come to learn you're a great many things.

Half mermaid, half human. Confused, strong, resourceful. Loving, caring, devoted, loyal. Sometimes skittish, occasionally downright weird. But above all, you're my friend and I don't make friends with monsters. The monsters are those who kill without remorse, those who seize girls because they think they own them, those who do horrible things to decent people without any care to what those actions do to their victims and the families of their victims. You hate yourself for what you did to Whistler, and maybe you should; but by hating yourself you're only proving you're better than he could ever be."

"You're just saying that because you're my friend."

She squeezed harder and my arms hurt. "I'm saying them," she said in a tremulous voice, "because if you let this eat away at you, you may as well have parted your legs and let Whistler do whatever he wanted, because he'll win. Even when he's been dead for five years, he'll still have won. He doesn't deserve to, Misako. Am I glad you killed him? No. Am I glad he's dead? Yes. If I could have arrested him without an uprising in that unit I was commanding, I would have done so and avoided all of this. Now come here."

She hugged me tightly, fiercely, and in that embrace I could feel her sorrow shudder through her body. Braal was worried for me, worried for me with the same degree of passion that I was worried that my revelation would have destroyed our relationship. And in that instant, I knew it did not matter. She had forgiven me, perhaps even believed there was nothing that warranted her forgiveness.

"I don't deserve you," I said with a struggle.

"Yeah, you do," she said, pulling away. "And don't ever think otherwise."

As she walked back to her horse, I said, "Braal, there's a theory about girls with red hair and blue eyes returning as vampires when they die."

She looked back, a little surprised. "Uh, OK."

"I'm just saying …" I inhaled to control my chattering teeth. "I'm just saying, I hope that's true. Because then you and I could spend an eternity together."

"That's sweet. Misako, could I ask you a question?"

"Sure."

"Why do people believe that? It's a bit silly. I mean, sorry if that insults your religion or anything."

"Faeries don't have religion. And, yes, it is a bit silly. But a lot of faerie mythology is silly. It doesn't mean most of it isn't true, though."

Entirely confused, Braal shook her head and resumed walking. A little lighter of step now that I had a few things off my chest, I slipped into place at my rightful place – beside her.

By the time night fell, we had not made it to the village Braal thought we would reach, so we prepared to set up camp for the night. I knew it would be awkward, for we had not really spoken all that much since our embrace. I knew Braal did not hate me, but she would still need time in which to work through everything I had said. It did not matter that she said I should not think of myself as a monster, the important thing was that Braal did not see me as one. That was something she would have to seriously consider, and I had found the best decisions were always made after a good night's sleep.

Unstrapping the blankets from the side of Braal's horse, as I had done many times over our travels together, I set about unfolding them upon the ground. Ordinarily by this point, Braal would be gathering stones and twigs for a fire, but instead she was staring at something in the distance.

"What's up?" I asked.

"Listen. What do you hear?"

I listened. "The birds."

"Misako, you have a faerie's senses. Tell me what's out there."

I had been living so long as a human, I had almost forgotten I had heightened senses. I could see nothing, so closing my eyes, I took a deep breath and cast out my mind. There was a strange scent to the air. It was not death, but it was pain. I could not quite describe what I meant by that, but the odour was of sadness.

Then I listened, as Braal had instructed, and found I could indeed hear something. It was screaming, or at least crying. It was not a battle, yet I could hear the clank of armour, of weapons, and the neighing of a horse.

I opened my eyes. "There are soldiers out there."

"That's what I thought, but I can't see anything in the darkness."

I had not even noticed night had fallen so quickly, but it was true.

"How far away are they?" she asked, still straining to see.

"Half a mile maybe, I'm not sure."

Braal was restless, for she knew what she had to do yet was talking herself out of it.

"Don't worry about me," I said. "Seriously. You do what you have to do."

"I'm a knight provisional and this is territory owned by Torbalia. If there are soldiers out there, they should be Torbalian."

"Don't convince me, just go."

"I'm not leaving you here with my horse. Come with me a little way. I'll assess the situation before I decide what to do."

I nodded. "And we can fight together."

"No." She looked at me with frightened eyes. "Whatever happens, you do as I tell you, understand? If I tell you to run, you run; if I tell you to fight, you fight."

"Then tell me to fight."

"Misako, I mean it."

"So do I."

She shook her head. "I don't have time to argue this with you. On the horse."

We both mounted Clippety and with a single command from his mistress, the horse charged through the darkness. Braal did not need any direction from me to know where we were headed, and I clasped her about the waist to hang on while we carved through the night with the knowledge that we were riding in to save someone's life.

Riding on a horse at full gallop was far different to sitting astride the animal while it marched. Initially, my stomach heaved at the jolts, as though I was on a ship fighting the waves; but after a few minutes I got used to the motion and it was more akin to flowing through a calm tide. I knew it was all perception, that my body and mind had simply learned to make sense of the unexpected motion, although I did not envy Braal having to ride in such a fashion on a daily basis.

There was a cluster of trees ahead and Braal did not slow, navigating her horse through the copse. The screaming intensified the more we travelled, and it was joined by laughter. Braal drew the horse to a halt and swung her legs smoothly over as she dismounted.

"Stay on the horse," she told me. "If anything bad happens, ride."

"If anything bad happens, I'm coming after you."

"Misako, no." Her eyes were intense but the fear was more for me than herself. "I can't go into this knowing you're going to be in danger. It'll make me lose focus."

I nodded, although I did not know whether I was being truthful. "I promise to do what you tell me."

"Good." Braal patted the side of her horse's head and placed a hand upon her sword without drawing it. She moved swiftly to where the trees petered out and I kicked my heels into Clippety that he might wander after her.

I remained hidden within the trees and saw Braal slowly moving ahead. There was a plain before us, in which there lay a broken waggon. It was a large wooden contraption I had seen many times before, with four massive round wheels and a horse to pull it. Two of the wheels were broken and the waggon had tipped over. The horse lay dying, a grievous wound tearing through his side and up into his neck. Blood gushed freely and it was clear the animal would not last much longer. The contents of the waggon had spilled across the ground and two laughing armoured men were picking through what it had contained, which seemed mainly to be bottles of something. There were six other soldiers – three women and three men – and they were laughing as they pushed around two girls slightly younger than me. The poor girls were terrified and were openly weeping at the cruel game. There was another man, lying against the overturned waggon. He was aged in his thirties and was no doubt the girls' father. Blood stained his shirt and one of his arms was twisted to his side. He was pleading with the soldiers, who only jeered at him and spat in his face.

"That's enough," Braal said as she warily approached. She still had yet to draw her sword, but stood with her shoulder facing the soldiers so she would be easily able to swing her weapon free. "What the hell do you people think you're doing?"

One of the men laughed as he shoved a girl to his fellow in their obscene game. "Look, guys, someone else to play with."

"Your uniform's Torbalian," Braal said, her voice filled with such fire that I immediately pitied those people. "What regiment are you from?"

"Regiment?" the man laughed. "Hey, Sarcasa, she wants to know what regiment we're from."

One of the female soldiers laughed. "Got your regiment right here," she said, turning to Braal and for some reason pulling down her trousers to show her bare backside. The soldiers found this hilarious and two of the men followed suit.

Needless to say, I was utterly confused.

Braal did not rise to their antics. "Knight Provisional Braal of the Second Battalion," she said. "I'm placing you under arrest for assault, destruction of civilian property, slaughter of a civilian horse, attempted murder and attempted rape of civilians. You really want to let those girls go and get on your knees and pray."

The man who had been laughing the hardest lost all his humour and drew his sword. It occurred to me then that these were Torbalians, these were Braal's own people. They were not enemy soldiers, they were defenders of the kingdom. They should have been protecting these civilians and instead they were defiling and killing them.

"Seems to me," the man said, "we're going to hang whatever we do. Seems to me the best thing we could do is slaughter us a knight provisional."

"Uh, Garon," one of the other men said, "I don't think that's such a good idea. The battalion knights provisional are …"

"Are what?" Garon barked. "Super soldiers? Able to take down entire hordes of demons by themselves? That's propaganda, Amack, and you know it."

"I just think maybe we should …"

Garon slapped him about the face. "When you're in charge, you can do the thinking. Until then, you do as I tell you. Now, go get her."

Amack reluctantly drew both a sword and a knife and moved towards Braal.

"Are you stupid?" Braal asked him.

Amack stopped. "Uh, no?"

"Is that a question?"

"No," he said more forcefully.

"You just told him you think I can kill all of you without breaking a sweat and, when he tells you he doesn't believe it, you're willing to attack me by yourself? If Garon there's so sure I'm not a threat, why isn't *he* attacking me?" She paused. "Because he knows I am and he needs someone stupid enough to prove it to him. Or, in other words, while I'm cutting you down, Garon's going to be using that time to run away."

Amack glanced back to Garon, uncertain. "Uh …"

"Get him," Sarcasa said with an angry frown. "Amack, stop being such a coward."

"Which means," Braal said, "she agrees with you as well. Why don't the two of you fight me together, Amack? Ask Sarcasa to come over here with you."

"Uh, Sarcasa, would you please …?"

"Are you kidding me?" Sarcasa asked angrily. "Amack, just do what you're told."

"Sarcasa," Garon said without taking his eyes from Braal, "attack her with Amack."

"What? Hold on, what are you …?"

"Now."

"But honey, I don't think …"

"And when *you're* in charge of this group," he snarled, "*you* can think all you like as well. What are the rest of you looking at?"

"The only coward in this field," Braal answered for them. "Even that horse has more courage than you. I mean, who kills a horse? Do you know how valuable horses are? You'd have to be a complete idiot to allow your people to attack a waggon and kill the horse."

"Enough," Garon said, drawing his sword and seizing Amack's from him so he could wield two. With a cry of rage, he charged Braal. She allowed him to come, sidestepped and thrust her knee into his belly. Garon staggered as he passed her and Braal dropped and spun, her foot catching his ankles and sending him crashing to the ground.

Returning to a standing position, Braal drew her own sword and twirled it experimentally.

Snarling, Garon flew to his feet and took a mad swing at her. Braal dropped back at Garon's every swipe, not once raising her sword or attempting to block his attacks. Garon expended so much energy over the following ten seconds that he would be far too slow to react when Braal finally did make her move.

That move came so suddenly that even my breath caught in my throat. As Garon's left-handed sword came down at her, she brought up her blade to smash it aside even as she twisted her body, bringing her sword about to grab the hilt with both hands as she plunged it directly through his belly.

Garon emitted a startled gasp as he dropped both swords. Braal pulled back her blade and kicked him in his wound, sending Garon falling in a gory convulsing mess upon the grass.

Facing the remaining soldiers, Braal held her bloody sword ready and said, "One more chance. Throw down your weapons and come quietly. If that man and his girls live, I'll even make sure you don't hang."

The soldiers stared for several moments in open-mouthed horror. Then Sarcasa said, "I'm taking over this unit. The one who kills her becomes my second. Go!"

The soldiers, numbed through the death of their leader and probably mindless to begin with, attacked as one and Braal fell back on her heel. I watched her tactics and was amazed, for it was the first time I had ever seen her fight. She used her sword as an extension to her body, and it was a body she knew better than anyone I had ever known. Her stance allowed her to pivot and spin as required, her perfectly honed muscles allowed her to deliver hacks and thrusts with maximum efficiency whenever she needed to. She used the flat of her blade to parry, the point to stab, and as I watched, awestruck, I decided all those stormy nights spent doing naked press-ups with her drill sergeant were worth it, for Braal was herself a single arrow which could take down an army with one release of the bow.

Other soldiers had fallen, either dead or wounded, I could not say, until only Amack and Sarcasa remained, and they were only standing because they had thus far avoided the fight. I watched as Amack picked up a sword, for Garon had taken his, and he stood with wavering courage before Braal.

"Stay back," he said as she walked towards him. "I'm warning you. Stay …"

Braal reached him and punched him full in the face, splintering his nose and sending him spinning backwards to slam into the ground.

Sarcasa had seized the opportunity to do something particularly cowardly, for she had grabbed one of the terrified girls and was holding her as a shield, a knife kissing her throat. The other girl was tending to her dying father, although the horse had ceased moving sometime earlier.

"Don't be an idiot, Sarcasa," Braal warned as she circled her like a killer whale eyeing a seal on an ice floe. "Let her go."

"Why?" Sarcasa asked, her laugh cracking in her throat. "So you can take me in and execute me? Or just cut me down here where I stand? We both know I'm not going to survive this. Not your way."

"What's your plan?" Braal asked in a bored tone. "To walk backwards for hours, dragging that girl along with you, until ... what? I'll only follow you. And you have to sleep sooner or later."

"Throw down your sword."

"What? Why would I do that?"

"Because I'll kill her."

"You'd cut through your own shield? You're a really bad soldier, Sarcasa."

Sarcasa was panicking, which was Braal's intent. I could not see what she would do, but trusted that Braal had this figured out. I wanted to ride down to help, but had promised Braal I would obey her. I could not interfere with her work and had to trust that she held the necessary experience to get the hostage safely away.

"I'll do it," Sarcasa said. "I'll kill her."

"So you've said. But the fact you haven't done it yet makes me think you won't."

"I ... I ..."

Braal heaved a deep sigh, then looked over Sarcasa's shoulder and slowly shook her head. I looked in that direction but could see nothing. I did not understand her intention, until Sarcasa also glanced over there.

Braal moved with the speed of lightning. She leaped through the air, grabbed the knife's blade with her gloved hand and as she yanked backwards, her other fist flew into Sarcasa's face. The hostage ran, sobbing, back to her family and Braal tossed away Sarcasa's knife. Blood dripped from between Braal's gloved fingers, but she did not appear to notice.

"Well, that could have gone better for you," Braal said.

From where she crouched upon one knee, Sarcasa began to laugh. Her laughter was so out of place that Braal stole a glance back to the hostage and her family. Shock appeared in her face and I followed her gaze to see half a dozen more uniformed soldiers appear in the clearing. One of them waved and in their wake half a dozen more appeared.

"Run," Braal said to the two girls. "Run. Now."

"Father …"

"He died two minutes ago. Now go."

The two girls did not want to leave, but to stay would have been a fate worse than death. Thankfully, their fear lent them stamina and together they fled into the woods, their laments going with them.

I watched them go before looking back to Braal. "Get ready, "Clippety," I said. "Braal's going to need us."

Braal moved from the waggon, keeping herself at the centre of the clearing. She parted her legs to give her the best possible angle for combat and readied her sword. Drawing her dagger, she kept both blades perfectly steady, as though she felt no fear. Yet I knew Braal and I could see she was terrified.

"Well, well," one of the new soldiers said. "What have we here? Looks like Garon's finally met his match."

"She killed everyone," Sarcasa said, rising groggily to her feet. She held a hand to her bleeding nose. "We still have the waggon of booze, but she cost us two girls."

"That won't do at all," the newcomer said. "I take it you're assuming command, Sarcasa?"

"Too right I am."

"And your orders?"

"Hurt her. Wound her. Hack off her arms and legs. Then have some fun with her before she dies."

A great roar of approval went up through the soldiers and Braal swallowed nervously.

"Ready," I whispered into Clippety's ears.

Braal looked directly at me, where the soldiers had yet to notice my presence. "Run," she said, her voice breaking.

"No," I said. "Braal, I'm not ..."

"Clippety, fly!"

With a neigh of protest, Clippety bolted. I screamed at the stupid animal, but he did not listen to me. He charged full tilt from the scene, ploughed through the trees and did not stop. I held on for dear life, for I knew I would surely die should I fall, and struggled with the reins. No matter how hard I pulled at them, however, the horse did not stop. I was not his mistress and he was a warhorse. He had received orders and he would obey them, just like any decent soldier.

It was miles before he even slowed down, by which point I was sobbing in the saddle. I had tried to turn him through sheer force, I had screamed vengeance at him and I had pleaded with him. Nothing had worked, and now, so far from Braal, Clippety stopped and I tumbled from his back. I shouted obscenities at him, flung dirt in his face, promised dark revenge upon him. Other than a little shying at the dirt, he did not react. He simply stared at me as though wanting something. It took me a while to realise what – his mistress was dead and now he was at a loss of what to do. He wanted orders, as though I had any to give.

I was too lost to know what I said to the beast. My mind was in turmoil, my emotions exploded within me and my heart was crying. I had met a lot of people since coming inland. Some were good, others were bad, but Braal had been like a sister to me. Braal had been the first person I had bonded with, the first human I had ever truly loved. It was like losing my mother all over again.

The sun had risen before I moved. How many times it fell and rose, I had no idea, for I had long ceased to care for anything.

CHAPTER FOURTEEN

I do not recall how I reached the lake, nor do I recall how long it took me to get there. Clippety remained by my side the whole time, waiting patiently for me to recover; it's possible the animal dragged me onto his back and carried me to the lake. However I got there, I stayed at that lake for a long time. A month, two, I did not care to know. The lake itself was large and was filled with fish. It was deep enough for me to lose myself, and almost entirely enclosed by hills. It was fed by several streams, with the water leaving the lake going through the hills. The surrounding lands were fertile and here wild grasses grew, with trees and bushes in abundance. I spent my days keeping myself busy in a variety of ways. I helped an otter build a holt, I chased fish and explored the lakebed. There were crabs down there, and sea snakes which had somehow survived away from the ocean. The lake was so large it was even home to dozens of bobbit worms, their vicious maws poking through the sandy lakebed, awaiting prey to float by oblivious before the animals struck.

Of Clippety, I saw little, mainly because I spent my time in the lake. I still had not forgiven him for what he had done, although he was clearly distraught over the loss of his mistress and did not know what to do. Whenever I did see him, he was waiting by the edge of the lake. Sometimes he was eating grass, other times he was wandering back and forth, but mainly he was just waiting. I cursed him from the water, threw stones at him and mud. I screamed at him, asked him what he wanted of me, told him to go away and leave me in peace. Yet still he was there more often than not whenever I came up to the surface.

Finally, I could take it no more and came to the water's edge, where I hauled myself onto the shore. It was the first time in ages I had changed my fish tail to human legs, although I did not intend to remain that way for long. My clothes were where I had left them when I had tossed them away to leap into the lake so long ago. I saw them then. The grass had grown around them, small animals had worried at them curiously, while the rain had covered them with mud.

"What do you want of me?" I asked, standing before him with my hands on my hips. "You've already killed the best thing in both our lives, what more do you want? Instructions? Advice? Braal said she paid insurance on you, Clippety, she said you were the property of Torbalia. Go back to Torbalia. There's an order for you. Go home and find someone new to betray."

The horse neighed although I did not for one moment believe he understood me.

So I struck him about the face. Hard.

He staggered but did not fall, so I hit him again.

"Go. Get out of here. I don't want to see you around here any more, you stupid horse."

He whinnied, uncertain, and I crouched to grab up a wad of mud which I hurled in his general direction.

"Leave," I shrieked. "I hate you. You murdered my best friend. Go."

Above me, the sky rumbled. It was something I had not managed for a long time. Inland as I had been, my powers to affect the elements were diminished, but at so great a lake I could feel my powers returning. Clippety backed away, distraught at what I was capable of.

I did not have to say another word, for at last Clippety understood. With a final pleading neigh, he turned and trotted off. My eyes followed him until he was gone, and then I collapsed to my knees and wept. Clippety had killed Braal and I hated him for that; but he had only been following orders. Braal was dead because she had protected me, because she had sent her horse away so I could survive.

My teary eyes found my discarded clothes again. They were all but embedded into the ground, a strange type of seed taking root in the hope of growing something decent. But there was nothing decent about me. I had abandoned my friend when she had needed me the most. It was not Clippety's fault Braal was dead, for he was just a horse who followed orders. Braal was dead because I was a civilian and she had been protecting me. Braal had been my sister and I would have fought with her, would have died for her if necessary. Yet she had never given me that chance. She had made the decision for me and now Braal was dead and I had to live with the fact that I had killed her.

I had killed her.

I had killed my best friend.

A Mermaid's Odyssey

Returning to the lake, I stayed there for a long time. In all, I do not know how long I spent at the lake, only that it must have been at least equal to my entire time thus far spent upon the land. I had come from the ocean, I had tried and failed to ingratiate myself into human society, and I was back in my element, albeit in a much smaller context. Of my father I had found no sign. Braal had tried for me, she had done more to locate my father than I had managed by myself the whole time I had been inland, but even she had found nothing. I had to surrender to the fact I would never find him, that during the nineteen years after which he impregnated my mother, he may well even have died. I had feared I might find him settled, having raised an entirely human family, but retained the hope I would discover him searching for me. Now, with the price of death staring me in the face, I knew I would have to face reality and ditch the fantasy.

If Braal could die, so too could my hopes and dreams. My mother ... Braal ... my father ... I had now lost everything.

The ecosystem of the lake was fascinating and I immersed myself in life there that I might forget I had ever attempted to be happy. Several times, I emerged from the lake in the hope of seeing Clippety on the shore, but I had chased him away and he was not coming back. Resolved to a life alone, my days were long and miserable. Without even meaning to, I took to singing sad songs, either beneath the water or while lying on a rock bare to the sun's warmth. I did not think during my time in the lake, could not focus; nor did I much care what happened to me. Life was a cruel joke and I no longer cared anything for it.

"Your song's beautiful, but so sad."

I started, not having realised there was anyone nearby. I was on my rock, jutting a little way into the lake, and my mermaid's tail was on show. I had been a fool not to have hidden myself, and it had taken my first human contact since leaving Braal to snap me back to the reality of the human world and all the caution that went along with it.

The woman sitting on the shore was a little older than me, I would have placed her at around twenty-one. She wore simple attire which denoted neither poverty nor wealth. She had by her side a wooden bucket, which suggested she had come to the lake in order to fetch water. That was odd, since I knew of no settlement nearby. She had short untidy red hair and dark eyes. Her appearance reminded me a little of Braal, especially in her smile, but Braal was gone and I could not transfer my emotions for her onto this stranger.

"I'm a mermaid," I said tiredly as I lay back down on the rock. "Go away or I'll eat you."

"Eat me?" she laughed. "Mermaids entice folk in for a roll around the riverbed. Sorry, you're not my type."

"I could still eat you. I haven't eaten human flesh in days."

"You sound like you're trying to convince yourself more than me. Do you mind if I fish?"

"Do I mind if you're a fish?"

"Fish," she said and I looked over to see she was holding some form of long rod. "You know, fish."

"Are you calling me fish?"

"No, I'm ..." She took a deep breath. "Wow, this is difficult. Would you, mermaid protector of this humble lake, perchance mind if I should cast my line into the waters here and remove its denizens for my supper? Fish as a verb, not a noun."

"Are you making fun of me?"

"Only a little."

"Well don't. It won't be healthy for you."

"OK. But can I ...?"

"Yes," I snapped, closing my eyes and lying back down, "go ahead and fish."

"Great. Thanks."

An hour passed. Neither of us spoke during that time. Nor did the stranger catch any fish.

"You're not very good at that," I said at last.

"Nope."

"Do you ever catch anything?"

"Sure."

"Then what are you doing wrong this time?"

"I'm not using any bait."

"Why?"

"Well, usually I put a worm on the end, but I figured if I did that, it'd be just the same as you using your voice to lure men in. I'm doing pretty much the same thing you do, you see. Cast, bait, lure, snatch, kill, eat."

I propped myself onto an elbow to regard her. "So why aren't you using any bait this time?"

"Because, no offence, you're scaring the bejeebies out of me. I mean, you're a mermaid sunning yourself on a rock while I'm taking fish out of your lake."

"Then what are you still doing here?"

"You told me I could fish, so I didn't want to offend you. I figured I'd stay here a few hours, then leave."

"Oh."

"I haven't offended you, have I?"

"Why would I be offended?"

"I don't know. But you're a powerful water deity and I could do without you gutting me, so I'm trying very hard not to upset you."

I look deeply at her for any signs of mockery. There were some, but not enough to cover her sincerity. "I'm not going to eat you," I told her. "And I'm not going to gut you or kill you or string you up by your toes and use you as a punching bag."

"I never thought you were going to use me as a punching bag. Is that a mermaid thing?"

"What's your name?"

"Ooh, that's your game."

"What's my game?"

"Names have power. If you tell a demon your name, they own your soul. You don't want my body, you want my soul."

"I'm not a demon."

"I thought faeries and demons were the same thing."

"Well, yes, they are. But demons are powerful faeries and they don't like that word."

"Like old people."

"Excuse me?"

"They're powerful in years but they don't like to be called old."

"You're saying demons are like old people?"

"Don't mind me. I'm babbling because I'm still not convinced you're not going to kill me any moment now. Would you mind singing again? You have a lovely voice and if I'm going to die, I could at least die happy."

"I'm not going to kill you, I told you that already." I was trying very hard to stay annoyed at this woman, but there was something about her which was lifting my spirit. She reminded me a little of Braal, but at the same time was nothing like her, and I found that refreshing. She was so unsure of herself, so afraid, yet conquered her fears purely because she was in love with my singing voice.

"What's *your* name?" she asked. "If you told me your real name, it might go some way to convincing me to give you mine."

"Misako."

"Oh, I didn't expect you to do that. I guess I have to give you my name now. Otherwise I'll have broken the pact we made and you'll drag me off to Faerie and throw me to the demons."

"Was your name in there somewhere?"

"No. Maya."

"That wasn't so difficult, was it?"

Maya patted herself down. "Well, I'm still in one piece."

"So are the fish."

"Yeah. Uh, Miss Mermaid, if you don't mind me asking, do you live here?"

"I suppose I do."

"Alone?"

"Yes."

"No wonder you sing such sad songs."

"What about you? Where do you live?"

"Here and there. I travel a lot. I prefer my own company. Actually, I just don't like paying taxes, but I don't tell people that. Oh my, was that some kind of mermaid thing you just did? Pulling that from my mind?"

"No, you just don't know how to shut up."

"I know. I tell myself that all the time."

"Do you get lonely?" I asked.

"Yeah. I'm always lonely, except when I don't think about it. You?"

"No," I answered quickly. "I like it here."

"Fantastic. Happy for you." She beamed as though she meant it. "Anyway, thanks for letting me use your lake, Miss Mermaid. Anything I can do for you in return?"

"No. Here, hold on." I slipped from my rock and plunged into the lake, resurfacing a moment later holding a fish in my mouth. Maya was startled that I had appeared right beside her, but she took the fish regardless, if a little reluctantly.

"Thanks," she said dubiously. "Great, you even left me tooth marks."

"I killed it under the water for you, thrashed it to death. So yes, I left tooth marks."

She dropped the fish into her bucket. "Well, I'll think of you when I eat it. You sure there's nothing I can do for you?"

"No." I paused. "Yes. Come back and visit sometime."

"Is that all? I can do that."

"And …" I bit my lip, debating whether to tread a road long since abandoned. "I'm looking for my father. I don't know his name but he's a knight with one green eye, the other brown and a scar across one eye."

Maya thought about that. "Sorry, doesn't ring any bells."

"Well, it was a long shot anyway."

Maya bade me farewell and left the lakeside, whistling merrily. I returned to my watery home and knew she would never return.

A week later, she was back. This time, she did not have to fish, for I was so thrilled to see her, I brought her the fish myself. We chatted and gossiped, and for a few hours I forgot all about my troubles. I remained in the water and Maya did not ask me to leave it, perhaps she did not know that I could. She told me stories of her travels, of the people she had met, and I told her what I had experienced out in the ocean.

"I love fish so much," she said, "I went to Mrinth a couple of years back. That's a fishing port. It's a hectic place, too many people."

"There are good people in Mrinth."

"You've been there?"

I had not meant to say that, for I was attempting to forget all my land-based experiences. "It doesn't matter. Have you ever been to Torbalia?"

"Sure. This is Torbalian territory we're in, so visiting the capital is a must for any traveller worth her salt."

"Why are travellers worth salt?"

"No idea. Maybe salt's expensive to import or something."

"What's it like?"

"Torbalia? Huge. Bigger than Mrinth."

"Did you see the battalions?"

"No. It's huge, how could I possibly have seen the battalions?"

"But you know who they are?"

"Sure I know who they are. A bunch of stuck-up soldiers who like to preach at people. Like soldier clergy or something."

"I thought they were supposed to be good people."

She shrugged. "Like I said, never met them."

We spoke of little more before Maya had to go. I waved her off again and noted her whistle was still merry. That night I sang and was pleased to note my song was a little happier. Then I felt bad, for I did not deserve to be happy when I had killed Braal, and I spent the remainder of the night weeping.

Maya did not return for a long time – so long, in fact, that I thought she had moved on. She was, after all, a traveller, and a traveller could not stay in the same place for too long. When she returned, however, my heart sang with joy, although I could see by her expression she was even happier than I was.

"What?" I asked. "What's happened?"

"Lord Tendoom," she said.

"Who is?"

"The knight with one green eye, one brown and a scar above one."

I blinked, unsure I had heard her correctly. "Are you sure?"

She nodded emphatically. "I asked around, I have a lot of contacts. Travellers have the best contacts, you know. Anyway, long story short, I've found him."

I took a deep breath to steady my nerves. "How can we be sure it's him?"

"We can't be, but I went to find him personally. They wouldn't let me anywhere near him, obviously, but I found his soldiers' camp, pretended to be an entertainer and wormed my way over to his tent. I waited there for ages and when he passed me by, I shouted out to him. I said, 'Hey, I got a mermaid who says hi' and he stopped in shock. His soldiers grabbed me and beat me a little, but he told them to stop. Then he looked me dead in the eyes without saying anything. It's not something he'd admit to, is it? Having an affair with a faerie. If anyone found out, he'd be struck off, arrested even. But he let me go, told the soldiers I was crazy with the pox and that I should be pitied. Anyway, he came to see me afterward and demanded to know what I knew. I didn't tell him anything but said I might be bringing someone to see him."

She smiled. "And here we are."

I did not know what to say. After so many months of searching, so many dreams shattered, so many hopes dashed, here was a genuine opportunity to meet my father. Of course, there was no guarantee this was him, for mermaids are a wily bunch and there was every chance he could have had liaisons with some other mermaid. But it was a hope, and hope was something I had thought long gone.

"Thank you, Maya," I said and meant it from my soul. "Thank you."

"I brought you something," she said and dropped a pack on the ground. She opened it to reveal clothes.

"Figured you'd need to wear something if you're going to go for a walk."

Climbing out of the lake, I changed my tail to legs and dressed without drying. My hands were shaking so much I found it as difficult to don clothes as I had that first day upon the trawler. Maya waited patiently, not saying a word, and soon enough I was ready to go with her. She had no horse, nor any transport other than her shoes – she said they were all she ever needed – and together we set off.

We travelled for two days, moving farther inland all the while. During this time, I plied Maya with questions about my father, but she did not have any answers for me. I asked her the size of his army, whether they were good people. I asked her what he looked like, how old he was. I wanted to know whether he was a good man, whether he would think I was someone to be proud of. Maya could not answer any of my questions and eventually made me promise to stop asking her.

After two days, we stopped. We had reached a point where several roads crossed in a main thoroughfare. About us were fields and trees and everything I had come to associate with human society, but no people. There was a sign at the crossroads, with various arrows pointing in every direction, but I could not read what they said. There was also a rusted cage, within which lay the crumpled heap of a skeleton.

Maya sat on a rock.

"What are we doing?" I asked.

"Waiting."

"My father's coming here?"

"We have a ride coming which will take us into his camp. You can't just stroll in, someone might see you're a faerie. These are trained Torbalian soldiers, Misako, there's no sense in taking the risk."

If they were anything like the soldiers who had killed Braal, it was best I did not allow them to see me. If they were the same ones, they might even recognise me. Dread filled my soul that my father could have been a party to what had happened with Braal, but I would not believe it until I had no choice but to.

While we waited, I asked about the skeleton in the cage, because the creak of the metal in the wind was drawing my attention that way.

"That would have been a criminal," Maya said. "A thief, maybe, or a murderer."

"This was an execution, then?"

"Yes. They put people in these cages and let the sun bake them to death. It's at the crossroads in case the corpse returns as a vampire and wants to enact revenge against his or her killers. The vampire won't know which way to go because vampires are rubbish with directions, supposedly."

"They are?"

"You tell me, you're the faerie."

"I've never met a vampire."

"No? Sit around here long enough and one might step out of that cage."

"Do people really think there are vampires roaming around lost because they can't read road signs?"

"You know, now you put it that way, I guess it doesn't make much sense to stick the sign right next to the cage. Hey, here's our ride."

A waggon was trundling along the road, with several more behind. I rose excitedly and noted it was a fairly large caravan. At its head, the waggon was being driven by two tired-looking horses, with a man seated behind holding their reins. He drew the waggon up before us and Maya rapped her knuckles on the door.

"It's us," she said and stood aside.

I waited impatiently for the door to open, and finally it did.

"Inside," Maya said and I clambered in, bowing my head due to the steepness of the climb and the darkness of the interior. Behind me, Maya slammed the door shut on me.

"What are ...?"

That was all I managed to get out before four people descended on me with clubs and fists. I went down hard, my shock refusing to allow me to fight back. The blows took me back to the pirate ship, but the betrayal resurrected nightmares of Whistler.

As the waggon resumed its rickety march, I lay bruised and bleeding on the floor in utter darkness. From the front of the waggon, beside the man holding the reins, I could hear Maya whistling her merry tune and knew I should have at least been clever enough to have taken that as a warning sign.

CHAPTER FIFTEEN

The waggon did not take me to my father, but then I was not stupid enough to believe Maya had met anyone of his description. When the caravan finally came to a rest, the door was opened and harsh light spilled in upon me. I raised an arm to shield myself from the blinding rays but was not given a moment to recover, for I was dragged outside and dumped on the ground. My clothes were stained with dried blood and my head pounded. Lying there on the ground, I had little intention of fighting back.

There were scores of people around me, although I could see I had not been taken to a town. A number of tents had been erected in the field, although in the main, people seemed to be living out of their waggons and carts. The people in whose company I had fallen were neither rich nor poor, and many were dressed flamboyantly, with bright stripes and top hats. I saw animals as well – a scrawny yellow cat whose once-proud mane was a scraggly shadow of its former self, and a great grey leather-skinned beast with massive ears and a long nose. White stumps showed either side of the animal's face, which struck me as strangely out of place.

I caught sight of several interesting people. One was no taller than my waist, another two were conjoined, while a fourth was as large as an ogre. Perhaps he even was one.

Something snapped close to my face and I jumped. Looking up, I saw a man standing nearby. He was garbed in a bright green suit, wore an extravagantly curled moustache and carried a whip. I wanted to tell him not to wear such a garish green suit, as wearing green offended the faeries. However, I had a feeling that was the reason he was doing it.

"Glad to have your attention," he said with a sneer.

Maya appeared by his side and offered me a sheepish smile. "Sorry, Misako. I do feel a little bad about deceiving you."

I wanted to kill her, but the desire passed in an instant. I had killed before and it had haunted me for a long time. Besides, nothing that had happened to me was beyond what I deserved. Shifting my weight where I lay, I got to a sitting position, although my body screamed in agonising protest.

"Up," the man said, indicating with his coiled whip. "Up, up, up, let's take a look at you."

I considered refusing, but there was little point. I rose to my feet. The sudden blood rush to my brain exploded my vision with black spots and I almost collapsed. Somehow, I managed not to vomit.

When my vision cleared, I saw the man was walking around me, appraising me carefully. "Not bad, not bad." He slapped my backside with his coiled whip and I yelped. "Not bad at all. You've done well, Maya."

"I think I was promised a bonus?" she asked.

"Yes, yes, of course." He reached into an inside pocket and produced a few coins. He handed them across absently and they vanished into one of Maya's pouches. "Maya, get her cleaned up, fix her something to eat, water her or whatever. Then strip her of her clothes and put her in the tank. I want to see what she can do."

"What I can do?" I asked. "What do you mean see what I can do?"

"My dear," he said, stepping away from me and raising his arms like a true showman, "you have the good fortune to have entered into the greatest circus in the land. Nolan Sharrock's Travelling Oddities." He grinned. "And you are going to be a top-price act."

I did not say anything until he was gone. Everyone was moving around us, paying me no attention at all. Most people were preparing food or erecting tents, although I knew if I was to make a break for it, I would not get far.

"Sorry, sugar," Maya said, "but I sold you out for money. Money is everything, you know."

"In human society, yes," I said bitterly.

"You need to be less trusting."

"My father?"

Here her face fell slightly. "Yeah, I do actually feel a little bad about that. I could see how much finding him means to you. It was the only thing I could think of to get you out of that lake, though. Nolan was so excited when I told him I'd found a real live mermaid. He began construction on the tank right away and told me to stall you."

"Then you didn't find my father," I said, needing to hear her tell me it had all been a lie.

"Lord Tundoom?" she asked. "As in Sir Tundoom? No? Certain doom? As in, what I was leading you to?"

"Oh, you're so funny. You'll be laughing even harder when I tear out your throat with my teeth."

"Hey, I'm just trying to earn a living here," she said nervously.

Again, I restrained myself from killing her. Away from the water, I was less powerful, which was something Maya had counted on. "What's a circus?" I asked.

"What's a circus? Misako, you wound me."

"Just answer the question."

"It's a travelling show. You ever taken in a show?"

"Once. In Mrinth. There was a stall with puppets. And there was another one, with actors on the street."

"Right. We're a little of both, I guess. We erect a great big tent, charge people to come sit or stand while they watch, and entertain them for the evening."

"How?"

"We have clowns, jugglers, dancers, an elephant, a lion – although we lost the lion tamer last week. Still, we have a lion."

"That man said oddities."

"The freaks, yes."

"The conjoined twins, the giant and the dwarf?"

"We also have a bearded lady, a skeleton man, a woman with two brains and a talking dog."

"A talking dog?"

"It's not really a dog, it's just a man who looks like one."

"Then you lie to your audience."

"Yep," she said proudly.

"And you exploit your workers."

"The freaks?"

"They're not freaks. They're human beings."

"Oh. Well, I guess, in some way they are. But they get paid, right?"

"And money's everything? Enough money can blunt the pain of having people point and laugh at you."

"That's the spirit," she enthused.

I thought I had known Maya, yet here was an entirely different woman to the one I had met by the lake. "Aren't you supposed to be getting me something to eat and … watering me?"

"Watering you, yeah," she said sheepishly, rubbing the back of her neck. "Nolan doesn't know anything about mermaids, sorry. He assumes you have to stay watered. Do you have to stay watered? Does being watered make your tail appear?"

"I'm not a carrot. I don't need watering. Now get me something to eat."

Maya led me through the camp. There was a lot of jollity amongst those people and from what I could see, they were not bad folk. They had split into several groups, there were no doubt friendly clusters within the circus, and they worked and laughed together. I watched a woman juggling flaming brands as she showed off to her friends, then placed one in her mouth. I thought she was committing suicide, but her friends applauded.

I entered my own tent, although it had not been allocated me because I was anyone important. Within sat a large glass tank filled with clear water. Upon the base of the tank was sand and there were a few fish and crabs thrown in for good measure.

"That's your new workplace," Maya explained as she opened a crate off to one side to hunt for something to eat. "There were more fish originally, but they keep eating each other."

"That's because you people know nothing of fish."

"That's something you're going to have to teach us."

I approached the tank and placed my fingers to it. It was cold to the touch. "Is this water warmed?"

"No. Why would it be?"

"Are you trying to freeze me to death?"

"Isn't the sea cold?"

I removed my hand. "Just give me some food."

Maya handed me something and I sniffed it experimentally. It was a long, thin piece of what appeared to be meat, contained within bread. "What's this?" I asked.

"What we sell to our paying customers. It's cheap and nasty, but the punters love them. Makes us a fortune."

I bit into it tentatively but it was foul. "This is awful."

"Yep," Maya said, sitting on a crate and biting into one of her own. "But you get used to it."

I took another bite but it was still bad. "I take it you expect me to climb into that tank and perform for your customers."

"Our customers."

"So I'm getting paid?"

"No. If you do well, if you bring in the crowds, I'll talk to Nolan about you drawing a salary. At the moment, you're a curiosity, but you haven't quite progressed to freak. You're a mermaid, see, which means you're technically an enemy in the war. If we paid you, it means Nolan would be committing treason by supplying the enemy with money. If he claims you're a prisoner, he'll wrangle it so he can keep you as long as he likes."

"Politics."

"You don't have politics under the ocean?"

"We have a hierarchy. It's much the same thing."

"Then you understand our position."

"Maya, why did you do it?"

"Kidnap you?"

"Yes."

"I told you, money. This circus needs fresh blood or we're going under. Most circuses don't last more than a couple of years, but Nolan Sharrock's has always been the greatest. As old acts leave or die, he replaces them with new and innovative performers. No one's ever had a real mermaid in their circus before, you know."

"What do you mean by real?"

"You … don't want to see that."

"See what?"

"Misako, I really …"

"Maya," I said sternly, "we're alone in this tent and I have twenty times your strength. Right now, the only reason I haven't crushed your skull is because the last time I murdered someone it made me feel bad. So, show me what you're talking about."

She stopped chewing her bad meat and swallowed unconsciously, which almost made her choke. Clearly, she had taken me to be a sweet and sad mermaid who had never harmed anyone in her life; but I was changing. The human world had changed me, my own mistakes had hardened me and I was becoming the monster everyone on both sides of the war saw me as.

"OK," she said, "just don't overreact."

She moved across the room and tried a few crates before she found the one she wanted. Opening the lid, she stepped back and motioned for me to take a look. What I saw shocked me more than anything I had thus far seen upon the human world.

It was a body, fit snugly into the crate. Its lower half was that of a fish, its upper half was the decayed, skeletal remains, partly mummified, of some kind of animal. Its arms were curled as though it had returned to the womb, and its empty sightless eyes started out, pleading. It also stank and I could not believe Maya was keeping the thing so close to the food.

"What is this?" I asked.

"A mermaid."

"That thing? You think that thing's a mermaid?"

"Hey, *I* don't think it is, no. It's a fish sown onto half a monkey. But the public think it's a mermaid and, since they pay my wages, it doesn't much matter what I think."

"I ... You're telling me you put this in front of people, claim it's a mermaid and everyone believes it?"

"Probably not everyone. But who wants to be the only naysayer in the group? If all your friends say they believe it, so do you."

"And people paid to come see this?"

"Yeah. Crazy, right? You can imagine, then, how Nolan reacted when I told him there was a real mermaid in the lake. You, Misako, are the best thing that ever happened to this circus. You're going to make us household names, you're going to make us famous."

I was still in shock and replaced the lid of the crate so I would not have to look at the thing any more. I already knew human beings were animals, but had never thought they could flock to gawk at the corpse of one of their enemies. I tried to turn the tables, to picture a dead human in the land of Faerie, being laughed at and prodded. I struggled to form an image of my mother taking me as a child to see the mummified ruin that had one time been a man.

"Just when I think I've known the depths of human depravity," I said, "I find something even more obscene."

"I know. But, like I said, you get used to the taste."

"I'm not talking about the fake meat in the buns, Maya," I hissed.

"Yeah, best not to. Anyway, you're fed and since you say you don't need watering, you need to take off your clothes and get into the tank. Nolan's going to be by soon and he'll want to see what you can do."

"I'm not a showpiece."

"Not until you're trained, no."

"Trained?"

"Sure. Nolan has so many ideas. He's setting up hoops above the tank. With your muscular strength, we reckon you'll be able to clear the hoops easy. He's even talking about setting them on fire. Once you get the hang of it, of course," she added quickly.

"Any other tricks he wants me to do for him?"

"Yeah," she said eagerly, mistaking my question for enthusiasm. She ticked them off on her fingers.

"There's seal-wrestling, spearing fish, holding your breath ... he's got so much lined up."

"And if I refuse?"

"Refuse? How could you refuse?"

"By saying no. You've never refused a man anything?"

Her brow darkened. She knew an insult when she heard one. "You're not going to refuse," she said darkly, "because if you do, the trainers will hurt you. They won't kill you, but they'll hurt you so much you'll want to be dead."

"And if I'd prefer to be dead?"

"Then die. See if I care. But for now, just take off your clothes and we can get started."

"No."

"No?"

I folded my arms. "No, I'm not going to jump through hoops for you, and you can't make me."

"Oh, can't I?"

I had her by the throat before she could so much as scream. My grip was tight but not powerful enough to kill her. Maya hung in the air, struggling to breathe as her legs dangled. I looked upon her with dispassion, at this woman who had treated me so foully, who had built up my hopes just so she could dash them.

"I've been through a lot lately," I told her flatly. "I've lost family, friends and any happiness I've ever known. I've killed two people already, Maya, and you know what? I was wrong. I thought that by killing you, I'd somehow be damning myself. But now I realise it's the opposite. Allowing you to live would mean leaving you to do what you've done again and again and again. So many others will suffer if you keep up your inhumane treatment. Inhumane." I smiled wryly. "I've learned that not all humans are bad, Maya, and I finally understand that term. There are good people in this world, just as there are bad ones. I once told someone the difference between good and evil was what humans did as opposed to how they perceived they did. I was wrong about that, too. There are good people and there are bad people." I squeezed a little tighter. "My friend Braal was good and I mourn her. You ... you're just a ..." And then I screamed, for Maya had worked something loose from her belt and plunged it into my arm.

I dropped her, falling back as I clutched my injury. My arm was burning, scarlet blisters had formed in an instant and were sizzling black. Maya stabbed out again and I was in too much shock to stop her. What she held was a simple rod, no longer than a finger, but as she pressed it into my flesh, I felt the torment of obscene gods burn through me.

Maya slammed her foot into my belly – I had not even realised I had fallen – and screamed her rage as she stamped upon me again and again. It was like being back aboard the pirate ship, where I had first suffered at the hands of human beings.

Her assault did not last long, and I watched as she staggered to rest against the water tank, holding her crushed throat and using the metal bar as a ward. That it was iron I did not doubt, and my burning body refused to allow me to attack her.

"Damned harpy," she rasped, fighting to breathe. "Damn near killed me."

"Not near enough." I rose on shaky legs. The pain her feet had caused stung and I could feel blood seeping into my clothes, but the injuries were not bad. The touch of the iron still sizzled my flesh, and I looked around for some water. There was some in a nearby crate and I winced as I doused my wound. It was spreading fast and threatened to consume my body like poison.

The tent flap parted and Nolan Sharrock entered. He cast a quizzical glance to Maya before looking at me with a satisfied sigh. "Marvellous. Truly marvellous." His brow creased. "Are you hurt, my dear? Let me see."

He approached and gently took my arm. Then he pressed his thumb into the wound and I hissed curses at him.

"You need to still your tongue, girl," he said as he backed away, his whip coiled in his hand and ready for use. "Maya, why don't you take the training of this one? You two seem to have built up an accord."

"Can't someone else take her?"

"No, I want you to do it."

"But, Nolan ..."

"I said," he snapped before pausing and smiling, "I want you to do it." I imagined this Nolan Sharrock fellow held a perpetual smile and that he wore that ridiculous moustache so the audience in the back could see it extenuated.

"Yes, sir," Maya said meekly.

"And get her clothes off," Sharrock said as he raised the flap to leave. "No one's going to pay to see a mermaid just standing there. Get her in the tank."

"You want me to wear some shells while I'm at it?" I asked.

His eyes widened as a grand idea came to his mind. "Shells. Shells! She can wear shells over her breasts. If we staged an adults-only show, she could do a dance routine and pick them off. It'll be the first mermaid striptease ever. Mergirl, we're going to make you a star."

And he was gone, skipping merrily along.

I looked to Maya, who was still rubbing her throat but who had recovered enough to pick up a larger piece of iron. "I have a lot of this dotted around," she said. "Looks like I was right to think I needed it."

For the sake of not being tortured to death, I decided I would have to comply with at least some of what Maya and Sharrock wanted. Perhaps, after everything I had done, it was all I even deserved.

CHAPTER SIXTEEN

Maya's training was brutal. Even though I was resolved to my fate, even though I believed I deserved it, a part of me continued to resist. Entering the tank did not prove a problem for me, and no one came to gawp at me except for Nolan Sharrock himself, and there was nothing lascivious or crude about him. His face was alight with the passion of his circus and in me he saw someone who could bring him a fortune. Yet I did not behave, could not see myself as one of his playthings. Often I would refuse to do anything, telling Maya I was tired or bored or that I wanted to just lie in the tank for a while and she could lump it.

It was at such times that I would discover Maya's cruel nature. One time, I stayed in the tank and told her I was having the afternoon off. She wrinkled her nose, then started doing something at the base of my glass prison. Knowing she could not get to me, I did not pay her any mind, until the water grew considerably warmer. I swam to the side of the tank and peered through to see she was stoking a furnace. Shocked, I bolted to the surface, to find a lid closing upon me. Maya had pulled a lever and the tank was sealed tight. No matter how much I pounded upon that lid or the sides, I could not break free. And slowly the water began to bubble as the temperature reached boiling.

Maya sat back, folded her arms and watched me emotionlessly.

I pleaded through the glass, begged her to let me out, told her I would do as I was told. The superheated bubbles brushed past my skin, the scolding water burned my flesh and I watched as I quickly turned an unhealthy red. My eyes stung with so much pain I soon could not open them and my insides felt like they were about to burst.

With grinding resistance, the lid was raised and I rushed to the surface. Clambering out, I fell from the top of the tank to slam into the ground beneath. Heat visibly rose from me and I writhed in scalding agony. Turning over, I vomited onto the ground, heaving again as another wave of heat struck me.

Getting to her feet, Maya said nothing and strode from the tent.

Another time, having recovered from my ordeal and more than a little wary, I refused again. In this instance, she did not bother with the fire, for that had not taught me my lesson. Instead, she hurled two iron rods into the tank before closing the lid. Again, I failed to reach the top in time. The iron bars must have been treated with some special chemical, for they fizzed even as they dropped to the base of the tank. Iron shavings flew freely from them and mingled with the water. For a time, I was able to stay on the other side of the tank, but after an hour the water was so filled with iron my skin itched all over. Another hour in and I was vomiting in the water and once more pleading for Maya's mercy. Again, she finally stopped sitting there watching me and raised the lid before leaving the tent.

I was testing Maya just as much as she was me and I had found her to be a cruel and loveless mistress. While I recovered from each ordeal, I would do as I was told, learn the routines Nolan Sharrock had in mind for me. Thus far, I had not been put on display, for he wanted my act to be perfect, my submission to be total, before he revealed me to paying audiences. He knew if I was not properly broken, I could spout abuse at him – or worse, his audience – and ruin the entire show.

Several weeks into my training, I was sitting outside of my tank, sharing a meal with Maya. I had behaved myself that day and had pirouetted well within the tank, had even jumped through two hoops placed above the water. Maya was pleased with my progress and as a reward she gave me some salmon to eat, for she had learned I had a liking for it.

"Nolan will want to see you do the hoops," she said while we sat on crates and ate.

"Am I going into the show soon?"

"No. You're still too wild for that. We'll be moving out soon, though. We've been in this field for a while now, training new acts. We're going to head west, away from Torbalia, maybe head for Sardius."

I had no idea where that was, but it sounded far away. "I want to play Torbalia."

"I don't much care what you want," she said as she ate.

"Maya, can I ask you a question?"

"OK."

"Why are you such a twisted, bitter cow?"

"Misako, do you like pain or something?"

"I'm not refusing to do anything, I'm genuinely curious. I get that everything I initially thought about you was just an act, but you're a really bad person and I'm just wondering why."

"I'm a really bad person?" she asked. "What are you, twelve?"

"Insults aside, what happened to you? How did you end up with this life?"

"I ran away to join the circus."

"You did?"

"Lots of people do that."

I could see in her eyes there was something else, something she was not telling me. "I don't believe you."

"Like I said, I don't care."

"Do you enjoy it?"

"Circus life?"

"Causing me pain and misery."

"No." She chewed for several moments in silence. "Look, Misako, I know you hate me, but I don't get off on seeing you suffer, all right? Nolan needs you broken, like a horse, and it's my job to do that. I've done it before, with animals, and to him you're just another animal."

"I'm more a freak. I'm a hybrid, you know."

"I know. But to Nolan you're on the animal side of things. If he saw you as a person, sure you'd be treated differently. But he doesn't. You need to be fed, you need to be provided with somewhere to sleep and you need health checks every so often. That's about it. Oh frel, I forgot about your health checks."

"I'd be fine if you stopped sticking iron rods in me."

"If you die, Nolan will throw a fit."

"I wouldn't be too thrilled about it, either."

"You wouldn't be much of anything, you'd be dead."

That much was true.

"I'll get a doctor in to look you over," she said. "First thing tomorrow."

"I don't need a doctor."

"We'll let the doctor be the judge of ..."

"I don't need a doctor," I repeated more forcefully. "I'm not a curiosity, Maya. I'm not a thing, or an animal. I don't want to be poked and prodded by some stranger."

Maya went back thoughtfully to her food. "I'll have a think about it."

The next day, the doctor arrived. She was a woman aged somewhere in her sixties and did not want to be there any more than I wanted her there. Maya briefly explained that I needed a check-up to make sure I didn't drop down dead and the doctor nodded, having performed similar checks often enough.

She made me sit and be still while she held a candle before my eyes. Whatever that achieved, I had no idea.

"I need its mouth open," the doctor said.

I opened my mouth and the doctor placed something on my tongue. It looked like a piece of wood, although it seemed the wood was just to keep my tongue down while she examined my tonsils.

"Any swelling or discomfort anywhere?" the doctor asked.

"I ..."

"No," Maya interrupted. I closed my mouth, for it was clear the doctor did not even see me as a person, or at least refused to. "She's fine," Maya continued. "I've never noticed any fever or anything, either."

"I don't tend to get ill," I offered. "Faeries have a high constitution for ..."

"Does it ever get ill?" the doctor asked.

"No," Maya said. "Faeries have a high constitution."

The doctor nodded sagely. "Why is it clothed? Remove its top."

Maya lifted my shirt from me – I did not feel like helping her. The doctor felt the muscles in my arm, moved her hands down my side, my breasts, my belly. "There's bruising and burning."

"She's still not entirely broken."

The doctor raised an eyebrow. "Maya, we'll be going to a new town soon and Mr Sharrock wants this act working by then."

"She'll be ready."

"If it attacks someone in the audience, he'll have your hide."

"She'll be ready," Maya insisted.

"Are you sure you're torturing it enough? You can never underplay a good bit of torture to get an animal to do what you want."

"I torture her plenty, thanks."

"And it still doesn't obey? I can prescribe an iron injection, if it'll help. Iron can be beneficial for people, but will burn that faerie blood to the boil."

"I'm good, thanks," Maya said. "Misako, put your shirt back on."

I did so, aware that the doctor was annoying her. The two women exchanged a few more words before the doctor left.

"I really hate that woman sometimes," Maya said. "But she's not wrong. We're going to move soon and you need to be ready by the time we get to wherever we're going."

"I'll perform, don't worry about that."

"It's not whether you'll perform that has me worried. The doctor's right, if you do something stupid out there, it'll be me that pays for it."

"And we wouldn't want that now, would we?"

She placed her hands on her hips and sighed. "Misako, what are we going to do with you?"

"You could always let me go. I haven't done anything to you, Maya."

"Misako, I've boiled you, blasted you with iron, pressed rods into your flesh and still you're defiant. What's it going to take to break you?"

"You can't break me, Maya. I'm already broken."

"This is about that girl again, isn't it? Braal. Gods, would you stop going on about her?"

"She was my friend."

"The way you keep harping on, you'd think she was more than that. If you cared that much about her, you wouldn't have got her killed and you wouldn't have tormented her poor horse like you did."

I regretted ever telling her that part of my story.

"I'm starting to think you're right," she said. "What say we make a deal? You promise not to do anything which might upset Nolan and I'll tell him we're done. If you act broken, we can concentrate on your training. Then, when it's showtime, he'll let you perform. You do your thing and everyone's happy. I won't have to hurt you any more and you'll get all the perks you want. Food, booze, guys, girls if you're into them. The works. The better you do, the more Nolan will let you have. We'll both have an easy life. What do you say?"

I did not want to agree, mainly because when a faerie makes a bond, she's stuck with it. I did not want to be in the circus, but I had nowhere else to go.

"I'm not making a deal," I said after much thought, "but I'll do what you ask of me."

"I guess that'll have to do. So, get into the tank and we'll try the hoops again."

I obeyed and for the rest of the morning and well into the afternoon I jumped through hoops as my mistress commanded.

CHAPTER SEVENTEEN

My costume was odd and no matter how much I adjusted it, I could never get it right. Floating in my mermaid's tank, I had been given a bra made of two shells. Keeping the thing on was a nightmare, for it was held together by a thin piece of string at the back, designed to appear invisible. I had practised my act while wearing the shells, but found it a struggle to keep them in place. I suggested losing them altogether, but Nolan Sharrock was concerned about me doing my act in the nude. Maya tried to explain to him on my behalf that faeries didn't see nudity as an abhorrent thing and he replied that this was one of the man things which made us an abhorrent species. Besides, he had said, there would be children in the crowd and he did not want parents complaining.

"But they just don't stay on," Maya protested vehemently.

"Then glue them on."

"Glue them on? What if that hurts her?"

"We must all make sacrifices for the sake of the show, my dear."

So we dispensed with the string entirely and the shells were glued directly to my breasts. They felt uncomfortable, cumbersome, and I knew they would hurt like a demon when it came time to peel them off. Maya even seemed apologetic as she applied the glue. We had settled at a town and the show was due to begin shortly, so there were dozens of people bustling around us. Some were in costume, others were getting other people ready. Animals were being led to and fro, while boys and girls travelling with the circus ran around performing whatever errands were needed. I sat upon a large white drum, encircled with yellow and red ribbons, while Maya finished up gluing my shells, and as I looked around, I could not help but feel excited.

"You look happy," Maya noted.

"Not quite happy, just not as against this as I'd thought I was going to be."

"You're looking forward to your time in the spotlight?"

I felt bad as I realised I was indeed looking forward to it. I had spent so long in Maya's company, had worked so hard training, that the torture which had led me there was a memory. Still, I had far from forgotten it. I had become used to such treatment from human beings, but I had promised to do my best out in the arena and that was just what I was going to do.

"You should get the rest of your costume ready," she said, tapping my legs. "No one wants to see a mermaid without her tail."

I got to my feet and adjusted my shells. They weighed heavily on me, but the glue was strong enough to keep them there. "Do you have an act, Maya?"

"Sure."

"What do you do? I've never asked you before."

"You'll find out when we get out there. Now come on, it's never good to keep Nolan waiting."

I returned to my tank, where two of the circus's strongmen, already in their costume of tight pants and nothing else, were putting my tank onto treads. They smiled at me and I winked at them as I removed my trousers – which, in hindsight, probably made them think I was flirting with them. They each extended a hand and I placed one foot in each before they propelled me up and over into my tank. By the time I struck the water, my tail had formed, and they set to wheeling me through the backstage area to where I could be taken into the arena.

I could hear the roar of the crowds through the curtain, could hear Nolan Sharrock introducing each act in his flamboyant style. He was a fantastic entertainer and I found my heart racing at the prospect of going out there. It was strange, for I was in effect a tortured circus animal, yet there I was with my elbows hanging over the side of my tank as I listened for my cue.

Jugglers, fire-eaters, trapeze artists ... they all went out to do their thing and I wished them well as they passed my tank. Then the lion went out, the poor scraggly beast which had been whipped and beaten so much its once-proud frame was bent low in meek surrender. Some of my excitement broke away at that point. When I saw the elephant trail a few minutes later, my excitement died.

"It looks so sad," I said, not even realising I was referring to the animal in an asexual way, just as the doctor had referred to me.

"It's an elephant," Maya said from the base of the tank. "Do you expect it to dance?"

"I'm surprised it doesn't. What are those white stumps next to its nose?"

"The nose is called a trunk. The white stumps used to be its tusks. Big teeth; I don't know if any animal in the water has tusks."

"Are they like a walrus?"

"No idea."

"What happened to them?"

"For some reason, the stupid elephant files them down. No idea why."

"That's so sad."

"We had a bear once. All it did was pace. It paced so much, you could see in its eyes it wasn't all there."

"What happened to it?"

"I think we shot it, if I remember rightly."

"That's terrible."

"It was a mercy for the bear."

The curtain parted and someone hissed to Maya.

"That's your cue," Maya said. "If these lovely strongmen would like to take you out, I'll leave you in their capable hands."

"You're not coming to watch?" I asked, crestfallen.

"I'm on after you and I have to get into costume. I'd say break a leg, but you don't have any."

I had no idea why people kept telling me to break my legs, but it was something I intended to look into.

I was a little sad to think I would be performing without Maya watching me, yet as the strongmen wheeled my tank into the arena, I could not help think back to those mistreated animals. Not so long earlier, that had been me. I had been defiant enough to be tormented, yet to save myself pain I had succumbed. I had not been broken like the lion and the elephant, I had sold out.

I wondered which was the better fate.

As my tank passed through the curtain, all these thoughts evaporated, for I was absorbed into the full majesty of the big-top arena. The performance area was a great circular stage set upon the grass of wherever it was we had pitched our tent. Within the arena were blocks and big balls, stands and wires: anything which would be involved in the various acts, and also big bold shapes to draw the attention of the crowd. And what a crowd it was, for the circular seating surrounded the entire stage, save where the curtain was through which I had just passed. Nor was there only the one row, for behind each row of seating was another, and another, all in rising tiers so that everyone present could see and enjoy everything. The acoustics of the tent would be amazing, the lighting was expertly designed – everything was perfect.

And within the centre of the ring stood the tall, grandiose figure of Nolan Sharrock. His back was straight, his bowler hat in place, his green suit striking against the lighting. He gestured to my tent and I could hear the rush of awed whispers running rampant through the crowd. My heart fluttered to think so many people had their attention upon me and I hoped I would not let them down.

"And now," Sharrock said, "ladies and gentlemen, I offer you something unique. Something no other circus has ever produced. Outside of this tent, there exists another world. It is a world of reality and politics, of life-and-death struggles against foul creatures of the night. But in here, within this tent, we seek only to amaze and confound. I give you, for your amusement and enjoyment, the fabulous Misako, Mermaid of Mystery."

The applause was light, for the whispers outdid them. Within my water tank, I took a deep breath, which caused gasps I had not even intended from my audience. It was, after all, proof that I was a living mermaid and not simply a woman in a fish's tail.

My tank was amazing, and a great deal of effort had gone into preparing it. Aside from my shell costume, the tank needed to look correct. More fish had been added, and crabs and lobsters. A ship's wheel was half-sunk in the sand and stones at the base, along with a chest containing gleaming treasure (all fake). Plants grew through the sand, a sea snake twisted through their waving leaves, while the water itself was clear and clean, all the better for my audience to see me.

My audience. This was my turn to amaze. I had the attention of the entire tent.

I began my act with some swimming, to show I was at home in the water. I twisted and turned, looped and wove. I did some underwater juggling with stones, tossing them upwards to dance about them as they slowly descended. That received a little applause, but people were mainly still in awe. Perhaps they were also contemplating the morality of applauding a faerie when there was a war on outside.

"And now," Nolan Sharrock declared, "our Mysterious Mermaid Misako will leap through hoops for your enjoyment."

He gestured and large hoops descended from the ceiling. There were three of them and I swam about as I watched them come. Then, with a kick of my tail, I swam upwards, broke the surface and passed through one hoop. The audience cheered at that and I afforded them a little bow.

Continuing my swim, I broke the surface again, passing through one backwards, much to the delight of the crowd. After this, I swam so fiercely in a circle that I churned up the water in order to gain speed; then broke the surface to soar through all three hoops in one graceful arc.

The audience were on their feet in applause and I could not contain the grin which spread wildly across my face.

"But what's this?" Sharrock said. "Is someone … no, they could not possibly be … but they are. Our mischievous fire-eater is setting the hoops aflame."

The fire-eater was indeed doing so, with the aid of the trapeze artists getting her up that high. I feigned indignation and as the fire-eater was at last settled upon the ground I wagged my finger at her crossly. The crowd found this amusing, which was good since it had been Maya's suggestion.

It pained me again to think of Maya not seeing my act, but perhaps she would have got into costume by now and was watching from behind the curtain. I still had no idea why I was being so forgiving of the woman who had tortured me, and I hated to think I could forgive, or even justify, her cruelty so readily.

The fire hoops was an act I had practised a great deal, mainly because if I got it wrong I would burn myself horribly. I had to make a show of not being sure of them, of being scared even. I had to pretend I had never even considered this act, even though I had successfully completed it a dozen times.

I approached it nimbly, leaping from the water and failing to get through the first hoop, almost scalding myself in the process. The audience released a gasp of horror, which was good because it meant they had learned to look beyond my faerie heritage and see me as one of the performers. My second attempt at the fire hoop was more confident, although still did I not manage to get through. I swam around for a bit longer, glanced to Sharrock, who was grinning broadly at my act, and taking a deep breath, I bolted directly upwards, over the hoops, did a somersault in the air, plunged back into the tank, propelled myself back out and passed through all three hoops.

The crowd screamed and whistled and I was certain I heard at least one proposal of marriage.

When they had settled down, Nolan Sharrock said, "Now, if the Mysterious Misako could possibly help us out a little …?"

I nodded and swam back to the surface, dragging my tail along to create a wave which blasted up far enough to douse the three hoops.

The audience loved that as well, which was hardly surprising.

"Ladies and gentlemen," Sharrock said with a flourish of his arm, "I give you, Misako, the Mysterious Mermaid."

Their applause was thunderous and I smiled at them from within my tank. Sharrock had told me not to come out, not to rest my elbows over the side as was my wont, but to bask in the applause as I received it. The glass and the water dulled some of the sound, but even through its constraints I could hear how much the people loved me.

I would have gladly performed an encore, but Nolan Sharrock had other acts to show. He did leave my water tank in the arena, though, and I kept fairly still so as not to detract attention from the next act, although I wondered what it was. I was hoping it would be Maya, since I still did not know what her performance entailed.

"And now," Nolan Sharrock said melodramatically, even a little shocked, "we come to the most dangerous act in the entire performance. The act which has so far cost three young women their lives and has left a fourth without a hand."

I assumed he was lying, but was still intrigued.

"You've seen the lion tamers and you've seen the great hunters. Now it's time for you to witness a beast in its natural habitat as we watch a mighty monstrosity stalk its prey. Stalk its prey and perhaps devour? Even I cannot say, which means in this next act, anything can happen."

I did not understand what he was introducing, but Maya ran into the arena and I was glad of that much at least. My smile faded somewhat when I saw what she was wearing, and she received a number of wolf-whistles from the crowd. Where the strongmen had been wearing nothing but pants, with their legs, arms and torsos bear, Maya's costume was little better. She wore furred boots, a brown furry loincloth and a brassiere of the same material. Upon her wrist was a bracelet of small bones, while about her throat was a necklace of teeth. In her hand she carried a spear, and she skulked like she was some primitive savage.

A Mermaid's Odyssey

I had never seen her in such a persona and began to worry what her act might be about.

Maya made a show of moving around the arena, dancing expertly while maintaining the air of a savage. She grunted loudly, sniffed at the ground, even sniffed under her arms and recoiled, to the amusement of the crowd. She pretended to dig for grubs and shoved a handful of grass into her mouth, which she chewed thoughtfully.

After a minute or so of this, Sharrock, who had kept some distance, said, "But what hunter would be complete without her prey? Yet which is the hunter, and which the prey?"

Something wandered into the arena then, something large and fierce. It was not the half-starved lion I had seen meekly crawling around the circus, nor was it the pitiable elephant which filed its own tusks in anxiety and depression. This was something of the faerie races, something I had never encountered, yet something even I feared.

Part pig, part goblin, the thing was known as a hoglin. They varied in size and shape, and this one was bigger than a horse. Its large bulbous body was formed of leathery dark blue skin, almost black. It moved around on strong hind legs, with the forelegs short so the animal's snout could better reach the ground. The creature did not possess ears, yet it did not need any, for it enabled the head to contain a larger mouth. Fiery red eyes blazed out from the rise of the snout and it focused upon Maya, opening its maw to reveal rows of razor teeth. Shark-like, it was not content with simply the one row although, unlike sharks, they did not necessarily snap off those in the first row before utilising the second. To the side of the maw, two stalagmite tusks rose, their strength enough to shear through metal.

Hoglins were a tool of the faerie generals in their armies, for they infamously ate anything. They were seldom sent into combat, but were reserved for clean-up operations. After a battle, they would be sent in to devour the remains of both sides. Some saw them as horrific monsters, but in truth they cleared the lands of disease and in this fashion performed an important part to keep survivors alive.

The one stalking Maya looked incredibly hungry, which was the natural state of the things.

I could not believe Nolan Sharrock had brought the creature into the arena and glanced over to see his reaction. He was behaving as though he was scared, although I could see it was an act. He had little reason to be scared, for the hoglin's attention was upon Maya. He would, however, find out just how monstrous the thing could be when it was done with her and moved onto his audience, perhaps even Nolan Sharrock himself.

Where he had been keeping the hoglin remained a mystery, but that did not matter. All I could see was that Maya was in danger, and she did not even understand the extent of what she was facing.

The shouts from the crowd told Maya to look behind her. Maya, in true performer's fashion, cupped a hand to her ear, scratched her head, found a louse there to chew on and with an exaggerated shrug, pointedly ignored them to return to her foraging in the grass. All the while, the hoglin moved closer. It did not care for the vast number of people around, for a hoglin knew no fear. Where it saw creatures, living or otherwise, it saw food, and being trapped inside a tent with so many bodies was like someone shoving it into a larder and sealing the door.

I had to do something or everyone in the tent was going to die.

Thumping on the glass of my tank, I tried to get Nolan Sharrock's attention. He glanced my way but only looked annoyed. It was as though he could not see the hoglin stalking Maya, or that he thought it was just a big pig or something. In horror, I realised he honestly thought he had the thing trained, that he had broken it just as Maya had attempted to break me. He considered the hoglin to be just another of his sideshow animals, not understanding it was nigh impossible to tame a faerie. If he had not learned his lesson with me, the mistake was going to cost him dearly.

Giving up on Sharrock, I saw the strongmen were still nearby and I hammered on the glass again. One looked to me and shook his head crossly. I tried to get my fear across to him, but again he shook his head. The other strongman simply ignored me.

If I was going to save Maya, I was going to have to do it myself.

Swimming to the top of my tank, I was about to climb out when the lid dropped. I was shocked and looked through the glass to see Nolan Sharrock moving his hand from the lever. Panicking now, I looked back to Maya, who had finally noticed the hoglin. Her face drained of all colour and her acting ceased. She raised her spear in trembling hands and her mouth opened and closed, but no shriek escaped her lips. Whatever she had been expecting behind her, the hoglin was simply a nightmare version.

With no other recourse, I slammed my fist into the side of the tank. I had attempted to break the glass before, several times when Maya had been torturing me, and never with any luck. Never had I even been able to put a crack in the thick glass. Back then I had been fighting for my own life, while here I was terrified for Maya's. That was a difference which not many people would have been able to understand, for there is something more primal, more necessary, when I see a friend in danger. My temperament becomes more violent, my emotions more primal, and as I pounded my fists again and again upon the glass, I wept that I could not break through.

The hoglin had drawn boos from the crowd and there was laughter as Maya stumbled away in fright. She raised her spear through instinct more than anything else, but it was a toothpick for the beast. It lunged and Maya thrust forward, but its teeth snapped the spear, which splintered into kindling. I punched the glass again, impotent to do anything. My knuckles were in agony and I saw blood flowing through the water from where I had cut and bruised them, but I ignored the pain, for all I could see was my friend about to die. This woman who had abused me, tortured me and forced me to jump through hoops of fire – for reasons which have always been my own, I still regarded her as a friend.

Maya fell, her legs at last giving out, and she backpedalled as the hoglin snapped at her. The crowd gave mixed reactions to this. Some were still booing, others were cheering, while many were baying for blood. I could not understand how Nolan Sharrock felt a nude mermaid was not family friendly, yet having a woman mauled to death by a faerie brute was.

Swimming back from the wall which I knew I would not be able to break, I struggled for another means to help Maya, but there was nothing I could do. The walls were too thick, the lid was held on by strong hinges and there was nothing else I could do. Panic and grief tore through my body and I wept, my tears invisible under the water.

I knew I was about to watch Maya die and no one else seemed to care at all.

Around me, the water bubbled.

For a moment, I thought someone had lit a fire beneath the tank, but that could not have been true. As the bubbling intensified, I watched the fish dart in fear and the sea snake hide himself as best he could among the grass. Even the crabs were scuttling behind the broken wheel and inside the treasure chest, reminding me of Mallok's method of catching them.

The water churned about me, slicing out but not harming me. It was as though a storm was brewing within the tank.

Then realisation struck me. My emotions could cause storms, but only where there was water; and there was water in my tank. I was so afraid, so furious, so frustrated that even in so small amount of water I was forming a tempest.

Muttering came from the audience, although I could see rather than hear them. The strongmen looked concerned and Nolan Sharrock narrowed one eye, a rare time in the ring when he failed to smile.

Looking at Maya being stalked by that hoglin, I floated freely in the tank, raised my arms to my sides and brought them before me so my hands clapped.

The water shot at the glass like an arrow formed of the hardest steel. Thick glass exploded outwards, the water spilling across the arena floor, spraying everywhere with its force. I was bodily carried out of the tank to slam into the ground before rolling. The audience erupted with passion for my move, but no one else knew how to react. Sharrock was too shocked to do anything, the other performers looked to him for instructions and therefore did nothing, either. But I did not care for any of them, for the hoglin had barely glanced my way, intent on its meal as it was.

Upon the ground, Maya stared at me in wide-eyed horror and perhaps a little hope. Above her, the hoglin reared itself up on its hind legs and squealed to the sky.

My tail gone, I leaped across the arena, propelled by powerful leg muscles, and caught the hoglin about the throat. Swinging upwards to sit upon its head, I grabbed its tusks and heaved. The hoglin grunted and squealed in protest as it dropped back to its four feet. It bucked and reared as it tried to throw me off its back but I held on tight, knowing that to release my hold was to be trampled or gored. Upon the floor, Maya was in shock and unable to move. In her primitive savage's attire, her bones would be smashed to pulp should the hoglin land a foot upon her, so I veered my weight to the side in order to make the hoglin move.

Squealing in protest, the hoglin put everything into one almighty effort and threw back its head. My hand slipped and I was flying over its side, my other hand losing its grip in the process. I hit the ground hard but rolled even as the hoglin's feet would have trampled me.

Coming up into a crouch, I watched the hoglin as it shook its great head. It was confused by what was happening, for no one had ever before been stupid enough to assault it directly, and as it locked eyes upon me, it decided I would have to pay for my transgression.

I got to my feet and parted my legs in a stance I had seen Braal use. She had not trained me in the art of fighting, but I had paid attention to everything she did, and with my superior strength I felt I perhaps had at least a slight chance of surviving the encounter.

The audience were thumping their fists in delight, screaming encouragement, wailing in ecstasy. It took me a moment to remember that my mermaid's costume consisted solely of two shells and that perhaps by reverting to my woman's legs I was giving them a show they had not been expecting, but if Nolan Sharrock had a problem with that, he could take it up with me afterwards.

Grunting, the hoglin pawed the ground and kept its head low. I knew this was going to be bad, but there was no chance to run. Maya had still not moved, and no one else was doing anything to help, which meant it was still all down to me.

With a squeal of rage, the hoglin charged. Tensing my body, I allowed it to come, fear striking through me but not ruling my actions. When it was within but a few paces, so close I could smell its foul breath, I pushed myself against the ground, leaped into the air and curled into a ball. The hoglin passed me by and I landed to its side. Disorientated, the hoglin shrieked at me and I stood ready for its next charge.

That charge came a moment later, and I tensed again. The crowd gave a sickening drum-beat in the build-up to our collision and I blocked them out as best I could. As the hoglin reached me, I dropped, rolled forward and pushed myself up with as much strength as I could. My fist slammed into the underside of its jaw and the hoglin staggered, shocked. Jumping to the side, I followed it through with a left-handed punch to its face, shattering one tusk with the sheer strength and ferocity of my blow.

The hoglin tottered on uncertain legs and faced me once more, its eyes burning with pure hatred. Already bleeding from my intense assault upon the glass tank, my fists hurt like the blazes, while my heart threatened to explode within me.

Again, I stood ready. The hoglin was making all the charges and was using up its energy, while I was reacting and conserving what strength I had. With a roar of rage, it attacked, and with a roar of equal intensity which burned from my very soul, I met the charge. As we collided, the hoglin split open its maw, its teeth raking my arm, its remaining tusk narrowly missing a goring blow to my side. My own fist struck it in the eye and as we parted, it was with both of us in pain.

Falling back, I assessed my injury. My arm was flowing blood from a dozen tears the animal's teeth had shorn through several layers of skin, but the pain was minimal. I knew that was due to my adrenalin and fear, which meant the pain would hit me just as soon as it wore off. I would have to end the fight quickly.

"Misako!" someone shouted and I turned to find one of the strongmen tossing me something. I caught it and found it to be a pole. It was not much of a weapon, but it was better than nothing.

The hoglin's squeal indicated it was attacking again. The ground shook with its charge and I brought the pole around in a wide arc, screaming with the effort. The pole slammed into the side of the beast's head as it came at me, splintering the pole but knocking the creature down.

The crowd loved that move, but I did not care.

"Misako!"

I turned to find the fire-eater tossing me a burning brand. I caught it and, an idea forming, shoved the brand into the splintered end of the pole. Rushing forward, I saw the hoglin attempting to rise and knew I could not allow it to do so. Leaping, I twisted the pole so the burning brand faced downwards. The fire attempted to rise, but a moment later I shoved it down with incredible force into the hoglin's eye.

The beast shrieked and flailed. I danced back, dropping the pole as the hoglin thrashed. One hind leg caught me upon the knee and I heard something crack. Falling to a crouch, I knew I was far too close to the beast and that if it managed to rise, it would surely crush me.

With a superhuman effort, the hoglin got back to its feet. One eye was a blackened ruin, the stench of cooked meat filled its immediate vicinity, and it glared at me with its one good eye. Opening its maw, it revealed its hundreds of serrated teeth, showing me how I was going to die. I had taken its tusk and its eye and now it wanted revenge.

"Misako!"

I turned a weary head to find Nolan Sharrock standing beside me. Surprised, I tried to tell him to run for his life, but my throat was dry and I could not form words. He was holding a bow, which was strung with a single arrow, and he smiled, although his eyes told me he was not happy.

Raising the bow, he kept a steady aim and, as the hoglin ran for us, he released. The arrow passed through the beast's remaining eye and buried itself so deep in the creature's skull that it pierced its brain. Sharrock dropped the bow and threw himself over me as the hoglin thrashed in its death throes. The beast fell at our feet, twitched once and lay still.

I looked into its two ruined eyes and took several moments to realise we were still alive.

Sharrock released me and removed his jacket. Taking me by the hand, he dragged me to my feet and draped the jacket about my waist. My crushed knee made me almost fall but Sharrock's eyes warned me against doing so.

Facing his audience, he raised his hat to a great tumultuous applause.

"Nolan Sharrock's Travelling Oddities!" he said without needing to shout. "The greatest show in the world. Tell your family, your friends, even tell your enemies."

He went on in this vein. One of the strongmen lifted me in his arms and carried me from the arena. I saw the other helping Maya, although she batted aside his assistance and hobbled off on her own.

We had won and we had survived.

I had a terrible feeling there would be hell to pay.

CHAPTER EIGHTEEN

The show ended shortly after, mainly because nothing could have topped that act. Emotions ran wild backstage. While the doctor tended my knee – which was thankfully not broken – she even referred to me as female, and not it, which was something of a step-up. I was congratulated by the clowns, hugged by the dog man and given three cheers by the conjoined twins. The strongmen had decided they were now my bodyguards and stood close by: that they had both become infatuated with me was obvious and I couldn't say I minded. I would not like to think I was a shallow young woman, but it's difficult not to favour the attention of two near-naked muscular mountains of male perfection.

The fire-eater slapped me on the back and I thanked her for helping me out, as I had also thanked the strongman. I thought I should at some point get their names and felt shallow all over again for not knowing them already.

The happiness backstage was infectious and my soul was lighter than it had been for a long while. Maya was, of course, my main concern, and I insisted the doctor looked her over. There was nothing physically wrong with her, she said, and the shock would wear off sooner or later. The doctor could be a very vague woman sometimes but I was beginning to see she meant well – when she wasn't suggesting people torture me more brutally.

When Nolan Sharrock finally appeared, my heart jolted, for I seemed to be the only one who knew he was going to be furious.

"Wasn't she amazing?" the fire-eater asked him.

"Wasn't she spectacular?" a clown added.

Sharrock stopped directly before me, ignoring anything anyone said to him. He slapped me across the face, hard, and jubilation backstage ceased. No one spoke a word, no one dared even to breathe.

"You stupid, vainglorious little slut," he said, striking me again. "I've spent my fortune, my life, building this show ..." Another slap. "And you seize centre-stage and threaten to destroy it all in one night." He pulled back his arm but held it there, trembling. My face ached, for his passion lent him strength, but I did not give him the satisfaction of seeing that he had hurt me.

"Nolan," Maya braved, "she saved my life."

"Your life," he spat the word, "was never in any danger. And unless it's scripted to save someone's life, it doesn't do it." He looked about the crowd, his people. "You do all understand that, don't you?"

Many looked away, not wanting to object or disagree. The fire-eater looked annoyed, the strongmen were upset, while Maya was simply shocked.

"But ... but she saved my life."

"*I* would have saved your life. *I* would have, don't you see? You were never in any danger, I wasn't going to let you die."

"That was a hoglin," I said from where I sat, barely controlling my rage. "You can't control a hoglin, Sharrock. You may think you're the master of oddities, you may think you can bend anyone to your will, but you can't break a hoglin."

"Are you questioning me?" he asked, his face a mask of darkness. "You're a faerie living amongst humans. You live – *live* – at our sufferance. If you weren't in the show, those people out there would tear you apart. That hoglin, as you call it, didn't need to be trained. It did not need to be broken. It just needed to chase Maya around the arena for a while before I shot it through the eye. It was all staged, and you had to ruin it."

"Your plan was stupid," I said, rising on an unsteady knee, "and if you seriously think it had any chance of working, you're an idiot."

His fist lunged for my face but I caught it and twisted. Sharrock cried aloud as he fell to one knee.

"Don't touch me," I said with narrowed eyes as I slowly crushed his hand. "Don't you ever touch me again."

Something appeared just beneath my chin. I cast my eyes down to see it was a long iron bar. Another crossed it, while a third appeared behind me. The clowns were standing with Sharrock, holding a clear threat upon me. I looked around to the other performers, although they were all meekly looking away. The fire-eater still looked annoyed and Maya was stunned, but even they were not going to say a word.

I released Sharrock and stood as straight as I could. He got to his feet, nursing his injured hand. He would have struck me with it if the blow would not have hurt him more than me. He was sweating with rage but could not find adequate words to summarise his emotions.

"Get this thing out of my sight," he told the clowns as he tore his cloak off me, leaving me naked again save for my pathetic shells. "Take it to a cage. Lock it up with the other animals. Maya!"

"Sir?"

"I want it to suffer. I want it to understand the wrong it's caused this circus, this family. I want it to know so much pain it begs for forgiveness."

Maya was stunned by the command and did not speak. Sharrock turned a glower upon her and she opened her mouth, but only a strangled gurgle came out. Clearing her throat, she said, "Yes, Nolan."

Recognising the futility of continuing the argument, I allowed the clowns to lead me away,. They took me to the area in which the animals were kept. The lion's cage was not much larger than a coffin, and the elephant could not even sit in its enclosure. There was an empty bell-shaped cage formed of strong bars and a square door. I had seen it before: it was apparently a birdcage, although the circus had no birds. It was smaller than me, which meant I would have to crouch the entire time I was in there.

I was also reasonably sure it was made of iron.

"I'm not getting in there," I said, equally as angry as I was afraid. "If I spend too long in there, I'll …"

A clown shoved me in the back with an iron rod. The metal sent waves of agony through my naked back, allowing the clowns to seize me and hurl me through the square door. I fell on my side, my shoulders striking the iron bars, and screamed. Scrambling to my feet, I burned no matter what I did, for I was not even wearing any boots. The clowns laughed as only clowns can and one shot down the bolt on the door.

Screaming in pain, I attempted to place my feet on the grass between the barred floor, but there was only room for me to stand on tiptoes. Remembering I was still wearing my shells, I tore them away in order to use them as shoes. The glue ripped apart my skin and my chest was afire with pain equal to the rest of me, but I dropped the shells and stood upon them. As I expected, I had to crouch, nor could I dare move. Every slight motion caught an elbow, a shoulder or my backside against the metal cage and as I stood in terror, I found myself hyperventilating.

I was left alone in that area, separated by a curtain. I was far from the other performers, with only the animals for company. I would have been furious, but my pain was too great for that, along with an overriding fear of the surrounding iron.

I remained that way for several hours, not daring to move. My muscles were aching, my legs had cramp, but I still dared not move.

Then someone appeared and I looked up, knowing this was Maya, come to torture me as ordered. I was surprised to find it was not Maya, but the fire-eater. She was carrying something and, while she still looked annoyed, she was also sad.

"Here," she said, passing something through the bars of the cage. It was a cloak, which I quickly used to cover the floor so I could stand on it. "I thought you might want to wear it, actually," she said.

"It's better I stand on it. This cage is made of iron."

"So?"

I turned my body slightly so she could see the blisters and burn marks across my back and arms.

"By the gods," she said. "Of course, you're a faerie. I didn't ... Wait a minute."

I watched, shocked, as she removed her shirt and handed it me through the bars. I took it, dumbfounded, as she sat and took off her boots and trousers. Within moments, she was down to her undergarments.

"You need them more than I do," she said.

It was difficult getting dressed, but she placed her hands through the bars to help me. I still brushed against the bars a couple of times, but once I was dressed, I felt far more comfortable.

"Thank you," I said as I sat, finally able to relax my tense muscles. "You're a life-saver."

"*I'm* the life-saver? After what you did for Maya?"

"I couldn't let her die."

"Why not? She's so cruel to you."

"I know, I ... I suppose I was just raised well."

She did not understand my reasoning, but nor did she question it.

"Sorry," I said, "I don't even know your name."

"Phillis. My stage name is Fearless, which is Mr Sharrock's little joke."

"Thank you, Fearless Phillis."

She shrugged uncomfortably. "I shouldn't hang around here in my undies. Good luck with everything."

"Phillis," I asked as she turned to go. "Why does everyone stay with Sharrock?"

"He has a vision," she replied easily. "He's a great man, just not a very good one."

Maya arrived at that moment and the two women almost bumped into each other. Maya took a step back, looked the fire-eater up and down wordlessly, but said nothing as Phillis left.

"What is it with people taking their clothes off lately?" Maya asked as she approached the cage.

"Maybe people are sympathising with the faerie," I suggested coldly.

"I know you're angry with me and I'm sorry."

"Angry with you? Maya, you could have stuck up for me."

"I know. I could have done a lot of things, but I didn't."

"And now you're here to torture me, to make me behave like a good little trained monkey."

"The monkey was the fake mermaid, Misako. Nolan can't tell the difference, that's all."

"When are you people going to stop making excuses for him?"

"He looks after us, all right? Keeps a roof over our heads, puts food in our bellies." She unhooked a bag from her back. "That reminds me." She passed the bag through the bars and I opened it to find food and water.

"What's the trick?" I asked. "It's filled with laxative or something?"

"No trick."

"You'll forgive me if I don't believe you."

"Oh for the love of …" She reached in, took the flask and drank from it before handing it back. "Happy?"

"I'm stuck in an iron cage which could kill me just from being too close to it. What do you think?"

"I'm sorry. I …" She began pacing, which was infuriating to watch. I drank a little water while she did so, but was too angry to eat anything. "Misako, you once asked me why I joined the circus."

"Is this going to be your life story?"

"I want you to understand what I do."

I had to admit I was curious, although I would never tell her that. "Fine. I'm listening."

"My family died in the war. We weren't soldiers, weren't faerie haters. We weren't really anything special. We were farmers, living a peaceful life. We paid tribute to the gods, we worked hard to sustain ourselves and we kept away from politics. We knew there was a war on, of course, but it never bothered us. I'd never met anyone who'd even seen a faerie before.

"Then, one day, a faerie force passed through my farm. Great walking tree-like things, as though an entire forest was on the march. They tore through my home purely because it was there, slaughtered my parents and all my brothers. I only survived because my father tore up a floorboard and shoved me headfirst under the house. He told me to be brave, he told me not to make a sound.

"I heard them die, heard the entire house come down, heard the army pass. When I was brave enough to emerge, I found them all dead, crushed to death by the march of the demon trees.

"I took to the road, I didn't know what else to do. Nolan found me, and I was lucky he did. I could have fallen in with any number of brigands or worse, but Nolan cared for me, raised me, made me a part of his family. That's what we are here: a family. So I do whatever he tells me to, and I trust him."

"Did you trust him out there today?" I asked. "Do you honestly think that hoglin wouldn't have killed you?"

She looked away. "I don't know."

"And what about me? I'm a faerie, so you had no problem abusing me like you did?"

"Your people killed my family, Misako. I couldn't forget that. So, when Nolan gave me the task of breaking you ... yes, I enjoyed it." She looked at me then, and her eyes were terribly dark. "I made you suffer just as your people made my family suffer. I tortured you just as your people tortured me by taking away my family. That ruse about your father? Making you think I'd found him? I delighted in that. At first."

"And now?"

"You saved my life."

"I didn't think your life was in danger?"

She angrily wiped away a tear. "I like you, Misako. I've tried not to, but I can't help it. There's something about you, something ... I don't know. You're not the way mermaids should be, you're not the way faeries should be. You're unique and I don't hate you for what happened to my parents."

"I had nothing to do with that, and if people on both sides would stop hating each other as a species, we might have peace."

"Peace?"

"I had a friend once, a soldier. She thought there could be peace between us."

Maya weighed this up carefully and in her eyes something changed. "Braal?"

"Yes."

"I wish I could have met her. She sounds like a very wise woman."

Silence hung between us for several moments.

"Are you going to beat me now, like Nolan wants?" I asked.

"I should. I don't know."

"You mean you're considering it?" I asked, shocked.

"Nolan saved my life."

"*I* saved your life."

"I know. Misako, if I opened the cage door, would you run away?"

"Run away?"

"I'm offering to let you go free. Just don't go after Nolan in revenge, it's all I'm asking."

"He'd be very cross with you."

"What's he gonna do? Throw me in a cage?"

I raised my eyebrows and shrugged.

"Yeah," she said, "I reckon he'd throw me in a cage. Still, I'm willing to risk it."

"I'm not running."

"Then you're an idiot."

"All I've done since coming to the human world is run away from things. When people catch me, they beat me up and then I run away. I'm done running, Maya. I'm getting out of this cage and I'm going to give Nolan Sharrock a piece of my mind. If that means punching him in the face, so be it."

"Then I really should torture you, like he wants." She produced an iron bar and stared at it, long and hard. She could have done a lot of damage with that, prodding me through the bars. "But I'm not," she said, tossing it aside. "I'm not going to hurt you any more, Misako. I think I've hurt you enough. I think our whole wretched species has hurt you enough."

"I'm not sure if it's appropriate to thank someone for deciding not to torture me," I said, "but ... well, you know."

Just then, raised voices sounded from behind the curtain and the two strongmen barged in, looking fierce. Behind them, Phillis the fire-eater was struggling to get a shirt on while she walked.

"Stop," one of the strongmen said to Maya. "Don't hurt her."

"I wasn't going to."

The other strongman plastered his back to the cage, shielding me. "We won't let you torture her."

"I wasn't going to."

"You'll have to come through us."

"I won't need to."

"Guys, guys," Phillis said. "Curb your enthusiasm, I don't think Maya's a threat."

They were confused and a little disappointed, but their hearts were in the right place, even if their heads weren't.

"Thanks, fellas," I said. "I appreciate it."

They smiled at me, pleased to have pleased me, and I suddenly knew what it was like to own a pet or two.

"As chummy as this scene is," Phillis said, "we have a problem. I overheard Mr Sharrock on my way out. Misako, he's going to sell you."

"Sell me? I'm not a piece of property."

"To him, you are."

"Why would he sell Misako?" Maya asked. "He wants me to torture her, to get her back into shape. She's his star."

"Every star burns out eventually," Phillis said. "Her single performance is going to have to suffice. He wants rid of her because he thinks she's trouble."

"Then why am I torturing her?" Maya asked, angry.

The strongmen went to reaffirm their position as my bodyguards should Maya mean that, but I said, "Because he hates me. He doesn't care about the war, but he does care about this circus. I'm a threat to that and he wants me punished."

Everyone exchanged looks, but no one spoke.

"Right," Maya said at last. "What are we going to do about it?"

"Do?" I asked. "You're not going to do anything."

"We'll break you out of the cage," Phillis said. "Dom, Dom-Dom, get the bars."

I had discovered the names of the strongmen and stifled a giggle. They seized the cage and I stopped laughing. "I'm not going anywhere," I said. "If Sharrock has buyers out there, running wouldn't do any good anyway. If he's convinced them there's a mermaid in here, I won't get far."

"Who's he selling her to?" Maya asked.

"I'm not sure," Phillis said. "But they looked mean. I don't think it's a rival show, Mr Sharrock wouldn't want to hand her over to the competition. I reckon it's a mob of faerie haters."

"They'll kill her," Maya said.

"They'll have to get through us," Dom (or possibly Dom-Dom) said.

"I doubt that would be a problem," Phillis said. "Misako's right, though. She won't get far. Maybe the four of us could hold them off while she ..."

"No," I said so harshly both Phillis and Maya backed off in alarm. "Sorry," I said. "It's just I've had too many people I care about protect me while I slink away. Mallok, Salla, Braal ... I don't know whether any of them survived. I won't have all of you on my conscience as well."

"Then we have no choice," Phillis said with a sigh as she placed her hands upon her hips. "We're going to have to have it out with Mr Sharrock."

"Are you nuts?" Maya asked. "None of us are expendable. He'll sack us. Besides, it won't help Misako. He'll just oust us as faerie lovers and Misako will still be killed. Horribly. Mercilessly. Choked with her own entrails, drowned in her own blood, pounded with her own ..."

"Not helping, Maya," Phillis said.

"Sorry, it's the showwoman in me. I spout weird stuff when I get nervous."

"Does anyone have any ideas?" Phillis asked. She looked to Dom and Dom-Dom, but shook her head in wonder of why she was doing that. She looked to me, but I had nothing.

"I can't ask you to do anything for me," I said. "It's great we're all getting along here, but if I'm going to die, you know what? I'm not that bothered."

"Are you serious?" Phillis asked.

"Yeah." I exhaled deeply and was surprised I meant it. "I came to the surface world thinking all I would find were monsters. Amongst all the beastly humans there would be one decent soul among you: my father. I didn't find him, but I did find a whole load of humans acting precisely as I thought they would. But I also found good people. Friends. Family. People I care about and people who care about me. People I could love." I smiled at each of them in turn. "I'm sure about this, I really am. I don't have anything to live for anyway, so if I'm not supposed to survive this, I'm OK with that. Just so long as you four are all right, I don't mind at all."

"Braal wouldn't want you to die," Maya said softly. "She'd want you to fight."

"And if I hadn't killed her, she could tell me that herself."

"You have to stop blaming yourself."

A knot formed in my throat but I refused to cry any more. "No," I said. "No, I don't. Maybe this is what I deserve, maybe it's just the gods having their fun with me. Maybe it has nothing to do with any of that and it's just one man's egotism. It doesn't matter. Whatever will be, will be. But thanks for trying."

One of the strongmen began to cry. The other patted him on the back and said, "There, there. The show must go on."

"Showwoman," Maya said with a frown. "Show must go on. Show ... Oh the gods, you people are geniuses!"

Dom and Dom-Dom looked to me and Phillis, back to themselves and did not understand. They were not the only ones.

"What?" I asked. "Maya, what?"

"We have this," she said. "We can do this. Dom, Dom-Dom, I'm going to have to ask something really big of you. It'll be hugely embarrassing, but ..."

"We'll do it," they said together.

"Great. Phillis, I ..."

"Why not?" She grinned. "Let's go sort out the details."

"You know what I'm thinking?"

"No idea, but it already sounds swell."

I asked them what they were planning, pleaded with them not to do anything foolish, but all Maya did was offer me a big wave as the four of them trouped out through the curtain. I was left alone, speechless, and not quite sure any of that had just happened.

It was a while before I found I was ravenous and consumed everything Maya had brought me to eat.

CHAPTER NINETEEN

I slept badly in the cage, for there was little room to curl up, and my dreams were filled with all the possible things my friends could do to try to save me. I saw images of burning brands, of chanting villagers, I could feel the flames tearing through my skin as they set me on fire. Beside me, I could see Maya and the others, all burning with me, with Nolan Sharrock standing to one side, laughing with all the uncouth villagers who hated me for the circumstances of my birth.

I awoke to find my ankle was touching the iron cage, which was why the burning in my dream had been so real, and I curled up tighter and prayed. I did not even know to whom I was praying, but it seemed fitting to pray when in the land of human beings, since their lives were so ruled by their deities.

It was not long before someone came for me. I had hoped it would have been Maya or one of the others, but it was the doctor. She unlocked the cage without a word and motioned for me to get out. She made no mention of the cloak lining the cage floor, nor the fact that I was fully clothed.

"Where am I going?" I asked.

"Mr Sharrock wants you."

"Have my buyers arrived?"

The doctor hid her shock well, but I could see it regardless. "You must be a witch," she said.

"That's right," I said. "I steal people's thoughts. "I stared at her hard and wrinkled my nose. "There. All memory of your little sister, gone forever."

"I don't have a little sister."

"My powers work well, then."

She shuddered and shoved me forward without another word. The more she spoke with me, the more she lost, and I felt glad to steal my moments of victory, no matter how small they were.

Beyond the curtain, I was met by the clowns. We did not have clowns in the ocean, unless you count clownfish, and never a more disturbing sight had I seen. They were people of both sexes and all sizes and ages. Some wore bright clothes, others dark, and most had their faces painted white, although other colours were also favoured. They each had their idiosyncrasies: one had a red nose which honked when squeezed, one squirted water from a flower on her lapel, another wore a collection of hats and a fourth wore long shoes with bulging ends. Their smiles were painted on, so a clown could be crying and would still look happy. They were like a slave race who were never allowed to show their true emotions, yet their masks were formed of paint instead of clay. Of all the people I had met upon my travels, it was the clowns which gave me the worst nightmares.

There were a dozen waiting to greet me, all armed with iron weapons ranging from simple bars to spades and nails. Holding my head high, I strode past them and noted they jeered and mocked me, while at the same time egged each other on to push me or prod me with iron. None of them dared such a thing, though, which told me they were cowards.

I was taken into the main arena, which looked so different now there was no audience. It was colder, for the tent did not contain the heat of a thousand bodies or the excitement of the performances to come. I noted much of the equipment was still set out, the giant blocks and balls, for instance. Even my fish tank was still there, although it had been covered with a curtain. I could see the glass had been fixed and the tank refilled with water, which had truly been quick work. I should not have put it past Nolan Sharrock to have several spare glass walls in stock.

Speaking of the ringmaster, he was standing in the arena, chatting to a score of unsavoury characters. They were agitated, aggressive, and Sharrock was having trouble keeping them calm. Upon seeing the clowns leading me in, one pointed and several raised knives and pitchforks. I clenched my hands tightly by my side but did not slow my pace. There was no sign of Maya and the others, but I knew they were up to something.

One of the clowns stepped before me and hooted her nose. It was then I began to wonder at them, for clowns provided the perfect disguise. Indeed, as I turned a casual glance at my clown escort, I saw that one of them was as large as a strongman, although I could not make out anyone's actual features.

The possibility gave me strength, so I took a deep breath and stepped forward.

"That's her?" one of the ruffians asked Sharrock.

"That is indeed Misako, the Mysterious Mermaid," he replied. "As a good citizen willing to do my bit to stand against the faeries, you may have her."

"We've already paid you, Sharrock," the ruffian replied, "so stop pretending you're the saviour of humankind."

Sharrock approached me and for once his face was unreadable. Gone was the smile, for his audience had departed, and even his twirling moustaches were drooped. "I was wondering whether I'd feel any regret," he said, "but I don't. You're not a woman, which is something I have to keep reminding myself. You're an unnatural thing, an enemy of my species."

"That's funny," I said. "I didn't realise lice had enemies."

"A parting joke, how droll. That man there is the leader of this crowd. His name's Lord Baron and he's the mayor of somewhere."

"Lord Baron the mayor? That's better than my joke."

Sharrock nodded to one of the clowns, who handed him some cuffs. "I'll place these on you, if you don't mind. They're not made of iron, don't worry about that, but I can't have you killing all these nice people."

"I don't see any nice people."

He snapped the cuffs in place on my hands and said, "For what it's worth, I hope they kill you quickly. You may be a freak, but for a time you were the most wondrous freak in my menagerie."

"Careful, Nolan, that's almost a compliment."

He grunted and motioned for the clowns to take me forward. I knew my moment was coming, when

Maya and the others would reveal themselves. I looked to the big clown and waited for a signal, but he just picked his nose and yawned. I looked to the other clowns, frantically searching for any recognisable aspect to them, but all I could see were the walking nightmares of false faces and cruel smiles.

My heart sank, for I knew whatever Maya had planned, it had failed. Perhaps she had abandoned me, perhaps that had been her intent all along. Maybe that was why she had not revealed her plan while in my presence, because she needed to tell everyone to forget about me and allow things to go back to the way they had been before my arrival. I had pinned my hopes on Maya and she had let me down.

With lowered eyes, I blinked away the tears I refused to shed and walked towards the ruffians. The first grabbed me by the arm and yanked me forward. Two more landed punches in my side, a fourth complained she could not get her pitchfork in for a good skewering.

"Hey, hey," Sharrock said, pulling me off them. "You're not murdering someone in my circus."

"It's not someone, it's a thing."

"You're still not killing her here. Take her back to your village and sacrifice her or something, just don't do it here."

There was a lot of mumbling about this, but Sharrock would not back down. Eventually, the Lord Baron grabbed me with his stinking hands and pulled me towards the exit.

"Yoo-hoo!"

We all stopped, for the voice had come from the fish tank.

After several moments of silence, the ruffian asked, "What was that?"

"Nothing," Sharrock said. "Just go."

"Yoo-hoo!"

"There it was again."

"It's nothing."

"Oh, boys!"

"It's coming from behind the curtain," Baron said. "Sharrock, what's back there? Is that another mermaid?"

"I don't have another mermaid," he said. "I don't know what it is, but I'll deal with it. Just go. Pay no attention to the woman behind the curtain."

"He's hiding another one," a woman said. "He's giving us this one so we don't find out he has a whole harem of the things here."

A great deal of commotion ensued, and Sharrock raised his hands in an attempt to placate it. "All right, all right, I'll go see what it is. Stay here."

The group had no intention of doing that and followed Sharrock, dragging me along with them. I had no idea what was going on, but could faintly see something moving in the tank behind the curtain. Sharrock ordered the clowns to pull the curtain down and we all stared in shock. There was a woman in there, floating calmly and swaying her hips. From those hips there depended a fish tail, which draped all the way down past where the woman's feet should have been. The woman was naked aside from two familiar shells covering her breasts.

"Maya?" I asked, startled.

"Cooee," Maya said from inside the tank. She was leaning over it, with her elbows resting on the edge.

"Maya," Sharrock barked. "What are you doing?"

"What is this?" the Baron asked. "You have another mermaid, Sharrock."

"I don't, I … this isn't a mermaid. Maya, come out of there."

Maya pouted. "But I've put in so much practice. I can even hold my breath for two whole minutes, Nolan. Granted, I can't beat Misako's three-minute record, but it's not bad."

"Holding her breath?" Baron asked. "Sharrock, what are you trying to pull here?"

"No one's holding her breath," Sharrock said, distraught. "Misako here's the only mermaid we have."

"That's cruel," Maya said, fighting back tears. "I know we only have the one tail to share between us, but I'm the one wearing it at the moment, Nolan. *I'm* the mermaid now."

Lord Baron looked to my legs and said, "She's right. We're idiots, this one doesn't even have a tail. And she's wearing clothes. She's not a mermaid, she's just a girl."

"We beat up a girl?" someone asked.

"Hold on," Sharrock said to the growing agitation of the mob. "I can explain this. Maya's … I have no idea what she's … Maya, what are you playing at?"

Just then, Phillis walked into the ring, juggling brands of fire. She was painted orange and had lengths of piping coming out of whatever ghastly and cumbersome thing it was she was wearing. "Sorry, Nolan," she said. "I didn't realise you had company."

"What's this now?" Baron demanded.

"I'm a firecrab," Phillis answered before Sharrock could think to say anything. "You've heard of firecrabs, surely? They're faerie monsters that come onto the beach and steal turtle eggs from their nesting sites. Firecrabs are huge, some of them are the size of cows, and they're on fire. Like, even underwater. Come on, everyone's heard of firecrabs."

"I've heard of firecrabs," someone in the mob said, which made several others nod in agreement. Needless to say, firecrabs were not real, or, if they were, I certainly hadn't heard of them. Phillis was clearly banking on people not wanting to look stupid, which was something of a human trait I had come to understand.

"Stop, stop, stop," Sharrock said, losing control. "You, out of the tank. You, stop juggling those things. You, go with these people and get sacrificed."

"Sacrificed?" Phillis asked, failing to catch one of her brands. It struck the floor and hissed, causing several ruffians to back off. "Nolan, what are you doing? Is this because she asked for a pay rise?"

"Oh come on," Maya said. "You're such a cheapskate. You do know why she wants that pay rise, right?"

"Pay rise?" Sharrock asked. "I ..."

"She's pregnant, Nolan," Maya wailed, throwing water into her eyes when she could not bring the tears naturally. "You got her pregnant and she's terrified to tell you. So she asks for a pay rise and you ... you ... Bwaa!"

Maya descended into a bawling mess and I had to admire the spirit she was putting into her performance.

"Is this true?" Baron demanded. "You play happy families with one of your performers, and when she gets pregnant, you get us to pay you for taking her off your hands? You want us to burn her so we destroy all the evidence, is that it?"

"No, it's not like that."

"Then what *is* it like?"

The ruffians were muttering more loudly by this point, and the pitchforks were still being shaken, but everyone was losing interest in me.

"She's a faerie," Sharrock protested, not knowing what else to say. "She's bewitching you, just as she bewitched these people."

"You're saying she bewitched you?"

"She must have. She …"

"Just because a girl's pretty," someone from the crowd shouted, "doesn't mean she's a witch, you moron. Why is it always the girl's fault when she falls pregnant, eh? Why doesn't the man take any blame?"

"I'm not to blame," Sharrock stammered.

"So she was having an affair," Baron said, "and you found out about it. Makes sense now why you'd want revenge on her."

"It's not like that. She ruined my night, ruined my whole image. Yes, I want revenge on her for making me look bad, but I …"

"Get him!"

The mob lunged for Sharrock, who shrieked and fell to the sandy floor. He raised his hand to ward off the blows, but Lord Baron's people were merciless and within moments they were kicking and punching him with great relish.

I glanced to Maya, who winked from her tank and offered me a thumbs-up. I looked to Phillis, who was busy stamping out the flaming brands, for if one is going to use dangerous equipment, one must be responsible for any damage they might cause. I looked to Sharrock, and even though he had been in the process of sending me off to a horrible death, I knew I could not allow him to die like this.

"That's enough," I said, pulling people off him and hurling them away. With my incredible strength, I had reached Sharrock in moments and grabbed him with my handcuffed hands to drag him from their reach. Standing between Sharrock and the mob, I said, "You're better than this."

"Why are you defending him?" Baron asked. "He was selling you out."

"Because ..." I remembered where I was, and that I had to get into the spirit of the circus and all the drama and fakery which went with it. "Because there was no affair. I made it up to make Nolan jealous. He's the only man I've ever been with, and I won't let you kill the father of my child."

Further murmurs ensued; it seemed the mob was willing to go along with any tosh people fed them.

"I'm sorry," Baron said, taking out the key which Sharrock had clearly given him. He unlocked my manacles and they fell away to the floor. "You're a good woman, Misako. And to think, we would have killed you if your friends here hadn't shown up at just the right ..."

Something else bounded into the arena then: two somethings, actually. My mouth fell agape, my eyes widened, and I was not the only one to suffer such a reaction.

"Misako, the Mysterious Mermaid," Dom said as he rose to his toes and badly danced his way towards us, holding his arms in a crooked position over his head as though he was a ballerina.

"And Maya, the 'Mazing Mermaid," Dom-Dom said, sliding in with one arm projecting forward, the other behind him. Or at least he was attempting to slide, when what he was really doing was making short little shuffles of his feet to make it look as though he was sliding.

"The faerie sideshow," Dom said.

"Where nude is not rude," Dom-Dom finished.

They stopped moving, having come to their final poses. Dom was standing with his back ramrod straight, his arms bent above him and his fingers touching his head. Dom-Dom lay upon the floor beneath him, one elbow resting on the ground, a rose between his teeth. Where he had been keeping the rose, I had no idea, for both of them were completely stark naked.

Once I recovered from my initial shock at their entrance, I reasoned if I was going to die, it wasn't an especially bad sight to go out on.

"Sharrock?" Lord Baron said. He tried to explode, but he was too busy almost having a heart attack to do that. "What …? I mean how …? Why, Sharrock? Why?"

"It's something we've been toying with, Lord Baron," Maya said from her tank. "Faeries don't see nudity as a bad thing, you know. It's how we're all born and, unless babies are obscene, we don't as a species have a valid argument against it."

"And," Dom added, "we're all naked when we bathe."

"For those that do," Dom-Dom added sagely.

"We're toying with doing the whole show like this," Maya said. "You know, each of us dresses up as a different faerie. Misako and I are mermaids, Phillis is a firecrab and these two," she said sourly, "are supposed to be ogres but they forgot the body-paint."

"Ah," Dom said. "We forgot the body-paint."

Nolan Sharrock was speechless, which was certainly the supreme oddity in his whole sideshow of oddities.

"We're leaving," Lord Baron said. I could tell he was not best pleased with anything that had happened in the tent. "And you, Mr Sharrock, have some very strange acts. You should be ashamed of yourself, but I doubt you are."

The mob stormed towards the exit but Sharrock finally found some resolve to reply to that. Perhaps he thought he would be taking some damage to his reputation otherwise. "This is a show of oddities, Lord Mayor, and what are oddities without the eccentric? We have chosen to embrace other cultures, for this show cares nothing for the war. We want people to know that when they come to see Nolan Sharrock's Travelling Oddities perform, they are leaving all their worldly problems behind."

Baron huffed at this and departed with his cronies. My joy almost overwhelmed me, but it was nothing compared with Maya, who was clapping frenziedly as she wept.

"You can knock it off now," Phillis said. "We pulled it off."

Maya sniffed, wiped away her tears, blamed the water and asked if someone could help her down. The water had nothing to do with her tears, although if that was her story, she was welcome to stick to it.

I reached up to take Maya by the hands and she clambered over the side of the tank, slipping on the edge and falling. I caught her, tail and all, and she threw her arms about my throat and hugged me. "I'm sorry, Misako," she said. "I'm sorry for everything."

"I forgive you."

"Great. Now, put me down."

I set her down gently and she shrugged out of the tail. She was wearing tight leggings beneath the tail, much as the trapeze artists wore, and she tossed it aside with glee.

"No offence, Misako, but I have no idea how you put up with that thing. Hey, you two can stop posing now."

Dom and Dom-Dom stopped whatever it was they had been doing. They were both extremely excited and clapped hands with one another.

"I'm sorry," I said, "but I have to ask. Why are they naked?"

"Why were they late, more like," Misako said.

"Sorry," Dom said. "We were rehearsing our script."

"Doesn't matter," Phillis said. "It was all sorted before you got here anyway."

"That's not entirely true," I said, seeing their crestfallen expressions. "I for one was certainly glad to see you two." I moved over to embrace them both. Dom picked me up in his strong hands and tossed me into the air in joy. Dom-Dom encircled us both in a hug and for a moment I couldn't breathe and thought I was going to be crushed to death by two very happy naked strongmen. Pushing them both aside, I extricated myself and at the same time reminded everyone present that I was stronger than both of them put together.

Phillis offered me a nod and said, "I'm not hugging you. I don't do hugs."

"Strangely, I never thought you did." Then I remembered Nolan Sharrock was still with us. I expected him to be furious, what with everything that had happened, but he looked more resigned than anything.

"You saved my life," he said. "Why?"

"You know," I replied, "sooner or later, that's the question everyone seems to ask me. Why? It's like human beings don't know anything, that you want someone to hold your hands through life and show you the way. Or maybe it's because you want to learn." I thought of Braal and the memory brought sadness to my heart, but warmth as well. "I've known people who've wanted to learn. But to ask why I saved your life ... That's not a question anyone should ever have to ask. I saved you because you don't deserve to die, Sharrock. You're an egocentric megalomaniac, and those are your good qualities; but you don't deserve to die."

He looked around at everyone in the tent and I could see him thinking. It was always good when people were thinking. It meant the world had the chance to become a better place. "I was ready to kill you," he said. "I was handing you over to a mob of faerie-hating monsters."

"I know. And I forgive you."

"You shouldn't."

"No. But I do."

Again, he looked around at everyone. Then he said, "Maya, would you be kind enough to gather everyone? I need to make an announcement."

Maya looked uncertain, but I nodded to her and she scurried off to comply.

"Misako," Phillis said, "are you going to be all right if I leave you alone with Mr Sharrock?"

"Sure. Where are you going?"

"I'm going to root out some pants or something for Dom and Dom-Dom. If Mr Sharrock's going to be making an announcement, I'll need to concentrate and they're putting me off."

The three of them departed. I could see no trace of the clowns and supposed they had fled the arena the moment things had turned sour for Sharrock. It meant the two of us were alone, although I was not afraid.

"Misako," he said, more dejected than I had ever seen him, "you have good friends."

"No matter where I go, Mr Sharrock, I always seem to make good friends."

"And enemies."

"Yeah, them too. I had a good friend one time; apparently I keep harping on about her. She was a soldier who thought there could be peace between two sides who had been warring for a thousand years or more. I've known you for just a few months, and that's nothing for a faerie." I extended my hand. "What do you say?"

"You'd shake the hand of the man who ...?"

"Mr Sharrock, just take my hand."

With a small smile, he did just that and we shook emphatically. "You know," he said, some of his roguish smile returning, "purely for the sake of interspecies diplomacy, if you wanted to make that pregnancy story a reality, I'd certainly be ..."

"Too far, too soon."

He laughed and released my hand.

Maya returned with the performers and they quickly filled the tent. There were a lot of people present and I had not realised there were so many who worked for Sharrock. As everyone gathered, I saw curiosity on their faces. There was a lot of talk among them, for no one knew why Sharrock had called everyone together. I was myself intrigued.

Sharrock did not stand upon a platform, for his voice could be heard clear across the tent, and his presence was so tall, all could see him. "Ladies and gentlemen," he said with an ironic smirk. "I don't have much to say, so I'll be brief. An hour ago, I was a jealous, vain, heartless man who wanted nothing more than to see a young woman suffer and die. Now, I'm a jealous, vain man who hopefully is not quite so heartless. There's a war going on outside in the world, but not in here. It's taken someone with a great deal of courage to teach me that. From now on, this circus will be devoted to the peaceful coexistence of all individuals, no matter their species, no matter their differences.

"I treat bearded women and conjoined twins with respect, yet I keep lions and elephants in tight cages. I am kind to the largest and smallest of humans, yet persecute faeries of similar stature. I torment mermaids who can turn their legs human, but," he looked to Maya, "I have ... great fondness for women who turn their human legs to a mermaid's tail."

There were a few whistles at that, a collective "Oooh!" and Maya turned bright red and swore at them all collectively.

"Nolan Sharrock's Travelling Oddities has been around for many years," he continued, "and it's always been a haven for those society has chosen to shun. That will continue, in earnest. We'll seek out any who are different and offer them a place to call home. They may turn us down, but they deserve the chance to be offered."

I thought about the man in the woods; the man whose carrot patch I had weeded and who had fled at the sight of me.

"Nolan Sharrock's Travelling Oddities will have to change its name," he said. "Henceforth, we shall be known as ... Nolan Sharrock's Travelling Wonders. That is, after all, what each of you are." He raised his hat. "Let's show the world just how amazing we can be."

Maya applauded, the sycophantic clowns joined in and within moments the entire arena was roaring with praise. Even Dom and Dom-Dom were hooting with joy, although, bless them, I don't think they fully understood why.

After a minute or so, Sharrock raised his hands for silence and, when he achieved it, said, "We have a lot of work ahead of us, but there's something more we have to do. This young, beautiful woman saved my life, my circus and perhaps my very soul. There are those who claim mermaids can bewitch, and to those people I say they can indeed." There were a few chuckles. Not from me. "So we have to do something for her in return," he said. "Some of you know this, but Misako is searching for her father. He's a knight with two differently coloured eyes and a scar across one. We have a wealth of history to us, and between us we may be able to remember something of him. If not, we'll keep our eyes peeled as we travel. For he's somewhere out there, in the world, and if we keep moving, it's only a matter of time before we find him."

My heart caught in my throat at his words. The performers cheered again and Sharrock got them heading back to work. I was only vaguely aware of them drifting out, for my brain was a roiling mass of excitement and disbelief. Soon enough, only Sharrock, Maya and I remained in the arena.

"Mr Sharrock," I said. "I don't know what to say."

"You can start by calling me Nolan. I only allow one other person to do that, you know."

That reminded me Maya was still there. I turned to thank her for everything she had done, certain I was now on my road to finding my father.

"That's swell, Misako," she said nervously, "but, uh, could I have a quiet word with Nolan?"

"Oh. Oh! Yes, of course. I …" I leaned in close to whisper, "He's not bad, is he?"

"If you left us alone," she whispered back, "I might get to find out."

Knowing a dismissal when I heard one, I departed the arena with a heart filled with song. Life, it seemed, could indeed be happy.

CHAPTER TWENTY

Three months passed, and they were glorious. Dom and Dom-Dom had become my devoted friends, and I trusted them so much I incorporated them into my act in a variety of ways. Phillis found something else to be annoyed about, but then Phillis was always annoyed about something, and the doctor avoided me, which was a bonus indeed. When they realised I was in Nolan Sharrock's good graces, the clowns started to fawn over me, although once I had chased them away a couple of times they stopped doing it. The animals were treated better, were fed more and kept in larger cages, although were also allowed to roam loose for certain periods of the day. It was still cruel to keep them confined, but they no longer hated their lives.

As for Maya and Sharrock, they were quick to develop a relationship and were both happier than I had ever seen them. Sharrock was older than her, of course, but I was told it was a trait of human nobility that young wives were not frowned upon. I was under the impression this was especially true in Torbalia, which brought to mind many fond memories.

We worked hard and travelled far. Sometimes one of the performers brought word of my father, but it always turned out to be false. Everyone was eager to help me, and it seemed the whole world knew I was searching for him. Sometimes we would even arrive at a town and discover folk waiting for us, claiming to have seen my father, claiming to know my father – some even claimed to *be* my father.

Of my father, however, there was never any trace at all.

As our caravan trundled along, moving towards our next venue, I stood upon one of our great waggons, waving to everyone we passed, while clowns walked beside, handing out leaflets. I still could not read them but the pictures imprinted on them were grand. Nolan Sharrock liked for me to stand there waving, and he was completely honest about his reasons. He said that even without my mermaid tail I was a captivating beauty and that people would flock to our show just to see me. I knew he was being kind, and I made sure he said equally pleasing things to Maya.

We were approaching a large settlement, and upon the horizon beyond I could see the ocean, with a large number of ships in port. The place was familiar and in my excitement I recognised it as Mrinth.

Leaping from waggon to waggon (much to the amazement of several passers-by who now simply had to come to the show), I made my way to the cart in the back of which Sharrock and Maya were lazing. They smiled as I dropped into their cart, which meant they had been expecting my arrival.

"That's Mrinth," I said.

"I thought you might like to go back," Sharrock said. "Maya tells me you made a friend there."

"Salla. I wonder whether she's still here."

"How long has it been?"

I thought hard. "I don't know. Half a year? More, maybe."

"We'll see."

We trundled into town with a fanfare, for Sharrock always sent his clowns on ahead to announce our approach. Men, women and children flocked the streets to greet us. They marvelled at the clowns, pointed at the elephant's trunk peering out the window of a waggon, and waved excitedly at me and anyone else they could see. I kept an eye out for Salla, but there was no sign of her anywhere. I did notice several of the town's militia and wondered whether any of them were among those who had chased me through Mrinth before I left. They would not recognise me, although my mermaid's act had become legendary, so it would not be too difficult for them to work out who I was.

We had already been allocated an area in which to set up, and soon enough we had arrived and were pitching our tents and setting up our equipment. It would take several days to get everything ready, for the big top alone was a truly impressive affair and for the sake of safety could not be erected overnight. We all worked hard to get things done, helping one another wherever we could. The elephant and the strongmen were of great help in getting all the heavy equipment moved and, due to my immense strength, I had proved an invaluable asset in that regard. We worked tirelessly for an entire day and, with all the heavy moving finished, I asked Sharrock if I could be excused for a while.

"Of course," he said, "although you need to be careful here. I'd like you to take someone with you."

"I'll be fine," I said.

Dom and Dom-Dom had overheard and stood either side of me. "We'll happily come with you," Dom said. "Maybe we can get some fish from somewhere. We like fish."

"That's very sweet," I said, "but I don't need looking after. I'm a mermaid, remember? I could take you both with one hand."

Maya stifled a giggle. When everyone looked at her, she said, "Like I'm the only one here with a dirty mind?"

"Please don't travel far," Sharrock said. "I know you want to find your friend, but I'm worried about you being here."

"Then why bring me here?"

"I didn't think it through," he admitted. "Maya asked me to do something which would make you happy, so I thought of Mrinth. It wasn't until I saw the militia on our way in that I realised I could have made a mistake."

"Would you people stop worrying about me?" I asked. "I'm a big girl now. I'm not the naïve little thing who wandered naked into this town from the shore. I've grown up, matured. I can take care of myself."

"I know," Sharrock said. "It's just, you don't have to any more. You have us to take care of you, just as you take care of us."

He was being kind, and I knew he worried. He was a far cry from the man who had tried to get me killed for being a hybrid freak, but sometimes he was smothering. Managing to convince everyone I would survive the tough streets of Mrinth, I waved goodbye and headed into the familiar port. The salty sea air was invigorating, the noise and commotion of the place was just as I remembered, and I walked boldly through the marketplace, searching for any vendors I might recall.

I had been away from Mrinth for so long, even the jewellery-stall owner had ceased trading, or perhaps he was simply not working that day.

With a destination in mind, I walked all the way to where Salla lived. Her building with the blue door was distinctive and even though it was midday, I saw several women outside. They could have been working, for they were certainly dressed for the role, although I knew most of their business was conducted at night.

There were no faces I recognised and none of them was Salla.

"Morning," I said to them. "I'm looking for Salla."

"Salla?" one of the girls asked. She was younger than me and I wondered whether I should have been pained to see someone so young engaged in such a profession. She did not look happy at my question. "There's no Salla working here."

"Well, you probably weren't around when I was here. Does anyone know Salla?"

"I know Salla," someone said. I noticed there was indeed a face in the crowd I recognised and my stomach churned as I also remembered her name. Mirna. The one who had given me up to the militia.

"Can I see her?" I asked.

Mirna spat on the ground. "No one sees Salla. She's a faerie lover, you know. Takes faeries to her bed and does wicked things with them." She spat again. "She started with a mermaid, and when the sea cow fled the town, Salla moved onto other despicable things. I caught her with a unicorn. You don't want me to go into the details about that."

The other women were nodding, some were muttering prayers. I could not believe what I was hearing.

"You didn't catch her with a unicorn," I said. "You're lying, about everything."

"Even the mermaid?"

"I ... No, the mermaid was real enough. But Salla never did anything with her. They were friends."

"We make friends by the hour," Mirna replied. "Salla just did what came naturally to her, but she did it with an unnatural beast." She spat again.

"Why do you keep spitting on your doorstep?" I asked.

"I ... That's a good point."

"Where is she? I want to see her."

"Good luck with that."

"Does she still work here?"

"No."

"Is she ... is she alive?"

"If you can call it that."

My fear threatened to overwhelm me, but it was my anger that got the better of me. I stepped forward and stared venomous daggers into Mirna's eyes. "I'll ask one final time. Where is she?"

Mirna cringed, although there was caution to her eyes as well. She recognised me from somewhere but could not quite place where. I wanted to keep it that way, but I also needed to know where Salla was.

"Petal sees her sometimes," Mirna said. "Don't you, Petal?"

"Salla was good to me," the girl younger than me said. "She took me in, taught me the trade. I think she was infatuated with me, kept feeding me strawberries."

"How old are you?"

"Eighteen."

I was surprised, for I had thought her much younger than me. It showed I was getting old, even though I was not yet myself nineteen. I was reminded of how Braal and I had been of the same age, but that I was a young and naïve eighteen-year-old, while Braal had been the old and experienced one.

"Please, Petal," I said, "take me to Salla."

Some of the women jeered at me as Petal led me away, although Mirna said nothing. She narrowed her eyes and rubbed her chin in thought, but did not say a word.

Petal led me through the busy streets with the precision of someone who knew how to dodge unwanted attention. I observed her closely and tried to find some of Salla in her, but they were not similar at all.

"How do you know her?" I asked.

"Salla took me in when I first got to Mrinth. I was young, didn't know anyone. She gave me a place to stay, something to eat. She asked me what I wanted to do with my life, what I was good at." She shrugged. "Nothing and nothing. So I ended up doing what Salla does. It's not pleasant work, but it beats living on the street and having people doing it to you anyway."

"Salla looked after you."

"She did." She looked at me strangely. "You're her, aren't you?"

"Who?"

"Misako."

"What makes you think my name's Misako?"

"Salla was in love with you. Did you know that?"

It hurt to hear the words spoken. "I kind of figured it out afterward."

"You never got a hint when you were with her?"

"I was new to the world, and I was overwhelmed with all the sights and sounds and smells."

"To the world? Then it's true you're a mermaid?"

I shrugged. "Salla didn't care."

"It's you being a mermaid that caused all her troubles."

"I didn't bewitch her, whatever Mirna says."

"You know Mirna?"

"Didn't like her before, like her even less now."

"Yep, you know Mirna."

"Petal, what happened to Salla?"

"It's best I show you. I visit her sometimes, but she thinks I'm you so I don't know why I bother."

"She thinks you're me?"

"You'll find out when you get there."

Our journey took us into the less-populated areas of the town. There were more soldiers around in those parts, but I refused to look away, for that would have made me appear guilty. Petal took me to a circular stone building, a tower of some sort, which had a few small windows set into it on the way up and a single door. Before the door was a guard, who was half-asleep at his post.

"Hey, Derk," Petal said.

"Petal," he said, brightening. "Appreciate the visit, but I'm on duty."

"Oh hush, Derk. I need to see Salla."

"Ah, that kind of visit. Sorry, I thought it was the other kind."

"You can stop talking any time you like, Derk."

He fumbled with his key and was clearly besotted with Petal. Unlocking the door for her, he tried to strike up a conversation, but Petal thanked him with a coy smile and took me into the tower. It was dark within, and cold. We traversed a winding staircase, passing several heavy wooden doors. I did not know where we were or why Salla was there, but eventually we came to a landing and Petal stopped at one door. It had a stout iron lock and a small barred window towards the top.

"You can talk to her through the wicket," Petal said quietly, "but not even Derk's ever given me the key to her cell."

"Why is she in a cell?"

"Talk to her. Hold on, I'll start. Salla? Salla, can you hear me?"

From within the cell, someone grunted; then cackled. I looked through the wicket and the stench of urine and an unwashed body struck me as a blow to the heart. The thought of Salla being in there, surrounded by wild beasts or homeless drunks, filled me with trepidation and remorse.

"Salla?" Petal called sweetly. "I brought a friend."

Within the cell, a shape shuffled. It was dark inside, the only light being from a window which was essentially just a very narrow vertical slit in the stone wall. My eyes were better than most, but even I was having trouble making anything out. As the form moved towards me, however, I recoiled. The stinking mess was like a shambling, louse-ridden dung heap, yet I knew it was Salla. Her hair had lost any shine and beauty, for it was a frizzy mass which had been neither combed nor cut for a long time. Her skin was pallid, her body gaunt from lack of food and water. Her eyes were wide and staring, bloodshot as though she never slept, while her lips, always ready with a cheeky smile, were a single line, a bare crack in her face.

"Salla?" I asked. "It's me, Misako. What have they done to you?"

"Misako?"

"Yes, yes, Misako."

Salla reached the door and Petal hissed for me to be careful, but I ignored her. Salla looked at me through the wicket and there was nothing in her eyes. There was no confusion, no despair, but there was also no love or passion. She was like a walking corpse.

"Salla," I said, fighting back tears. "It's going to be all right. I'll get you out of here. I'll look after you."

"Misako ..." She laughed, cackling toothlessly as she danced about her cell before finally collapsing into the corner, sobbing.

Blinking back my tears, I rounded upon Petal. "What happened? What's she doing here, why doesn't she have any teeth?"

"Her teeth started falling out when she stopped caring for herself. They removed the rest because she kept biting her wrists."

"Who's they?" I was about ready to kill someone and was not hiding it well.

"You shouldn't get so angry," Petal said with narrowed eyes. "It's your fault she's here."

That shocked a lot of the aggression from me. I looked back to where Salla was harmlessly rocking on the floor of her cell, arms hugging her knees while she sang about strawberries.

"Please," I pleaded with Petal, "tell me everything."

Petal inhaled deeply and some of her own anger dissipated. "It began a month or so after Salla took me in. She was good to me, she loved me. Or at least she said she did. In reality, she loved you, but you'd rejected her."

"I was innocent. I didn't realise she loved me."

"Whatever. Anyway, Mirna started making trouble for her. She'd spread a lot of rumours about the two of you. The constabulary were satisfied that you had Salla under a spell or something and they'd left her alone, and Mirna didn't like that. I don't like Mirna. Salla always defended her, said there was something wrong with her mentally and that her maliciousness wasn't her fault. But then that's Salla for you, always ready to see the good in people.

"Things were strained for a while. Salla didn't do anything about the rumours, but the more people heard them, the more people talked. Every few days, Mirna would come up with something new. I think she'd convinced herself they were all true, as well."

"The unicorn," I said.

"Yeah, the unicorn was the oddest one. Salla laughed about it, but I told her it wasn't funny. She said unicorns didn't exist, so why would people believe Mirna?"

"They exist," I said. "You'll never see one. They're like faerie gods, although we don't have any gods."

"You're not helping."

"Sorry. Go on."

"Salla began losing trade. No one wanted to go with a woman who cavorted with faeries, they didn't know what they were going to catch. Most of her regular work dried up, and since her regulars were in the militia, that meant rumours were circulating through their ranks as well. It wasn't long before they came for her. I'll never forget it. They sent a dozen men to bring her in and Salla just looked at them and said, 'I haven't had any trade from you guys for weeks and you all turn up at once? Looks like I can start paying my back-rent.' She was always laughing, always happy, although she knew why they'd come.

"I didn't see her for a month, they didn't allow anyone near her. They took her off for treatments. She had been declared unclean, said she needed curing. I don't know what they did, but there are marks all over her arms, so she must have been injected with something, over and over. From talking with her, it's difficult to be sure, but I think they forced her to drink and eat things they thought could cure her. Garlic, wild roses, small quantities of hemlock and wolfsbane. And they shoot lightning through her. I can't quite figure that one out, but apparently they have a method to do that."

"But why?"

"Because they think she's tainted. They think she has sexual relations with faeries and it's made her indecent."

"So they dragged her away and drove her mad?"

"Pretty much."

"There's nothing wrong with her, there's nothing that needs curing."

"I know. But people hate faeries, that's never going to change. Our people are at war with yours, Misako. They're afraid, afraid you're turning our women against us. Everyone knows the rumours about faeries stealing babies and replacing them with changelings, everyone knows the faeries are a dying species and are looking to replenish their forces with human-born children."

"Is that what people think?" I asked, aghast.

"Look at you," she said snidely. "You have a foot in each world."

I trembled at what she was telling me and moved back to the wicket. She was right. I was to blame for everything that had happened to Salla. I had caused her misery. If I had never walked into Mrinth, she would have been leading a happy life.

"Is there any hope for her?" I asked Petal.

"No. She won't relinquish you, that's her main problem. She loves you, keeps talking about the wonderful vision she met one day, the most beautiful creature in the world who took her from her misery and made her happy for just a short while."

"That's the madness, surely?"

Petal fixed me with a steely glare. "She's been infatuated with you ever since the two of you met. Even when she took me in, she used to talk about you with such a smile to her eyes that I knew I could never put there. Do you know what it's like to make love to a woman who closes her eyes and pretends you're someone else?"

"No," I whispered.

Petal did not say anything and I could tell she was not only angry, but grieving.

"You love her," I said. "Don't you?"

"Yes. She doesn't love me, I know that. She loves you and just pretended I *was* you. But that doesn't matter, because I'm all she has. I may be sloppy seconds, but in her current state she doesn't realise I'm not you. I can never be with her, can never kiss her or even touch her, but I can talk with her. So that's what I do. As often as I can. Because the real Misako abandoned her and I've taken her place. Like a reverse-changeling."

"I'll break her out," I said. "The lock and bars are iron, but if I do it quickly enough, I can …"

"No. Don't you see, there's nothing you can do for her. You've done enough, Misako. She needs care, she needs love and constant support. I've convinced them to stop the treatments. For the last few days, I've been using a simple, non-intrusive means of saving her. I don't know whether it will work, but the peaceful approach is the only thing that can save her."

It broke my heart to leave Salla in the cell, but Petal was right. "Salla," I said softly through the bars. "Salla, I'm sorry. I'm sorry I did this to you."

"Misako?"

She rose, her eyes curious, a shadow of cognisance returning as she shuffled towards me.

"Salla?"

"Misako, is that really you?"
"Yes, Salla. I came back for you."
"That's nice. You're not wearing your pearl."
"No. I ... it's at home."
"Home. Must be nice to have a home."

She tried to smile, but the effort cost her dearly and her eyes hazed over again. She returned to wandering the cell, chatting to herself. Then she began to wail.

"You're upsetting her," Petal said. "I think you should leave."

The thought that I could ever upset Salla was repugnant to me, yet Petal was right. I had done enough damage.

We returned to the street and Petal dropped back into her playful persona to thank the guard at the door for his time. He made some comment about coming to see her later and she said she would look forward to it.

"Petal," I said while we walked away from the tower, "you're not afraid that's going to happen to you one day?"

"If Mirna starts any rumours that my love for Salla has infected me, it probably will. You turning up again isn't going to help me any."

"And who will you have if you end up in there as well?"

"No one. But I'm not abandoning Salla." She stopped and I could see there was finality in her eyes. "I'm not abandoning her when she needs me the most. I may be Misako, but I'm not you. Now, please don't come back. I have to get ready for work."

She walked off, leaving me alone and miserable.

I started back for the circus, knowing Sharrock had been right and that I never should have gone anywhere in Mrinth. My thoughts turned briefly to Mallok, to what might have befallen him on the trawler after I dived into the sea. I wasn't sure I wanted to know – I didn't think I could have lived with myself if I had destroyed the lives of Salla, Braal *and* Mallok.

I had not gone far when a woman stepped out before me, with soldiers pouring onto the street to surround us both. She was wearing the armoured uniform of the local militia and I recognised her at once.

"You got away from me last time," she said, "but now you're going to pay for everything you've done."

"And what *have* I done?" I spat. "I haven't done anything. I spent a day in Mrinth, a glorious, wonderful day with a good woman. We ate strawberries, we shopped down the market, we laughed and we joked and for a single day we forgot this stupid war existed. If those are crimes, kill me. But I've done nothing wrong."

"Oh, don't worry," the woman said. "You'll be killed eventually. But first there has to be a trial. Then, once every man, woman and child has had their piece of you, you're going to hang."

She motioned for her soldiers to close in. There were only twenty of them and I knew it would be an even fight; but I had no desire to resist. Salla's life had been destroyed because of me and if this was human justice, I was in no position to deny them anything. If I fought back, I would likely only destroy other lives, kill more people I cared about.

I closed my eyes and allowed them to come at me with their clubs and blades.

"Misako!"

I opened my eyes. The soldiers had yet to reach me, for they had problems of their own. Barrelling through them were two mighty man-mountains, while behind them danced an annoyed woman wielding flaming batons which kept the soldiers back. I stared, stupefied, mute.

"Misako, come on," Maya said as she grabbed me by the arm and pulled. I did not move. "Misako!"

"Leave me," I said. "I don't deserve to be rescued."

"Leave you? Nolan didn't like the thought of you out here alone, so he sent us to watch over you. Good job we did, now come on."

"She's up in that tower, Maya. Insane, tormented, tortured. All because of me. I ruined her life. It would have been more merciful to have killed her."

"Salla?"

I nodded.

"You can explain it all back at the tent, but I'm sure it's not your fault."

"How can you be sure?"

"Because when you left her, she was happy. Anything these people did to her after that was because they're the monsters, not you. Now, I'm not saying this again. Come on."

It was not the first time someone had told me I was not a monster, nor was it the first time a human had said other humans were more monstrous than I. It was, however, the first time I perhaps believed it.

Uncertain of anything, I knew only that if I did not leave, Phillis, Dom, Dom-Dom and Maya were going to be battered, beaten and arrested. For that reason and that reason alone, I fled the street with my friends. Beyond that, I had no thoughts at all.

CHAPTER TWENTY-ONE

"Well, it's certainly a mess," Sharrock said back at the tent. He was pacing, which was never a good sign, and he was holding his hands to his moustache, almost covering his mouth while he thought, which was also never a good sign with him. He had a problem and did not know the best way out of it. I knew the best way, but he was refusing to entertain that possibility.

"We need to leave," Maya said. "We need to leave right now."

"Let's not be hasty," Sharrock said. "To get all the equipment packed up will take time, and they'll cotton on to what we're doing."

"Then we leave it behind," Phillis said. We had all of us gathered in one of the smaller tents, with Dom and Dom-Dom watching the entrance for us.

"Leave everything?" Sharrock asked. "But this is our livelihood we're talking about."

"And it's Misako's life," Phillis replied coldly.

"Nolan's right," Maya said. "We can't abandon everything."

"No," I said, "you're not going to. I'll give myself up. They won't care that the rest of you assaulted their soldiers. I'll say I had you under my spell and they'll settle for you leaving Mrinth forever. It's me they want. If they can get me peacefully, they'll be more than happy."

"Out of the question," Sharrock said. "And that's the end of that particularly stupid discussion."

Maya gave my hand a squeeze where we sat together and offered me an encouraging smile. It was nice Sharrock now had my back on things and I put most of it down to his relationship with Maya. However, sentiment would get them all killed. "That's swell of you, Mr Sharrock, but you have to think of the rest of the family. I'm not going to be the one who brings the house down."

"The show must go on?" he asked. "Misako, you truly are getting into the spirit of the circus."

"This isn't funny."

"And I'm not laughing. Misako, do you recall that announcement I made before the whole arena that time?"

"Of course I do."

"That wasn't a show, I meant every word. This circus is a haven for the downtrodden and abused. We celebrate differences and we don't give a damn about the war. I'm not going to surrender those beliefs just because some jobsworth soldier wants to arrest you for a vague collection of crimes you supposedly committed months ago." He paused. "Did you actually commit any crimes? If you did, we probably should know about them."

"I stole a homeless man's jacket," I said. "I didn't mean to, but Salla threw it out the window so I didn't get to give it back."

"I don't think that particular offence is punishable by public flogging and execution."

"This isn't about *you* any more, Misako," Maya said. "If we backed down from this, we'd be telling the world Nolan Sharrock's Travelling Wonders is just a stage name for a bunch of cowards who turn on their own when things get bad."

"That, too," Sharrock said. "I reacted badly last time you sullied my reputation, Misako, so I wouldn't advise doing it again."

My argument was done, for none of them were backing down. I could breathe a little more easily by that point, although my heart was still pounding. "So, what do we do? If they come for us with their whole army, everyone here's going to be beaten up and I'll still be taken."

"They have a town militia," Sharrock said, "not an army. And we have an elephant and a lion, don't forget. A well-fed, strong lion who really knows how to roar."

It was funny how the powerful roar of the lion now drew in far more of an audience than the underfed creature had when all it did was jump through hoops.

"We'll have a little time to prepare," Maya said. "That captain will have returned to her garrison and will be drumming up support, but her superiors are going to be wary about a full-scale attack on a circus. For one thing, they don't know our capabilities; but it would also look bad for their image. If other travelling entertainers stopped coming to Mrinth, the town would lose a lot of revenue. This will have to be taken up by whoever's in charge of the military here, and then a report will be made to the mayor. A committee will be consulted, arguments and counterproposals will be tossed around, there will be important business lunches conducted. It'll be a while before we have to worry about ..."

"Boss," Dom said from the tent flap, "we have a problem."

Sharrock departed the tent and the rest of us followed. Dotted around the field were all our other tents, along with the big top and any equipment which had been left out in the sun. Performers milled around, uncertain as to what was happening, as a great armed force a hundred soldiers strong marched directly across to us. At their head was the captain who had tried to arrest me back at the tower, and she looked as smug as a well-fed shark.

She stopped around twenty paces from us and her soldiers stopped with her. "Captain Teth of the Torbalian militia stationed at Mrinth," she said in a voice loud enough for us all to hear. "Nolan Sharrock, you have in your possession a faerie soldier in the army of our enemy. I am under the belief you are keeping the creature as a curiosity, if I have the right word. An oddity. A thing which dances for our amusement."

I looked to Sharrock fearfully, but he stepped in front of me. "Good day, Captain Teth. Might I say, the sun favours you in this light and certainly brings out the shine of your eyes."

"The mermaid, Sharrock," she replied through gritted teeth.

He thought a moment. "No. No, I don't believe we have anything matching the description you gave, Captain." He raised his hat and turned from her. "Good day."

"The mermaid," she replied sternly. "Now."

"No," he said, whirling to face her. It had been a while since I had seen him angry and the sight shocked even me. "No, Captain, you don't come into this field besmirching my performers and using bully tactics to get what you want. You asked me for a thing, a curiosity, an oddity. I have no things here, Captain, I have people and I have animals."

"An animal, then," she said, losing her patience at last.

"A step up from a thing, but the only animals we have are an elephant and a lion."

Teth rolled her eyes. "Misako, the Murderous Mutant Mermaid, or whatever you call her." She pointed directly at me and my knees would have given out had not Maya, beside me, clasped my hand in hers and squeezed. "That creature right there," Teth continued. "I'm taking her, Sharrock. Stand aside."

"No."

"No? This is a direct order from the supreme commander of Mrinth's militia. You can't say no."

"I want documents, paperwork. I want the supreme commander standing here before me. Until the supreme commander is here, right before me, I'll not hand over anyone."

"And if I could get the supreme commander?"

"Then you'd have to make an appointment, because I'm a very busy man." He made a show of looking around. "I don't see the supreme commander, so unless ..."

"I *am* the supreme commander," she interrupted. "Here in Mrinth we take matters of our species' survival very seriously. Harbouring a faerie is a war crime, Sharrock. Hand over the mermaid or I'll arrest you, and anyone who attempts to stop me." Her eyes narrowed. "And you'll all hang."

Some of the performers shifted dubiously on their feet, the clowns looked as though they were about ready to bolt for the hills. Some of my friends clenched their fists, although I could see not even Dom and Dom-Dom were willing to make a move. Everyone looked to Nolan Sharrock for their orders.

"Oh dear," he said with an exaggerated sigh. "It looks as though you have an argument to counter everything I put forward, Captain. You leave me with no choice."

Captain Teth raised an arm and her soldiers produced clubs and staffs. It seemed they did not intend to slaughter us, probably because of the bad image Maya had spoken of.

"No choice at all," Sharrock said sadly. "Sorry, Misako, you're going to have to go."

Maya gasped so hard she almost crushed my fingers. Phillis looked more annoyed than I had ever seen her and Dom began to cheer, until Dom-Dom nudged him with an angry shake of his head. Even the clowns looked sad, for I had grown to like them over our time together.

"You're handing her over?" Teth asked with a frown.

"Of course I'm handing her over. What, you think I want the rest of us beaten with clubs? No, if this is the only way, you can have her."

Teth took a step forward.

"However," Sharrock said, "my contract has her down as an employee. I pay her a wage, you see. I stopped treating her as a thing a long time ago. If she's going to break her contract and leave the circus early, I'll need compensation."

"The town will pay it," Teth said sourly.

"And I'll need her signature to say she's agreed to it."

"Then fetch the paperwork."

"Ah, but Misako can't read. In the spirit of keeping everything above-board, I'd like the chance to teach her how to read her contract, so she can fully understand what she's ..."

"Nolan Sharrock," Teth said icily, "you are to hand over that mermaid immediately, or my soldiers will take her by force."

"Really?" He looked them over, his action exaggerated. "But you only brought a hundred soldiers."

"I know a thing or two about faeries, Sharrock. They have the strength of twenty people. I think a hundred soldiers can handle her."

"I'm sure they could," he said, uncoiling his whip. "But first they're going to have to get through me."

"You?" Teth asked with a smirk.

"I'll have you know, my ego is the size of that big top over there. Just clambering over it will take you all afternoon."

The smell of burning wood wafted past me then and Phillis was beside him, holding a quarterstaff she had set alight at both ends. She twirled it before her like a fiery halo on its side.

"Oh yes," Sharrock said, "I also have a woman who's trained with fire her entire life. She even eats it, you know. And I have Maya. She doesn't have a particularly valuable skill set for this fight, but I love her just the same."

Maya smiled cutely at him and offered a little wave.

"And us," Dom said. "Mr Sharrock, do we have to take off our clothes again and do that little pose?"

"Uh, no."

"Enough," Teth snapped. "You people are insane. That's a monster right there among you and you're willing to hang for her?"

"The only monster I see," Sharrock replied, "is bigotry. It doesn't have a physical form but infects everyone on all sides like a plague. I'm warning you to leave, Captain."

"And I'm done warning you, Sharrock. Take them."

The soldiers charged, but several tripped and one hopped around as a tiny clown clung to his leg. I had not seen the tripwire the clowns had laid out, but at least a dozen of the soldiers were floundering upon the floor as the clowns descended upon them with foam mallets. What good they thought foam mallets would do against armoured soldiers, I had no idea, but the attack would certainly have put the fear of the gods in me if I was one of those soldiers.

The trapeze artists leaped into the air, curled themselves into balls, caught one another's hands and flew horizontally into a row of soldiers, knocking them down also. Soldiers behind them grabbed the artists, but they were nimble and danced away.

A roar filled the clearing, accompanied by a tremendous bellow, and Teth shouted to her soldiers as the lion and elephant ran at them. The lion's teeth were back to being sharp, his coat was shiny, and even the elephant's tusks had regrown, for he had stopped filing them down. The lion clamped his jaws upon a soldier's arm and tried to worry his way through the woman's armour, while the elephant tossed soldiers right and left with his powerful trunk.

Teth was shouting for her soldiers to re-form and they concentrated their efforts in a more controlled manner. Three soldiers wrestled with the lion and I watched one of the clowns disappear beneath the clubs of our enemies.

Within minutes of the fight being sparked, it was already becoming a blood bath.

"Mr Sharrock," I said, running over to where he was keeping the soldiers at a distance with his whip. "Mr Sharrock, you have to stop this."

"Don't be ridiculous, Misako. Hya!" His whip slashed out, catching a soldier across the cheek and opening up a nasty wound. She fell back but two more moved in to take her place.

"Mr Sharrock, people are going to die."

"You're going to die otherwise. Just keep fighting. If we can bloody their noses enough, they'll retreat. By the time they come back, news will have got out about this and public opinion will be so much against the soldiers we won't have to do anything to save you. Look, the crowds are already forming."

He was right, for there were a lot of people gathering about the edge of the field. Ordinary people, people who were frightened by what was happening. People who did not understand what we were fighting for.

Three soldiers were suddenly before me and I jumped back to evade their clubs. They swung again and I raised an arm. The heavy wood slammed into my shoulder but I ignored the pain and grabbed the club from the soldier's hand, tossing it aside. The other two came at me and I punched out, smashing the nose of the first, before grabbing the second by her shirt and hoisting her through the air. I tossed her clear across the field and saw her crash into a water trough, making the crowd cheer.

To them, it was not a fight, but entertainment.

That was how the war was seen by some, and it sickened me.

"Misako, move," Phillis said and her fire almost singed my hair. She thrust it into the general vicinity of a soldier who was trying to knife me from behind. The woman dropped her blade and fell back, screaming. "Misako, you need to be more careful."

"Phillis, we have to stop this."

"Misako, down!"

I ducked, throwing my hands over my head as Phillis spun her flaming quarterstaff. Another trio of soldiers fell back, wary of her weapon, and she ran at them, laughing hysterically.

All around me, people were fighting. Soldiers were shouting, animals were roaring and performers were doing their best to stay alive. I saw the dog man on the ground, trying to protect his face from two soldiers who were beating him, while one of the conjoined twins appeared to be unconscious. Dom was hurling soldiers in every direction, while Dom-Dom had a terrible gash to his forehead which was oozing blood into his eye.

All around me, people were suffering, and it was all because of me.

"Misako, move," Maya said, almost barrelling into me. "Don't just stand there, you have to keep moving."

"Maya, our people are being killed."

"Nah, the militia isn't stupid enough to kill anyone. It's why they brought clubs. Nolan says we just have to hold out a while."

I looked to the jeering crowd. Some were horrified, were hurrying their children from the scene, while others bayed for blood. I watched as Nolan Sharrock spun his whip about his head, keeping all the soldiers at a distance. They were trying to time their movements, but every time they darted towards him, he would snap his whip and keep them back, for he was an expert with the thing. Sooner or later, though, one of them would get through.

"Misako, snap out of it," Maya said.

I heard a cry from behind and saw Phillis lose control of her staff. It dropped to the ground and a soldier stamped on the flames, setting his trousers on fire in the process. Phillis flailed with her fists, but soldiers poured atop her and she disappeared.

"I have to go help her," Maya said. "Misako, keep your head in the game."

I watched Maya run to Phillis, screaming as loudly as she could in order to cause confusion. Two of the soldiers were startled enough for Phillis to momentarily clamber out from among them, but the others faced Maya with their clubs and I knew she would not stand a chance against them.

All about me, my friends were being beaten to death. It was happening again. I had caused pain to the people I cared about. I had once more become the downfall of everything I cared about.

Never again.

I reached the decision without even being aware of it. Balling my fists and drawing on an unknown power deep within me, I ran for Maya. She was already down on one knee and a solider stood above her, club raised. With an inhuman cry, I lowered my shoulder and slammed into him, sending him staggering into one of his fellows. I could see no sign of Phillis, yet as I tore into the soldiers around me, I knew she had to be somewhere.

"Misako," Maya said as she got back to her feet. Her sleeve was torn and there was blood down her arm. There was a nasty purple bruise forming on her forehead, but she did not seem to notice. "Come on, we can do this."

"No," I said. "I'm sorry, Maya, but I can't. I appreciate everything you've done for me, everything you're prepared to do for me. I'm sorry faeries killed your family and, for what it's worth, I forgive everything you did to me when you took me in."

"Misako, what are you saying?"

"I have to go."

"Go? You're worrying me."

"Tell Nolan … I don't know. Just tell him something. Make it up, it'll sound better coming from you anyway."

"Misako," she said, grabbing my arm as I started to run. "Where are you going?"

"Away," I said, my eyes moist, the word catching in my throat. "If returning to Mrinth has taught me one thing, it's that everyone's lives would have been far better if they'd never met me."

"Misako ..."

I shook off her hand and backed away. "I'm sorry, Maya. Goodbye." I turned and fled without hearing what it was she shouted after me. There were soldiers ahead and I crossed my arms before me to crash through them. I heard cries of other soldiers to stop me, to knock me down, and my fists flew indiscriminately. Then I saw the person I was after. Captain Teth stood not ten paces away.

"Mermaid," she hissed.

"You want me, Teth, come get me."

I ran. I did not run towards her, but followed my nose and ran towards the fresh, clean scent in the air. Teth shouted commands to her soldiers and they broke away from attacking the performers. I could hear Sharrock shouting at me, but blocked him out because I didn't want to hear his words, either. If I stopped to listen to anyone, I would likely lose my resolve, and that was all I had left.

Running from the plain, I saw the townsfolk make a frightened path for me, for they did not know the power of a mermaid and did not want to find out. I ran through the streets, crossed the marketplace and leaped a fruit stall which sold orange fruits called apricots. I passed a familiar building with a blue door and saw Mirna waving a fist at me and shouting uncouth and racist words. I did not stop for any of it, for as I rounded the next corner, I found what I had been searching for.

The harbour was ahead, as was the pier beneath which I had hidden, naked, so long ago. I slowed to a fast walk and crossed the pier to stand upon its end. The ocean was before me, the call of gulls music in the air, the crash of the waves the warm beckoning of tidal hands welcoming me home. But I was not ready to leap into the water and instead stood upon the end of that pier, soaking up everything of the life I had left behind so long ago. There I awaited the arrival of Captain Teth.

I did not wait long.

"Misako," she said. Turning my back on the ocean, I saw the captain tentatively stepping onto the pier, a strung bow in her hand, an arrow already nocked. Behind her, the militia held back. They had all left the circus, which meant my friends, my family, were safe.

"Captain Teth," I said. I was not calm and wondered whether I appeared to be at all. "Why can't people just live in peace?"

"Because we're at war," she replied easily. "Because between faeries and humans there can never be peace." She raised her bow and pointed the arrow at my heart.

"I'm not a soldier."

"You're not a soldier yet you can single-handedly take down a regiment of my troops. Imagine, then, what your actual soldiers can do."

"I don't have any soldiers."

"You know what I mean. You're a faerie, Misako. Personally, I don't dislike people for what they are, but I can't allow a faerie to run around Mrinth. I'm a soldier; I don't have the luxury of doing what I want, only what's best for the people."

"What's best for the people is peace."

At this, she laughed bitterly. "You're an idealist, Misako. Stand down or I'll kill you. I'd prefer to take you in, but since you're going to hang anyway, it doesn't much matter either way."

A commotion sounded amongst the soldiers and I could see some of them pushing the crowd back. People were gathering behind them, others were stretching out across the beach. I could see faces appear in the windows of the buildings over the docks and there were even curious people on the boats.

"I don't mean you any harm," I said. "All I want is to live."

"And all we want is for you to die."

"I'm not just a faerie," I said, my emotions churning within me. "My father is human, my mother was a mermaid. I'm just as much human as I am faerie."

"Then you're damned in both worlds."

Above me, the clouds gathered. As close to water as I was, I was able to draw it into a storm, but I was reluctant to do so. There would not have been any point.

"This arrowhead is forged of iron," Teth warned. "I can kill you with one shot."

"Then do it," I said, the thunder rumbling, but the only rain came from my eyes. "If I can't live anywhere, Captain, kill me and be done with it."

Teth drew back her arm and concentrated. I tensed, waiting for her to fire, but she did not.

"What are you waiting for?" I asked.

"I don't know."

"You know this war is wrong, Captain. You know we can't hate each other just because of how we're born. I never chose to be what I am. I was created because of the love between a faerie and a human. I was created by both species, yet I belong to neither. It's nature's cruel joke. I could be used as a template for how we should be, for how we can peacefully coexist; but all anyone of either side wants to do is kill me."

"I don't want to kill you."

"Then don't."

"So long as we're at war, I don't have a choice."

"Then lay down arms and end the war. If everyone on both sides laid down their arms, there wouldn't even be a war. Please, Teth, I'm begging you. It can start with one person. Then there'll be another, and another. If we all work together, we can …"

She released the bowstring and the arrow thunked into my shoulder.

I jolted in shock, my shoulder went instantly numb and I tasted blood in my mouth. Looking at my shoulder, I could see the wound already blistering, festering, with blood coursing down my arm to fall as crimson rain upon the wooden pier. My shirt was stained red and I felt blood pooling in my mouth, falling from my lips. I looked up at Captain Teth, who lowered her bow. There was pain to her eyes, but also the stern belief that she had done what was right, what was necessary.

Then the pain hit me, tore through my body, as the iron went to work. I took a step back and my foot slipped from the pier. An instant later, I was tumbling. The world spun about me, my mind became an agonising haze, and I hit the water, plunging into the depths, swallowed by the ocean which had been my home for so many years of my life.

I did not close my eyes, for I wanted to see death coming for me. As I lay just beneath the surface of the water, I could see the vague shapes of everyone above me, gathering on the edge of the pier. Some would be cheering, others may have been angry. All would be relieved that the faerie among them was no more.

My legs changed, became the mermaid's tail with which I had been born. In my final moments of life, I was returning to my natural state, and I was glad I would die in that form.

As consciousness drifted from me, I decided none of it mattered. I had tried to live in the human world and I had failed. Nor could I return to the water. I saw my mother, her smile just as I remembered; and I saw my father, with his unique eyes and his scar. They called to me, like a mermaid enticing a lover, and I felt light. The pain disappeared and I allowed myself to go.

There was nothing left for me in either world but memories.

CHAPTER TWENTY-TWO

The sun's rays warmed my body and the gentle rocking of the waves provided a steady, pleasurable rhythm which soothed my mind. There was a dull ache in my shoulder, but otherwise I felt calm, at peace, at one with both worlds.

I opened my eyes to stare into the bright blue sky. The clouds were white, the gulls were noisy and there was a salty tang to the air which made me homesick.

Looking around, I saw I was lying in a wooden rowing-boat. It was a small thing, barely large enough to contain two people. At the oars, rowing steadily, was a woman my own age, wearing a blue uniform. Her blue eyes shone with radiance, her long red hair was combed to perfection and her smile was the sweetest thing I had ever known.

"You're awake," she said. "I was beginning to think you were going to sleep all day."

"Braal?" I asked. "But I killed you."

"Funny, I don't remember it that way."

I sat up, joy coursing through my veins. Then I realised I couldn't be in a rowing-boat with Braal on the open sea. Braal was dead. Then I recalled the iron-tipped arrow and knew I was dead as well.

I felt at my shoulder. My wound had been tended to, for there was a bandage wrapped expertly in place.

"I've had a lot of experience removing arrows from people," Braal said as she rowed.

"Am I dead?"

"Do you want to be?"

"Yes."

"Charming."

"What do you mean?"

"I go to all the trouble of saving your life and you want to be dead."

I sat watching her for some time. She continued rowing without saying a word. There was so much I wanted to say, so much I wanted to tell her, so much I wanted to share. But there was only one thing which really mattered.

"I'm sorry," I said. "For everything."

"I'm told you say that a lot."

"Maybe I'm just a sorry person."

"I have a few other words for you."

"Any of them pleasant?" I asked with a wince.

Braal stopped rowing. "Misako, you really don't get it, do you? You bring so much joy into this world, so much love into people's lives, and all you ever see are your faults. The world doesn't accept you? Screw the world. You need to accept yourself, you need to believe in yourself, and you need to look to the people that matter and forget about everyone else."

"I ruin people's lives, Braal."

"You make people's lives worth living, Misako. You're like everyone's last meal before execution, everyone's third wish from a magic lamp. You're the reason we might one day find peace."

"I thought that was you."

"It can be both of us."

I did not like to tell her she was wrong, especially since I'd killed her once already.

"I saw my parents," I said. "Under the water. I guess I'm still there."

"Misako, you're not dead."

"Of course I'm dead."

Leaning over, Braal poked me in the shoulder. Pain exploded through me and I released a string of curses at her.

"Someone's been listening to soldiers too much," she said, sitting back down.

"Gods, that hurt." The pain was subsiding, and with it came a realisation. "Hold on a minute, if I'm not dead, that means … it means you're …"

"Alive, yeah."

Squealing with delight, I threw myself at her with such force I almost capsized the boat. She was warm and soft and smelled of roses, but some of that could have been in my imagination since I was a tad delirious. As she pulled away, she took up the oars again, although her face was filled with delight.

"Was wondering when you'd get around to that," she said.

"But what happened?"

"I pulled you out of the water, removed the arrow (I have experience in saving faeries from blood-poisoning) and …"

"No, I mean with you. You were being attacked."

"There were only a dozen of them. I'm a battalion knight provisional, we're not just ego and bluster. Clippety found his way home, by the way, but without you."

"Oh no, I punched your horse."

"Really? That wasn't a nice thing to do."

"I … How did you find me?"

"After I fought those guys at the woods, I went looking for you, but I couldn't find you anywhere. When Clippety came back, I tried to get him to take me to you, but he was a little skittish about that. I suppose because someone punched him in the face. Anyway, I had to return to Torbalia to make my report about the battle, which was where we were headed before we got separated. I was hoping you'd reach the city by yourself, but you never came."

"I was in a lake, moping."

"I know."

"You know?"

"After reaching Torbalia, it was one thing after another. I asked my high commander for special leave to go find you, but he needed me around for a while. When I finally got permission to go, I searched everywhere. Then I began hearing about Misako, the Mysterious Mermaid, so I followed the circus all the way to Mrinth."

"You were at Mrinth?"

"I couldn't reach you in time. I saw Captain Teth shoot you, but I was too far away to do anything. So I hijacked a rowing-boat and came out after you."

"How long have we been at sea?"

"A couple of days."

"You must be dehydrated."

"I have my water flask and a few provisions on my belt, but yeah, it's been tough. And I smell ripe."

"You smell of roses."

"Aaand you're back to being creepy. It's like we're meeting for the first time all over again."

I smiled, despite the situation. "Where are we going?"

"To Mrinth."

"Mrinth? But Captain Teth …"

"Is waiting for us."

My joy faded. "You're handing me over to her. I … No. You wouldn't do that, which means you have a plan."

"Not really," she said. "Not a plan, as such."

"What, then?"

"You'll see."

The shore was in sight, but we still had an hour or so before we reached it. I told Braal everything I had done since we had parted company and she recounted a little of her own life. It was strange, being back with Braal, but also comforting. It had been so long since we had seen one another, it was like an old friend dropping in. But it was not the same as it had been. She was pretty much the old Braal, but I had changed, I could feel as much within me. I was not the innocent girl I had been when I had stripped before her and excitedly waded into the pool, thinking she was a mermaid. I had matured to such a degree that I could not imagine doing something like that now.

Perhaps I had become a little more human.

We arrived at the shore to find some soldiers waiting for us. There were not many civilians, although there were certainly a few looking on curiously. Captain Teth stood at the head of the soldiers. She looked grumpy and frustrated, and I could not help but notice one of her eyes was swollen shut and black.

Braal moored the boat and we climbed onto the shore. The soldiers were tense in my presence and I could not say I was pleased to see them, either.

"Captain Teth," Braal said jovially. "So good to see you. Any more of my friends you want to shoot, or do you like seeing out of that other eye of yours?"

"I respectfully request you hand over the prisoner, ma'am."

"I don't have any prisoners, Captain. I have a friend. Misako, Captain Teth has something she'd like to say to you."

"No," Teth said, "I don't."

"I think you do."

Teth bit her lip and I could see the hatred blazing in her one good eye.

"Wait," I said. "If Braal's making you apologise, I don't need to hear it. We each do what we do because it's what we feel is right. It's just in your case, Captain, you were wrong. Instead of apologising, reflect on it and learn from your mistake."

"We're at war," she said simply.

"I'm not."

Braal took me past Captain Teth and I was amazed at how much authority Braal's rank carried. I was still not entirely certain what the Torbalian battalions were, but if their knights provisional could order around militia captains, I could only imagine how much power their high commanders had.

We strolled through the town as though we had all the time in the world. Braal chatted to me along the way, bought some fruit from a stall and even tried on some jewellery but didn't buy any. It took me a while to realise what she was doing. She wanted people to see us and to think it perfectly normal that a human soldier and a faerie could be the best of friends. Once

I understood, I chatted back and ignored the mutters around us.

Braal led me to the edge of the town. I saw the touchstone marking the boundary but could not recall whether the old man had said it absolved sins by touching it on the way in or out, so I did not chance it.

"What now, then?" I asked Braal. "You've got me out of Mrinth, and I'm grateful, but I don't have anywhere to go. I don't have a home, Braal. I'm back to being all alone in the world."

"That's not what I hear." She looked to the south and I followed her gaze. There was a cart there, pulled by two horses, behind which sat Maya. In the cart sat Dom, Dom-Dom and Phillis, while Nolan Sharrock stood outside, a great smile plastered across his face.

"Misako!" he boomed and I ran to him, embracing him and allowing my tears to spill forth. For the next few minutes, I hugged and kissed my friends. We laughed, we cried and we hugged all over again, until I was exhausted.

"How?" I asked Braal.

"I got to the circus while the fight was still going on," Braal said. "Nolan told me what had happened and I raced to the pier to find you already in the water. Like I said, I commandeered a rowing-boat and went out after you. But I didn't spend all my time out there. I came inland to clean your wounds and there these guys filled me in on everything. I only took you back into the sea because it was safer for you there until you woke up."

"Braal saved you," Maya said. "She's every bit the hero you made her out to be."

"Oh shucks," Braal said, scratching the back of her head in mock embarrassment.

"The caravan's waiting a couple of miles out of town," Sharrock said. "Hop into the cart and we'll be on our way. The circus isn't complete without you, Misako."

"We'll be back to the way we should be," Maya said.

I was overwhelmed, but there was something in my head screaming at me, telling me this couldn't be. "I'm not going with you," I said.

"What?" Maya asked. "Misako, you have to be kidding. Why?"

"I'm a trouble magnet. Look what happened here. It could happen anywhere we go. So long as I'm with you, you're all in danger."

"What's your alternative?" Sharrock asked. "Live a life alone just so you can't hurt anyone?"

"Pretty much."

"Great idea," Maya said. "I think I'll live a life alone as well. I might do it wherever you're doing it."

"I think the whole circus might do it," Sharrock said.

"Guys, guys," I said, "I mean it. I'm a danger to you and I'm not doing it."

"This war's funny," Braal said. She actually laughed, which was entirely inappropriate. "It can end, I truly believe that. I've been fighting politically to end it, but never get anywhere. But you know what? I still think we can have peace. And do you know why? Because it can start with one person and spread to another, and another, and another."

"You heard what I said on the pier?" I asked.

"No. But there are a lot of people in Mrinth who did, and they're talking. Oh, they're talking."

"It won't end the war."

"No. It won't. But talking is the first step on the road to peace, and you're the one that set that in motion, Misako."

"I want to accept what you're saying, Braal. But the world isn't a good place."

"No," she admitted, "but it has good people."

"That'd be us," Maya said. "Come on, Misako, you have a family here."

I bowed my head. "I'll let you down."

"You?" Sharrock said. "Misako, you've taught me more than anyone ever has. Plus, you've turned me into someone Maya can love, and that's not a bad thing."

"As for me," Maya said, "you've taught me not to judge a species by the actions of a few. You've taught me that although faeries murdered my parents, not all faeries are bad."

"Hey," Phillis said from the cart, "you've taught me not to be annoyed at everything all the time."

"Misako," Dom said. "We love you. Come home."

"I was going to say that," Dom-Dom said. "I had a speech prepared."

"Then say it."

"Misako," Dom-Dom said. "We love you. Come home. Maya needs a bridesmaid."

I looked to Maya in shock. "You mean you and Nolan …?"

"Well," Maya said, "it sort of makes sense. I was going to save this for later, but, uh … you're going to be an auntie, Misako."

"But I don't have a sister."

"Hey," Maya said crossly. "Don't ruin my moment."

"You mean you ...? Maya!" I hugged her so fiercely she had to push me away. "All right," I said, happy beyond words. "I'll stay. I'll stay, if you're sure."

"There's something else," Nolan said. "Braal there pulled some strings. Our circus is meant to be a haven for the oppressed now, so we've picked up a couple of strays."

"Strays?" I asked Braal.

"Salla," she said. "I signed her out of prison. Some girl called Petal insisted on coming along and Salla didn't mind. They're back at the circus. You can take care of her, maybe even get her on the mend now she's not being pumped with a cure."

"I don't know what to say."

"How about not saying again that you don't have a sister." Braal thumped her chest. "Hurt me too, you know."

"Would it be all right to have another hug?"

"Hmm. Sure."

We headed south to meet up with the caravan. Clippety was there, too, and I took a few moments to apologise to him, although I don't think the horse accepted it. Braal provided us an escort for a few days and asked where we were thinking of going.

"Sardius," Sharrock said. "We were moving that way at one point. We never quite reached there."

"Then take care," Braal said. "It's a rough part of the world."

"And you?" I asked.

"Back to Torbalia for me. I have work to do. Press-ups in the rain. Shame I don't have someone who controls the storm."

"I'll drop by sometime," I said.

"I'll hold you to that. Oh, I spent the last few months asking about your father. Nothing, sorry."

"That's all right," I said. "I think I prefer to live with the memory of the hero I think he was, rather than face the truth. My mother painted him as a courageous knight, but the truth can often be blurry. If he's alive, I'm sure I'll find him. I'm just not sure I care to any more. After all, he abandoned me before he even knew whether I'd been created, and I have a real family now."

Braal smiled and gave me one final hug before mounting her horse. "Good luck, Misako. Have a good life."

"And you."

I watched her ride off and brushed away a tear. Braal was our hope for the future, and she was my friend. But I had found more than friendship, for with the circus I had a family and a chance at a happy life. In sending me after my father, that was all my mother had wanted for me. If she could see me from wherever she was, I hoped she would be proud of me. For the first time in my entire life, I was proud of myself.

"Come on, Misako," Maya said. "If it's all right with you, I'd like you to teach me to sing. They say if you sing to a child in the womb, it helps them develop."

I placed my hand to her belly but it was far too early to feel the baby kick. Within her womb was a child who would be raised in the belief that everyone was equal, that war was horror and that peace was the greatest triumph anyone could ever achieve.

"I'll teach you to sing, Maya," I promised, "but you won't ever have to, because I'm not going anywhere. I'm going to be the best auntie ever."

Whatever the future had in store, the world was already a far better place indeed.

AVAILABLE NOW IN PAPERBACK AND EBOOK

Sheriff Grizzly Ultimate Omnibus volume 1 of 3

His town: Grizzleton. His name: Bear. His secret: He's a grizzly bear wearing a sheriff's uniform ... but doesn't realise.

Collecting the first 4 Sheriff Grizzly stories. Join Bear, Deputy Rake and Doc Rum Tinkly as they protect Grizzleton (population 36) from outlaws, varmints and strange animal folk who turn up from time to time.

First, Bear and his posse must face the outlaw gang of Dirty Salvatore, who besets their town with a British invasion; a group of bally chums determined to bring the civility of cricket to the Wild West.

Then Bear has to deal with a bounty hunter who arrests Doc Tinkly's friend for horse theft. Tinkly and Deputy Rake (who'd do anything for her) sneak out to mount a rescue from neighbouring Townton: a lawless settlement with a penchant for hanging suspects without trial. Along the way, Tinkly suffers the effects of blue ice lollies, while Deputy Rake falls foul of the fictional folk hero Bandit-Man.

In book 3, Grizzleton's bank is robbed by the Coyote Colt Kid and one of Bear's deputies faces the blame. Only the Kid's former lover, Grizzleton's priest Father Yarek, can provide any hope to clear the deputy's name.

If you're still with us by this point, Deputy Rake and Doc Tinkly go to the circus while a mysterious lion-like stranger from Bear's past is determined to murder the poor sheriff.

All the while, Bear – a five-foot bundle of fur, fangs and feral fierceness – really can't understand why people seem to think he's a grizzly bear.

A Mermaid's Odyssey

March of the Demon Trees: A Knights of Torbalia Gamebook

The Second Battalion of Torbalia. Knights, thieves, barons, mercenaries ... the Second Battalion is formed of unlikely allies. In each Knights of Torbalia gamebook, you take on the role of a different soldier. Can you master them all?

An attack from an army of yggdras separates you from the rest of your battalion. Lost and alone, you must work your way through the yggdras-infested lands and reach the rendezvous point. Only in the safety of your battalion do you stand any hope of survival.

Taking the role of Braal, you must determine your own course of the story, deciding who to trust, who to fight and above all how to survive.

A gamebook of 57 paragraphs.

There are 10 Knights of Torbalia gamebooks available.

The Faerie Contract

Lisa Vale is an ordinary fifteen-year-old girl from a quiet rural village. She drinks at parties she shouldn't be at, has a tattoo her father doesn't know about and endures an annoying nine-year-old sister named Jenny.

When a strange girl named Aris protects her from a boy at a Christmas party, Lisa runs home in a panic. The following morning she discovers Aris has kidnapped Jenny in payment. To get her back, Lisa must convince Mayor Aldman to return the Christmas tree proudly displayed in the village square. For Aris is a hamadryad, a wood faerie whose very life is tied to the tree the mayor has invaded the faerie kingdom to acquire. Until Aris is returned home safely, she intends to keep Lisa's little sister in the faerie kingdom, slowly turning her into a creature of myth.

As Lisa investigates, she discovers the history of her village, and how the lineage of Aldmans and Vales stretches back many generations, to a terrible time when a deal was struck between man and faerie – a contract that neither can ever afford to break.

The Trojan Ant

Lost on a world of giant ants, Amy Garris is searching for her missing lover. Accompanied only by her boss, military scientist Anthony Grant, the two of them explore the strange world of unnatural insects. Having developed a pheromone which not only enables them to communicate with the ants, but also to make the ants believe they are members of their own colony, the two scientists fall into the company of General Allisira, a soldier ant steeped in duty and devotion.

A fungoid disease called cordyceps is turning the ants insane, destroying their lives and exploding spores from their brains to potentially infect the entire colony. Allisira's focus is purely on finding a cure, but Garris knows it is only a matter of time before the general realises the scientists have ulterior motives.

As the search for Garris's lover continues, she begins asking questions and comes to realise that both he and her boss know more about the strange world of ants than either of them should. Facing a world infested with intelligent bats and millipedes, and with a fungal killer lurking in every shadow, they are secrets Garris fears they shall all be taking to their graves.

Dinosaur World Omnibus

4 stories set on the quarantined dinosaur world of Ceres:

Excavating a Dinosaur World: Recently divorced and fighting a custody battle, Sara Garrel accepts an assignment to protect an archaeological expedition to the dinosaur world. Her charges are a stuffy professor, a spoiled rich gentleman and a flirtatious young student. But Garrel would put up with anything if it means earning enough money to win back her daughter.

Dinosaur Fall-Girl: When Professor Marigold Harper illegally enters Ceres in her search for the cure for cancer, a military unit is dispatched to bring her back. Separated from her unit, and with her escape shuttle wrecked by curious dinosaurs, Corporal Autumn is forced to drag the professor miles across hostile territory.

Dinosaur Prison World: Ashley Honeywood becomes the greatest dinosaur pit-fighter the Ceres penal colony has ever known. When her lover Garret Seward, the owner of the only decent eatery in the bayou, vanishes in a dinosaur attack, Honeywood heads out to find him.

The Dinosaur That Wasn't: A prison is seized by the inmates and Aubrey Whitsmith and Dexter Valentine find themselves in charge. When three soldiers arrive, they realise their dominancy might be about to collapse. But the soldiers are more interested with what's pursuing them through the swamp. For there is something out there, stalking them all.

Token Love

Best man on a stag party, Mark Fletcher has arranged a few days in the seaside town of Glazton. There amongst the flashing lights and empty promises he discovers Sandie Ford – a local young woman working at the prize counter of an amusement arcade. When Mark asks how many tokens he would need to exchange for her phone number, Sandie tells him ten thousand in an effort to get rid of him.

Mark, along with the stag Bill and their entire party, undertakes the mission to reach that goal.

Sandie's actions are applauded by her employer, Derek Reynard, who offers her a bonus if she leads Mark on, for every token earned is money spent. Feeling ashamed of her actions, Sandie attempts to find consolation in her colleague, Ruth; but Ruth – a stunning girl with her sights set on Vegas – does everything she can to support the venture, while at the same time trying her own luck with Mark.

As time runs out, Sandie faces the possibility that Mark might succeed in her challenge and agrees to meet with him so they can talk away from the gaudy deception of the arcades. Glazton may represent a holiday romance for Mark, but for Sandie it is a way of life; and a life perhaps she might be willing to change.

Everything depends on how determined Mark is to win the grand prize of Glazton.

Operation WetFish, Vampire Detective Ultimate Omnibus Volume 1 of 4

Police incompetence, witness intimidation, expensive lawyers. There are many reasons the guilty walk free of court. For Operation WetFish, a legal and entirely unorthodox department of the London police, the courts never have the final say. Frame-ups, alerting rival gangs or simply making the bad guys disappear ... Operation WetFish employs a variety of methods to clean up the mistakes of the courts.

Charles Baronaire lives for the thrill of making the streets safe. But Baronaire has other things on his mind. He's stronger, faster, more agile than ordinary human beings; he can focus his mind to alter people's perceptions, can establish command over nature's baser creatures. And he has an insatiable appetite for human blood.

Collected here are books 1 – 13 of the 50-volume Operation WetFish saga.

Have Imagination, Will Travel

Heather Tarne is not a witch – she just knows enough about the world around her to make sense of all the unexplainable things that happen in life.

This does not, however, stop Tarne and her friends from bouncing around realities, going from past, to future, to present and back around to the past in a series of bizarre stories which happily stop midway through and later pick up where they left off.

If that sounds confusing, imagine what it's like for Tarne. One moment she's negotiating peace treaties for a mediaeval king, the next she's playing a futuristic game of stick-in-the-mud with mutant snake people.

As the stories become stranger and stranger, Tarne begins to suspect this is not quite how life is meant to be. When a mysterious figure suggests there might be a reason for all her bouncing around between realities, Tarne looks to her group of friends and suspects one of them could be the cause of all her woes.

From spaceships to pirate ships, from detective agencies to super heroes, from Dark-Age brothels to reptile universities, Tarne's travels through reality are limited only by her imagination.

Ever trying to keep a level head, she's still (pretty) sure she's not a witch.

Detective's Omnibus: 7 to Solve

Seven self-contained detective stories.

Detective's Ex: Lauren Corrigan's former lover, Detective Carl Robbins, refuses to look into the murder of a kind old man, so Lauren decides to solve the case herself.

The Murder of Snowman Joe: Cut off by an intense snowstorm, rural detective Felicity Hart calls in a retired big-city detective to catch a killer trapped in the village with them.

Murder While You Wait: A colleague is missing, so two detectives abandon their workload for what becomes their most bizarre investigation ever.

One-Way Ticket to Murder: Businessman. Teacher. Runaway. Ticket Inspector. One murder – four witnesses. All have a train to catch.

The Murder of Loyalty: Constable Caroline Lees lies to protect her boyfriend after a drunken brawl. When a body turns up, Lees fights to escape her own web of lies.

The Woman Who Cried Diamonds: Investigating a diamond theft, Detective Blake calls his ex-lover, former jewel thief Shenna Tarin; but soon suspects she may already be involved.

Chasing the Shadow Man: When an armed robbery goes wrong, a young girl is kidnapped and D.I. Jonathan Hope must team up with an old colleague if he's to get her back alive.

Printed in Great Britain
by Amazon